"W[...]D,

"I'm trying t[...] and held her arms w[...]

She stumbled to her feet, water streaming down her body—her *body*, because the tight black stuff she had on was virtually transparent. She was like an angry goddess rising from the sea, full breasted and glorious in her rage.

"Are you trying to save me or just make me crazy?" she shouted at him.

"I'm trying to—"

And then he forgot what he was trying to do, because she surged forward and he surged forward, and they came together in an explosion of pent-up desire. Right there in the middle of the bathtub in the penthouse of the Beverly Pacific Hotel.

"Damn," he gasped, shocked by her slick hands on his bare back. "I never intended—"

"Shut up and kiss me," she ordered in her throaty voice, "because I *did* intend."

So much for that lousy commandment from the boss about clients and bodyguards not getting involved....

Dear Reader,

I love stories about people trading lives. I like to think, read and write about living in somebody else's shoes. I've never done it, but the concept fascinates me.

That's what drew me to *Trading Places*. What would happen if a deserving but everyday woman had a chance to live the life of her boss and exact opposite, a beautiful and notorious adventuress? Would it turn out to be a dream come true or would it be a disaster—perhaps even a dangerous disaster?

Alice gets the opportunity, whereupon things go wrong in bunches: car bombs, threatening phone calls, bullets, ex-husbands she's never met—you name it. Fortunately, she has Jed by her side; *un*fortunately, he has no idea who she really is. How will he react when he finds out?

I hope you enjoy reading *Trading Places* as much as I enjoyed writing it. And I suggest that the next time someone you know well acts…just a little off…you take a closer look.

We see what we expect to see, as Alice learned.

What do *you* expect?

Ruth Jean Dale

Trading Places
Ruth Jean Dale

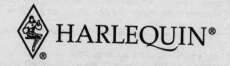

HARLEQUIN®

TORONTO • NEW YORK • LONDON
AMSTERDAM • PARIS • SYDNEY • HAMBURG
STOCKHOLM • ATHENS • TOKYO • MILAN • MADRID
PRAGUE • WARSAW • BUDAPEST • AUCKLAND

ISBN 0-373-70992-7

TRADING PLACES

Copyright © 2001 by Betty Duran.

Visit us at www.eHarlequin.com

Printed in U.S.A.

Trading Places

PROLOGUE

SHARLAYNE KENYON threw back her head and let loose her trademark laugh, deep and sexy and somehow bawdy. "*That's* what you want to call my book?" she asked when she could speak again.

Linden Wilbert, fifty-two-year-old head of the small and eccentric New York publishing house that bore his name, regarded this magical creature with a mix of disapproval and fascination. He could well understand the power she wielded over the men in her life and those who *wanted* to be in her life. Much married adventuress, occasional actress, sometime model and internationally popular personality, Sharlayne was, quite simply, dazzling. She had traveled furtively to Linden's Long Island estate to discuss her latest incarnation: author.

The book deal, also furtive, had been struck more than a year ago after they'd happened to meet at a cocktail party.

To this day Linden, scion of old money and the ideals of another century, could not fathom why she'd chosen him to pilot her autobiography through the literary shoals. He understood even less his own willingness to publish a tome so at odds with his usual list, which tended to be long on quality and woefully short on sales. All he knew was that he'd surprised himself by leaping at the opportunity.

His only excuse was that publishing the memoirs of one of the most famous—perhaps the proper word was *notorious*—women in the world appealed to his sense of the absurd.

Now Sharlayne turned her enormous blue-gray eyes in his direction and he melted. She was even more beautiful in person than in photographs or on film. Her face was a flawless oval, the skin creamy and unmarred by lines or dullness. Long lashes framed those incredible eyes, also accented by impeccably arched brows. The straight nose was as perfect as the rest. Full lips glistened pink and tempting.

But her hair—that glorious soft blond mane that was her signature style—had been chopped into a short, curvy cap. It bared dainty ears and gave her an innocence he wouldn't have imagined possible in a mature woman of her background and age, which he guessed to be early forties, although she didn't look near it. She herself would only say she was "twenty-nine and holding." Gazing at her, he could almost believe it.

He refused to let himself think about her famous body. At least, he tried valiantly.

She leaned forward, her expression one of mild alarm. "That's a very funny title, really," she said in her throaty voice. "But I like mine better—*The Story of My Life* by Sharlayne Kenyon." She lifted graceful hands as if framing a movie shot.

Linden gave her an indulgent smile. "Old hat, Sharlayne. You've led an exciting life. You deserve an exciting title."

She pouted prettily. "Isn't there any way I can convince you?"

He could think of many, but he'd vowed from the offset not to fall into this woman's clutches. She'd never have any sincere interest in an aging, balding, boring, widowed publisher. "No way whatsoever," he said firmly. "Shall we move on to more immediate concerns?"

"Oh, you." She sat upright, throwing him an exasperated glance. "I've almost finished the manuscript, if that's what you want to know."

"Really." He carefully concealed his astonishment. He'd expected it would take her years to write her life story without professional help. He'd offered her any number of collaborators, but she refused to even consider an "as told to" book. She insisted that this was her life and she'd write about it her way or not at all.

She smiled, all sunshine again. "I knew you'd be surprised." The smile faded. "But there's a tiny problem."

"Such as?"

"The media frenzy that awful woman has whipped up."

"What awful woman?"

Her mobile face registered surprise. "You don't know? Gina Godfrey, of course. That witch refuses to leave me alone. The other barracudas of the press I can take or leave, but Gina's out to get me."

"Ah. Then Gina Godfrey is a journalist?"

"God forbid! She's head entertainment muck-raker for the *U.S. Eye*. And she's devoted to making my life a living hell."

He regarded her kindly. "That sounds almost paranoid, Sharlayne."

"Just because I'm paranoid doesn't mean nobody's out to get me." Her brilliant smile flashed again. How did she do that? "The problem is, I'm beginning to think I'll never finish the book if I don't find a little peace and quiet. To be perfectly honest, I don't know how I got this much done."

"Frankly," he said, thinking about all the times he'd read her name in newspapers and seen her image on magazine covers in the past year, "neither do I. But peace and quiet aren't your only problems."

Her eyes widened. "They're not?"

"You have several ex-husbands who may not *want* you to finish the book."

"Oh, them." She waved dismissively. "Every single one adores me. At least, the live ones do."

"Even the senator?"

"Him, especially. He cried like a baby when I divorced him."

"At his age, he could have been crying from relief. What was he, eighty?"

"Oh, you." She tossed back her head. "Age is nothing more than a state of mind."

"Then what's the state of mind of those near and dear to your most recent husband?"

She somehow managed to frown without marring the perfect smoothness of her forehead. "Oh!" Understanding dawned. "You mean because to John, *family* had a whole different meaning. But…John's dead. I didn't divorce him—he died. I'm a widow."

"Did it ever occur to you that with him gone, there's no one to keep his family in check?"

She laughed. "Family? You make him sound like some Mafioso. John was a very classy man."

"He was also head of one of the biggest crime families in New York. Might you not be in considerable danger, my dear? After all, you promised to reveal the unvarnished truth in your book. That could conceivably make certain parties very nervous."

"I'll tell the truth or not publish the book at all," she said with dignity. "Besides, once it's out, what can anyone do?"

"Plenty," Linden said darkly, "but there may be those who'd prefer to stop it from being published at all…as in seeing you get cement overshoes and a quick trip to the nearest deep body of water."

"Really, Linden." She leaned back into the overstuffed flower-patterned chair in his library, her body graceful in simple black.

Simple *clinging* black.

She tapped perfect fingernails on the chair arm. "On the outside chance that I've overestimated my charms, I've come up with a scheme—oh, dear, let's call it a plan. A plan to give me time and space to write while lulling everybody into a false sense of security, you know?"

He felt the first stirrings of concern. "I'm almost afraid to hear this."

"Don't be. It's very simple. I'm going to pay someone to move into my new house in Beverly Hills. Did you know about it?"

"Everybody knows about it. You did take a television crew from a national show on a tour."

"I did, didn't I." She looked pleased. "Anyway, I'm going to pay someone to move in there to impersonate me while I hole up somewhere far away and work in blissful solitude. It shouldn't take more than a couple of months to finish if I don't have to fight off the vultures of the press and deal with all life's other interruptions."

"Let me get this straight. You think you can find someone to impersonate you, one of the most famous and distinctive women in the world?"

She looked delighted. "Well, aren't you sweet," she said, traces of her Arkansas beginnings showing through. "I know it's a long shot, but with proper prior planning—you're familiar with the seven P's?''

''I don't have the first idea what you're talking about.'' Most of the time, in fact.

''Proper prior planning prevents piss-poor performance. My first husband used to say that. A lot, actually.'' She rolled those fabulous eyes. ''He said it. He didn't live by it.''

''Are you telling me you've already found someone who can pass as you?''

She nodded, suddenly very serious. ''Not a perfect match, of course—that would be asking too much. But she doesn't have to be a clone or anything. With a haircut, a makeover, a little careful instruction, she can pass for me.'' She frowned. ''At least from a distance. I'm sure of it.''

''Never.'' He shook his head decisively. ''You'll never get away with it.''

She looked hurt. ''Why not?''

''Well...people know you.''

''So?''

''So they'll see right through her, whoever she is.''

''Not necessarily.'' All business, she began ticking points off on long, slender fingers. ''Number one, I'll move her into my new house with a new staff. None of them will have a clue.

''Number two, I'll put out the word that she's— I mean, that I'm—not feeling well. What's a disease I can have that isn't disfiguring or fatal?''

"Why...I don't know. Mononucleosis?"

"No, that's catching. Don't they call that the kissing disease?" She shuddered. "I definitely don't want anything like that."

"Oh. Then...there's always exhaustion. You hear that a lot—celebrities checking into the hospital, suffering from exhaustion."

"But I'm not checking into a hospital," she pointed out reasonably. "Think of something else."

"How about a broken bone?"

She considered, finally shaking her head. "I don't want to get into casts or anything like that," she decided. "Been there, done that."

"I've got it!" He snapped his fingers. "Laryngitis. You can't even talk on the phone."

Her eyes lit up. "That's perfect. I can set up this decoy in my house, surround her with strangers—except for Tabitha, of course—and then I'll be free to hide away and write my book. Simple."

The mention of her personal assistant produced a grimace from Linden. Why the beauteous Sharlayne had hooked up with the formidable Tabitha Thomas was a mystery, but he knew they'd been inseparable for a decade at least.

"Where will you go?" he asked, then caught himself, realizing that now even *he* was treating this cockamamy idea as if it might actually work.

"I haven't figured that out yet," she said serenely, as though she recognized the precise instant she'd overwhelmed his objections. "Somewhere I can be completely anonymous. A mountain cabin, an isolated ranch—something like that. You wouldn't have any ideas, would you?''

When she turned that luminous gaze on him, he didn't have an idea in his head. He licked his lips. ''I...might come up with something.'' He pulled himself together. ''If you really intend to try this—''

''I'm not going to *try*.'' She gave him a reproachful glance. ''I'm going to do it.''

''In that case, you must provide this poor woman with some kind of protection.''

''Protection from what?''

''From all potentialities—ex-husbands, any ex-lovers lurking about, kooks who might wander by, everything.''

She considered. ''You know,'' she said at last, ''that might not be a bad idea. You mean, like a bodyguard?''

He nodded.

''This bodyguard could keep people at arm's length, so they don't get close enough to notice the switch.''

''He could possibly do that, yes.''

''That's a good idea, Linden.'' Her lovely mouth curved up. ''Thank you, darling. As long as the press doesn't find out that I've already signed a publishing contract and that the book is practically finished, there shouldn't be any problems.''

''From your mouth to God's ear.''

''Exactly.'' She turned on that smile like a neon

sign. "This will work. All I've got to do is convince my stand-in."

"Stand-in or stooge?" he wondered aloud. "Sharlayne, I don't actually believe you've found a woman who can pass for one of the most photographed women in the world—and who is also dumb enough to be talked into such a scheme."

"O ye of little faith," she said, softly mocking. "Finding her is the least of my problems. In fact, at this very minute she's in your kitchen, trying to convince your cook to treat butter, which is practically my only weakness, like poison."

The wink she gave him curled his toes, even as it enlisted him in her mad scheme.

"Cheer up, Linden." Leaning forward, she cupped one smooth hand around his cheek. "This will work."

"It won't. The first person she meets will see right through her."

She shook her head with absolute certainty. "Not so. And you know why? Because we see what we expect to see. If she's living in Sharlayne Kenyon's house and wearing Sharlayne Kenyon's clothes and jewels and you expect to see Sharlayne Kenyon, that's exactly who you *will* see when you look at her."

She was so sure she almost made him believe it, too.

CHAPTER ONE

How many husbands are too many?

We have it on excellent authority that Sharlayne Kenyon has flown East for a rendezvous
with potential husband number seven. Be
careful, whoever you are! You could end up
as an addendum in the book she keeps threatening to write—you know, the one that will
name more names than the telephone book....
                              Gina Godfrey, *U.S. Eye*

ALICE WYNN LOVED working for Sharlayne Kenyon.

It was beyond a doubt the best thing that had
happened in her thirty-two, mostly hard-luck, years.
Not only did she love the job; it paid very well
indeed.

That did not, however, mean that Alice was beyond having a little fun at her glamorous employer's expense. With a dead-on knack for mimicry, which she'd had since childhood, she'd easily
perfected a takeoff on Sharlayne that never failed
her. It was a wonderful means of relaxing strangers

and getting her own way in circumstances such as the one in which she currently found herself.

Mr. Wilbert's cook, it had turned out, was not interested in listening to special requests from *anyone*. When Alice made her perfectly reasonable request that butter, cream and all other high-calorie substances be excluded from Sharlayne's meals, the cook had pinned the interloper with a stern gaze.

"Don't tell me my business, young woman," she said. "I've been preparing Mr. Wilbert's meals long enough to know what I'm doing."

"Oh, yes, absolutely," Alice agreed, aware of the averted gaze of the young kitchen helper chopping vegetables at a butcher block table in the middle of the enormous kitchen. "It's just that Miss Kenyon has very delicate digestion. She simply can't handle rich foods—although she loves them, she truly does."

The cook's helper said eagerly, "I haven't seen her yet. Is she really as beautiful as she looks in all those magazines?" She put down her knife and waited with breathless attention.

"More beautiful," Alice declared. "And sweet as pie." Usually. "It's a joy to work for her except for this one little thing—about her meals, I mean." She gave the cook an apologetic glance. "She gets really testy when she can't find anything she can eat. You understand."

"I suppose." The cook spoke grudgingly, apparently not in the least bit mollified. She turned her glare on her helper. "Get to work! We don't have all day here."

"Sorry." The young helper picked up the knife and held it poised over a carrot. "Are all the stories about her really true?" she asked Alice.

"Most of them," Alice said. She switched easily to a deep-voiced near drawl to add, "And you don't know the half of it, honey. Nobody does." She winked.

Even the cook had to laugh at the impersonation, and was still laughing when the butler entered. He looked around with a guarded expression, which quickly turned to a frown. "Where is she?" he demanded. "I distinctly heard Ms Kenyon's voice."

The laughing girl with the paring knife laughed harder. "You heard Alice," she said. "She does a great impression of her boss. Do some more, Alice."

"Well…" Alice glanced at the cook, who was no longer laughing. Better jolly her along a little more. "If you insist. Have you ever heard the story of her first wedding anniversary?"

"Which husband?" the cook inquired.

"First. He was a garage mechanic, the only poor man she ever married. According to legend, he took a gift to his beautiful young wife on their first-week anniversary."

"One week?" Even the cook was interested now, while the butler, although pretending not to pay the least attention, had an ear cocked to catch everything.

"And a good thing, too," Alice retorted, "because the marriage only survived about six months." She lowered her voice to a conspiratorial level. "Guess what he got her."

"A diamond?" the kitchen helper guessed.

"Candy and flowers," the cook predicted.

"Wrong on both counts." Alice loved this part of the story. "He handed her a pretty box, and when she ripped off the wrappings she found...a blender."

Alice recoiled in perfect imitation of Sharlayne's own frequent telling of the tale. "And Sharlayne said, 'If it's not something to put on *this* body, I don't *even* want to touch it!'"

Her audience of three roared with laughter, which cut off abruptly. With a sinking feeling, Alice knew before she even turned around that this time she might very well have gone too far. The best job she'd ever had, and now she'd be out on the street because she just couldn't pass up an easy laugh.

But turn she must. Sure enough, Sharlayne stood in the doorway, beckoning to her like the spider to the fly.

But why was she smiling?

Alice had had an uneasy feeling from the moment almost a week ago when Sharlayne had announced that she and her two assistants were flying East. She didn't know why, since she frequently traveled with her employer. She just knew she'd been nervous about the whole thing for no good reason.

Now she knew why. She'd had a premonition of doom.

MR. WILBERT LED Sharlayne and Alice into an elegant room with floor-to-ceiling bookshelves. He certainly appeared to belong in these rich surroundings, not too surprising. Sharlayne had said rather calculatingly that he came from old money.

Lots of old money.

Alice spared a glance around, admiring the leather-covered tomes with gilt edgings, the heavy dark furniture, the brocaded draperies. How many of these books had Wilbert's own company published? How many of the items in this room were family heirlooms?

How long could Alice avoid the inevitable?

Taking a deep breath, she turned—and stopped short at the sight of Tabitha, who was just entering the room. Sharlayne's personal assistant wore her usual disapproving expression. Alice didn't take it personally, supposing that the woman simply didn't want *anyone* invading her turf.

Was she about to get her fondest wish?

Alice sighed and said a tentative, "Sharlayne—"

"Before we begin," Linden Wilbert put in, "may I offer everyone a glass of wine?"

"Nothing for me," Alice said quickly. "I'd just like to get this over with, if you don't mind."

"We do mind," Sharlayne said sweetly. "Thank you, Linden. That would be lovely." She gestured for Alice to take a seat.

Thoroughly confused, Alice chose a brass-studded leather chair beside a fireplace cold in May. She'd seen Sharlayne lose her temper only once and it wasn't a pretty sight. Why was she pussyfooting around now? Being the kind of person who'd rather get any unpleasantness over with as quickly as possible, Alice was nonetheless forced to wait until the wine was duly delivered.

Then she said, "I apologize, Sharlayne. I wasn't making fun of you, honest."

"No?" Sharlayne's brows arched above guileless eyes. "Who *were* you making fun of?"

"No one." Alice made it a point not to look at Tabitha, who was probably purring by now. "I just wanted to score brownie points with the cook. She wasn't real happy to hear about your dietary requirements."

Mr. Wilbert seemed distressed. "I should have spoken to the cook on your behalf, Sharlayne," he apologized. "She does tend to be testy."

"I was only trying to get on her good side," Alice explained, trying not to sound defensive, "but I shouldn't have used you to do it." Sharlayne said nothing, so Alice added a resigned, "If you're going to fire me, let's get it over with."

Sharlayne's eyes widened. "Is that what you think? That I'd fire a good and loyal employee over a little thing like that?"

"Well, actually…yes. I know loyalty is really important to you. I also know I was out of line."

"As you have been on many other occasions, and I didn't fire you then, did I? You've been doing that takeoff on me almost from the day I hired you."

"You knew?" And then Alice understood: Tabitha, blank faced and superior, was a stool pigeon.

Sharlayne smiled that dazzling smile. "You should know better than to believe everything you read and hear about me, Alice. I'm not really all *that* dumb."

"Lord, if there's one thing I never thought you were, it's dumb," Alice said fervently. "This is a real relief. I owe you big-time. How about I promise I'll never let myself get carried away like that again, for starters." She lifted her right hand, palm out, to verify her vow.

"Oh, dear," Sharlayne said. "That's not what I want to hear at all."

"You don't?"

Sharlayne shook her head.

"Then what?" Alice leaned forward, aware that Tabitha was doing the same. Whatever was going on, she wasn't a party to it, either.

But Mr. Wilbert was. "Sharlayne, do you really think you should go forward with—"

"Shh." Sharlayne kept her level gaze on Alice. "I won't deny it hurt to learn that you, my trusted friend and employee, were making fun of me behind my back."

"I wasn't," Alice protested. "Imitation is the sincerest form of flattery, after all."

Sharlayne sighed. "I was *not* flattered. But you see, something's come up where your knack for mimicry may come in handy."

"I can't imagine what."

"It's very simple, really. I need some space to finish my book and I can only think of one way to get it."

"You mean there's some way I can help? Of course. Name it."

An almost cunning expression appeared on Sharlayne's lovely face. "Oh, good," she said. "That's what I hoped you'd say. You heard her, Linden. You're a witness, too, Tabitha."

Tabitha let out her breath in a short hiss. "What are you up to?" she asked sharply. "What can Alice possibly do for you that I can't?"

Sharlayne's smile was beatific. "Alice can be me," she said. "And now I know she will."

DINNER WAS ANNOUNCED before Alice could do more than say a thoroughly confused, "Huh?" Sharlayne and Mr. Wilbert ate in the formal dining room; Tabitha had a tray sent to her room; and Alice grabbed a sandwich and took it outdoors to eat on the terrace overlooking a lovely formal garden.

What in the world was Sharlayne up to now? *"Alice can be me,"* she'd said, yet that must surely be a joke. No one could be Sharlayne Kenyon, but most especially not Alice Wynn.

For openers, Alice was relatively unsophisticated. A registered nurse, she'd spent nearly a decade caring for an invalid grandmother in her small Nebraska hometown. Only after her grandmother's death had she been free to look around for a job— and a life—of her own.

Hooking up with Sharlayne had been a stroke of good fortune. Alice had gone to visit a distant cousin in California, and when she'd happened upon an automobile accident, had gone to the aid of the injured. One of the victims was Sharlayne, who'd suffered a broken leg and a terrible scare: she'd thought at first that her face might be scarred.

In her matter-of-fact way, Alice had reassured Sharlayne. When Sharlayne was released from the hospital, she'd hired Alice to tend to her at home on a temporary basis. That had quickly evolved into full-time employment, with Alice in charge of meal planning and the general health of the household. She'd set up an exercise schedule and saw to it that Sharlayne, who had couch potato tendencies, stuck to it. From the beginning, Sharlayne had also used her new employee for general gofer duty, which hadn't bothered Alice in the slightest. She hadn't spent ten years fetching and carrying for a crotchety old lady for nothing.

The job was fun, the surroundings elegant, but the biggest plus was a generous salary that helped defray the staggering hospital bills for Grandma's final illness. With a light finally visible at the end of her personal tunnel, Alice settled in for a long run.

She'd never imaged being so close to so much glamour. For a little girl from Nebraska, it was dazzling. Through Sharlayne, Alice had met many beautiful people, among them a gardener with whom she'd had a brief but passionate affair. Strangely enough, perhaps, she'd never met any of Sharlayne's rich and famous ex-husbands, although she'd heard many stories about them.

Yes, she definitely owed her boss. The method of repayment, however, eluded her.

When Sharlayne summoned Alice later that night, she went with some trepidation. Again, she entered the library to find the same three waiting for her. She sat down without invitation, her knees suddenly rubbery.

Sharlayne's smile would set a garden statue at ease. "I'm sure you'd like an explanation," she said gently.

Alice nodded.

"You know I've been trying to finish my book," Sharlayne said. "It's going quite well, actually, when I can find the time to work on it. That's where you come in.''

Alice waited.

"I want you to pretend to be me so I can slip away to some hiding place and finish the manuscript," Sharlayne said, as if proposing nothing out of the ordinary. ''That's all.''

"That's all?'' Alice and Tabitha said in unison.

Tabitha threw in a scathing glance. ''You can't possibly be serious.''

"I'm deadly serious," Sharlayne said calmly.

"Nobody," Tabitha said flatly, ''will ever believe this Plain Jane is *you*.''

Alice sputtered, searching for words to defend herself that didn't come. She'd be the first to admit she was no Sharlayne Kenyon but neither was she a Plain Jane.

"When I get through with her," Sharlayne said with total confidence, ''her own mother will believe she's me. It's not that big a deal, Tabby.''

Tabitha huffed and puffed, muttering ''Hopeless'' and ''Ridiculous'' and ''Insane.''

Sharlayne laughed. "No, seriously." She turned back to Alice, who sat speechless with astonishment. "This will work," she said. "How tall are you?''

"F-five-eight.''

"Me, too. Our bodies are also basically the same. They should be—we do the same workout every day. I'm a bit more buxom—''

"An understatement," Alice observed, looking pointedly at Sharlayne's generous cleavage.

"That's why God invented push-up bras, dear."

"But—but—you're blond."

"Ever hear of bleach?"

This suggested she probably wouldn't be swayed by the fact that Alice's hair was twelve inches longer. That's why God invented scissors. "Our eyes aren't exactly the same color," she stated as though she'd finally settled upon a valid difference.

"That's true. Yours have less gray in them. But nobody will notice that unless they see the two of us together, which they won't. Blue is close enough."

"Okay, then—" Alice began again, grasping for straws. "My nose is shorter."

"Again, unless we stand side by side, who's to know? Besides, makeup will go a long way toward negating that."

"Sharlayne." Tabitha's tone was agonized. "This is insane. She'd never get away with it."

"She will if I put out the word I have laryngitis," Sharlayne said triumphantly. "If I set her up in the New York apartment, there could be a problem. But we won't do that. She can move into the new house in Beverly Hills, where nobody's met me. You'll be with her, of course. Everyone knows that where I am, you are, too, Tabby."

"No!" Tabitha turned on Alice in a fury, as if

the situation were her fault. "I should be with *you*, Sharlayne, wherever you're going."

Sharlayne shook her head. "Impossible. If you're not with her, nobody will accept that she's me." Leaning forward, she squeezed Tabitha's hand. "You'll do this for me, dear. I can't imagine you'd ever let me down."

The uncharacteristically mute Linden said into the sudden silence, "I'm beginning to see how this could actually work."

Alice turned to him, wide-eyed. "You can?"

He nodded. "There are certain basic similarities. If no one gets close enough—"

"Aha!" Alice gazed at everyone triumphantly. "There are always people around you, Sharlayne. How could *I* keep them away?"

"You won't have to. I'm going to hire a bodyguard to run interference for you."

"A bodyguard! I couldn't put up with a bodyguard. Besides, how do you know you can trust him to keep the secret? Something like this could be worth a lot of money to a scandal sheet like the *U.S. Eye*."

"He can't sell information he doesn't have. He'll think he *is* guarding me, of course. Everybody will. You'll put on that act you do so well for the help, then lay low until I finish the manuscript and come back. You'll have the run of the whole house, the pool, the tennis courts—everything. You'll live in the master suite and be queen of all you survey. It will be the experience of a lifetime.''

''She'll never pull it off,'' Tabitha reiterated.

''Damn it!'' Alice was getting sick and tired of hearing that. She glared at Tabitha. ''If Sharlayne thinks I can—''

''I know you can,'' Sharlayne said quickly. ''Do this, Alice. When it's over, I'll be *very* grateful.''

''You will?''

''So grateful that I'll pay off the rest of your grandmother's medical bills.''

Alice was stunned. She had no idea Sharlayne was even aware of those bills. ''Be careful,'' she said a bit uneasily. ''You're talking big bucks.''

''I'm aware of that. I know your debts to the penny.'' She leaned forward, hand outstretched. ''Let's cut to the chase. Is it a deal?''

Alice looked down at the sleek hand, with its faultless manicured nails, then at her own competent hand, which resembled a paw next to all that perfection. Ever since she'd met this woman, she'd wondered what it would to like to be so beautiful, so famous, so sought after. Now, out of the blue, she had a chance to find out. Even so...

Tabitha gave a grunt of disbelief. ''I'm warning all of you, this is a ridiculous idea. It will never work. Alice won't be able to carry it off and disaster will—''

''It's a deal,'' Alice said abruptly, tossing in a hostile glance for her nemesis. ''If you think it can work, Sharlayne, I'm willing to give it the old college try."

"I knew I could count on you."

Sharlayne's relief was palpable, and a shock to Alice. Somehow she got the feeling that something else was going on here, but what could it possibly be?

"SHARLAYNE." Linden took her hand between both of his, forgetting that she was more than an hour late for breakfast. "You've never looked lovelier."

She smiled and patted his cheek, her touch lingering. "How sweet of you to say so."

"Hardly sweet." He drew her toward the table set up in the sunroom—at 11:00 a.m., to the cook's horror.

Sharlayne settled gracefully into the chair he offered. "Did you sleep well?" she inquired, dropping the linen napkin into her lap.

"Not particularly. I was thinking of your double."

"Alice kept you awake?" She reached for the silver coffee carafe and poured for both of them, an almost smile tilting those bewitching lips.

He would not be put off. "I'm not sure Alice understands what she may be getting into. I'm not sure *you* understand what we may all be getting into."

Sharlayne's beautiful face remained clear and untroubled. "You worry too much, Linden," she scolded, simultaneously teasing and enticing. "None of us is getting into anything except a little plot to deceive the media and the busybodies of the world. It's a little game, that's all."

"Be that as it may." He offered her the basket of fresh croissants, now grown cold. "With your permission, I'll arrange for the bodyguard right after breakfast. When do you want to leave for your hideaway?"

She considered. "Next Friday," she finally decided. "That should give me time to remake Alice and get her set up in the new house."

"All right. I'll handle the arrangements."

"No one is to know *I'm* not really being guarded," she said quickly. "You understand that? Not the bodyguard, not the agency—just you and me, Alice and Tabitha."

"I understand." But he didn't like it. "I only hope you understand what you're doing."

"Trust me, darling."

When that dazzling smile fell upon him, what else could he do?

SEVERAL HOURS LATER, Linden dialed 1-800-HERO and waited patiently for the voice to announce, "S. J. Slade Insurance Agency," then asked for Samantha Spade Archer.

"I'm sorry, sir, but Mrs. Archer doesn't speak to

anyone,'' the woman said, sounding stunned that anyone would suggest otherwise. "Her daughter might be able to help you."

"I don't think so," Linden said. "Mrs. Archer is a personal friend. Please tell her that Linden Wilbert is in need of a bit of insurance."

"If you say so, sir." She obviously didn't believe him.

Mere moments later, Sam's husky voice exploded in his ear. "Linden, as I live and breathe. Long time, no hear, sweetheart."

"Too long." He found himself smiling. He could picture the elegant Samantha, dressed in ankle-strap heels and tight little forties suits worn with pearls. "Tell me, how's Mr. Samantha Spade?"

Her throaty laughter sounded indulgent. "That's Mr. Wil Archer to you, buster—and he's fine. So are the daughter and son-in-law and grandson."

"Delighted to hear it."

"Yeah, but it's not the reason for this call."

"True. I'm in need of your professional services."

"Looking for a little insurance, are you?"

Insurance: her euphemism for *bodyguard.* Sam carried discretion to new heights.

"Not me," Linden said. "A friend of mine. Perhaps you've heard of her? Sharlayne Kenyon?"

Sam gave a bark of laughter. "Yeah, I've heard of her. Who hasn't? So what's the story?"

"She needs someone to run interference for

her," he said. "Someone to keep the press at bay, to hold back the throngs—that sort of thing."

"Sounds like she needs a press secretary, not one of my highly trained operatives."

"She wants someone she can count on in an emergency," he improvised. "Not that she expects an emergency, but you know how it is with a woman as famous as this one."

"Yeah," Sam said dryly, "I know how it is. When do you need this glorified errand boy?"

"Now, Sam, don't talk that way. Sharlayne is a highly strung, artistic individual. She's exhausted and needs peace and quiet, which is what she's hoping your guy will help her get. Can you do anything for me?"

A long silence followed. Then she said, "Of course, sweetheart. Just tell me when and where and I'll have your man standing by."

THE QUESTION WAS, which man?

Samantha Spade sat at her desk, staring at two folders before her. The agency was overextended already. Business was booming and she didn't have a whole lot of choice here.

Two operatives were available. One had just returned from a harrowing assignment that required him to spend several days piloting a desperate senior citizen through Florida swamps in an ultimately successful attempt to avoid his vengeful heirs, eager to collect sooner rather than later.

The other was brand-new, bright eyed and bushy tailed; he had just signed on and trained and was waiting for his first assignment.

She flipped open his folder. Jed Kelby, thirty-three. Heir to a winery in California's Napa Valley. Six years an officer in the U.S. Marine Corps. Might have made a military career if his father hadn't died, requiring his presence at home. When his younger brother had stepped forward to take over Kelby-Linus Wines, Jed had looked around for something to do that might offer a little adventure.

Samantha, who'd known the senior Kelby in the wild days of her youth, had been taken aback when Jed knocked on her door one day and asked for a job. Not that she'd found anything wrong with his credentials; far from it. The tall—six foot two—Jed, with his straight, short dark hair and piercing eyes, was a true poster Marine. He was eager for the opportunity and ready to work hard to deserve it.

Still, she'd had reservations that she couldn't quite pinpoint. Maybe it was that he seemed too good to be true, too much a straight arrow. People in Sam's business sometimes had to stretch a point or two, without being told *officially* that they should. If she had one real concern about Jed, it was that he might be too much by the book and not innovative enough to protect his life and that of his charge.

Would it be fair to make his first charge a man-eater like Sharlayne Kenyon?

"YOU'VE BEEN ASKING for it, sweetheart, and you're about to get it—a chance to prove yourself."

Jed's pulse picked up, but he held himself at ease. "What's the job?" he asked casually, as if it didn't matter.

"Guarding a beautiful woman."

"Anyone I know?"

"Someone everybody knows. You have heard of Sharlayne Kenyon?"

"Jeez." He sucked in his breath. "What is it? Kidnapping threat? Blackmail? Stalker?"

Samantha laughed, but he didn't think she looked entirely comfortable. "None of the above. She's tired. She wants someone to fend off the press and public so she can get some rest."

"She wants—" He stared at his boss, in the grip of bitter disappointment. "You've been saving me for *this?*"

"You might be the only man in America who'd object to being cooped up with Sharlayne Kenyon for a few weeks. Just don't get too cocksure, okay?"

"Cocksure about what?"

"About your ability to treat her like just another client. Of course, that'd be a stretch for you, since she'll be your first client."

"If that's your subtle way of telling me to keep

my hands off, save your breath. I'm a professional." He grimaced. "Okay, a new professional, but everybody starts somewhere."

Sam nodded as if satisfied...or resigned. "Just remember the rules according to me. *Thou shalt not get involved with thy client.* It can get thee both killed."

He gave her a thumbs-up. "I got it, Boss. Don't give it another thought." He grinned, determined to make the best of the task. "From what I hear, she's too old for me anyway."

Samantha's great guffaw rocked the room. "Oh, you fool!" But she said it affectionately. "You don't know women like this one. She'll chew you up and spit you out if you're not careful."

"Naw," he scoffed, "not me. I'm not a skirt chaser."

"No," she agreed, "what you are is an idiot if you try to match hormones with an adventuress like Sharlayne Kenyon. But what the hell. Boys have to grow up someday."

She opened the file, all business again. "Now, here's the deal..."

CHAPTER TWO

Sharlayne update:

Sharlayne Kenyon's gone into hiding at her glamorous new digs in Beverly Hills, where, according to the smart money, she's working on her autobiography. Half the rich and/or handsome men in California are expected to head for the hills, should this prove to be true....

Gina Godfrey, *U.S. Eye*

JED CALLED HOME Thursday before leaving for Los Angeles. He'd be driving down from the agency headquarters in San Francisco in his old Ford pickup, only a six- or seven-hour trek. Before he left, he figured he should tell his family where they could reach him.

His brother, Steve, answered. After the usual chitchat—they needed rain, Mom was still flitting around Europe with Aunt Margaret, their sister Dana was expecting her second kid in the fall—Jed finally got around to the reason for his call.

"Hey, great, man," Steve said enthusiastically.

"I know you've just been waiting for that first assignment. Who and what?"

"I'll be guarding Sharlayne Kenyon."

"Say that again?"

"Sharlayne—"

"Jeez! You mean the one who's been married about a dozen times? The one who's been in movies and magazines and—"

"That's the one, all right," Jed confirmed dryly.

"You always did have all the luck."

That surprised Jed, who didn't think he ever had *any* luck. "How so?" he challenged.

"You're gonna be guarding one of the most famous bodies in America. That's not luck?"

"I'm guarding it, not making moves on it."

"Yeah, right."

"Steve, she must be ten years older than I am." He figured the photos in his briefcase must have been taken fifteen years ago and extensively retouched.

"Fifteen years older and twenty years smarter," Steve shot back.

"You think so? Look, little brother, guarding some flighty celebrity isn't my idea of a plum assignment."

"Everybody's got to start somewhere, my man."

"That's what I figure, so I intend to make the best of it. The body of Sharlayne What's-Her-Name will be guarded like never before, but that's all— *guarded*. This is strictly business."

"Knowing you, I believe it." Steve sounded disgusted. "Good old straight-arrow Jed." He sighed. "If it were me…"

"It's not. If you need me, use my cell phone number. I'll be at her place in L.A.—Beverly Hills, Bel Air, wherever."

"Okay. Have a good time."

"Fat chance. This is work."

"Speaking of work…" A pregnant pause followed, and then, "We really could use you around the old homestead, Jed. If bodyguarding doesn't pan out, you can always come home."

"It'll pan out. Give my love to Dana."

"Will do, and you give my love to Sharlayne Kenyon."

Jed hung up on a long, low whistle.

Steve must be losing it, he thought, tossing his sea bag into the back of the pickup. What did his brother know about this Sharlayne Kenyon that Jed didn't? He'd seen pictures of her, read her file. She was just another glossy blonde.

Wasn't she?

ALICE SAT AT the makeup table in the master suite of Sharlayne's Spanish-style villa in Beverly Hills. Practically in a state of shock, she stared at her reflection in the lit mirror.

Her own face stared back at her, bare of makeup but topped with Sharlayne's hair: a pale baby blond in a sexy, short cut. Sharlayne, who was also reflected in the mirror, tugged at a strand, testing the texture between her fingers.

"Well?" Alice inquired breathlessly.

"Not bad," Sharlayne responded grudgingly. "Your hair's finer than mine—less body. But Kathy did a great job, I have to admit."

"It went just the way you said it would," Alice said. "I asked for your hairdresser when I made the appointment, then gushed all over her about how much I loved your hair. I asked her to do mine exactly the same and this is the result."

"And since you went in sans makeup, she'll never put two and two together," Sharlayne said with satisfaction. "Okay, time to complete the transformation. Show me what you've learned in the past week."

Alice herself wasn't sure what she'd learned. Sharlayne had bombarded her with information and instructions, including the art of makeup. Although Alice had painted her eyes, modified her lip line, shadowed her nose to make it appear longer and allowed Sharlayne to change the shape of her brows, she'd never done everything all at once.

This would be the acid test.

With trembling hands, she reached for the jar of Sharlayne's custom-blended foundation. Picking up a sponge, she looked herself in the eye, took a deep breath and began.

Thirty minutes later, she was so racked with nerves that she really couldn't see the forest for the trees: all the parts that went together to create Sharlayne Kenyon. Everything about Alice gleamed and glowed with color and new shapeliness, but did it add up to success?

She shifted on the bench and fixed a plaintive gaze on Sharlayne. "Well?" She held her breath.

Sharlayne looked…stunned. Stepping forward, she put her hands on Alice's shoulders and turned her back to face the mirror. What Alice now saw was two Sharlayne Kenyons—*two*. For a moment, she didn't know which one was her.

Sharlayne said in a strangled voice, "I'm the one who thought this would work, and even *I* don't believe it."

"Neither do I," Alice gasped. "I never dreamed—!"

"I realized there were a lot of similarities." Sharlayne had pulled herself together, although she still appeared rattled. "Do you suppose we're twins separated at birth?"

Alice laughed. "Not likely, since I'm thirty-two and you're—"

"Older. A tiny bit older." Sharlayne grinned at her own intervention. "Actually, when I look closer I can see the differences. Your upper lip is longer…see?" She pointed to her own mouth. "Your nose is shorter, your cheeks fuller. That's why I showed you how to contour. Your neck's shorter, too." She preened her head from side to side to demonstrate.

"I see it when you point it out," Alice agreed. "Without all the camouflage we don't look that much alike at all." She rose. "Now what?"

"Now you get dressed. Wear that." Sharlayne pointed to garments laid out on the silk-draped canopy bed and strappy high-heeled sandals sitting on the floor.

Without a word, Alice stripped off her jeans and T-shirt. Beneath them she wore a thong—which was driving her crazy—and a demibra of lace and satin, artfully constructed to make the most of her assets. The underwear was new, selected and purchased by Sharlayne.

"You can wear my clothes and my shoes," she'd said. "You can even wear my jewels. But *no way* will anybody wear my undies. Since you have a penchant for cotton underwear and no one on the planet would believe Sharlayne Kenyon would wear such a thing—"

"But no one will see my underwear," Alice had protested. "What difference does it make?"

"Plenty," Sharlayne snapped. "*You'll* know and you won't feel like me in cotton underpants—trust me. Besides, what if you got hit by a car? Then everybody at the hospital would see. It would ruin my reputation."

"I'm not going to get hit by a car."

Sharlayne had got that sneaky gleam in her eyes. "There are other occasions to show one's underwear. You could have a mad passionate affair with your bodyguard.''

''I had a mad passionate affair with one of your gardeners. Remember that? It didn't work out so well. I won't be trying that again any time soon.''

''José was cute,'' Sharlayne said, ''but the language thing was a problem. I'm still not sure if he was kissing you off or inviting you to go back to Mexico with him.''

''Whatever. I was sorry I ever got involved.'' Alice stepped into white jeans and hauled them up over her hips. She had to take a deep breath to get them snapped, then to pull up the zip.

She'd never worn anything so tight in her life. ''Good grief,'' she gasped. ''How do you move in these?''

''They're denim. They stretch.''

''I hope.'' Alice tugged the black T-shirt over her head. Short and just as tight as the jeans, it reached only to a couple of inches above the waistband, baring her navel.

She stared in the mirror at her exposed bellybutton. ''You're kidding,'' she said faintly.

''You know better. You've seen me practically every day for two years. You've seen me wear *that*, as a matter of fact.''

''Yes, but...I don't know.'' Alice shook her newly blond head.

''Good,'' Sharlayne said approvingly. ''That petulant look is dead-on. Hurry up, put on the shoes.

Your bodyguard should be arriving any minute and you'll have to greet him.''

Alice's stomach clenched into a knot of terror. ''Sharlayne, I don't know—''

''The hell you don't! Put on those shoes!'' Sharlayne pointed with a stiff finger. ''Then put on that ruby tennis bracelet and the diamond earrings I laid out for you.'' The roar of an automobile engine interrupted and she frowned. ''What the...?''

Alice, closer to the second-story windows, walked over to peer out. ''It's an old pickup truck,'' she reported.

''Probably a delivery,'' Sharlayne grumbled, coming to check for herself. ''Tabitha must have authorized it.''

The driver's door opened and a man stepped out. And what a man: slim hips and shoulders to die for. When he looked up unexpectedly, both women leaped back as if caught doing something they should be ashamed of.

They faced each other, wide-eyed.

Sharlayne said, ''The bodyguard. Got to be.''

''Do you think so?'' Alice whispered, wondering how she got so lucky.

''I'm sure of it.'' Sharlayne grinned. ''Maybe I should hang around and send *you* off to finish my book.''

''Maybe you should,'' Alice agreed, wondering if what she felt beneath her feet was really quicksand.

"Go on, Alice," Sharlayne scoffed. "I mean, *Sharlayne*. That guy's a real hunk and his only interest in the next several weeks will be guarding *your body*. Let him earn his money. Remember, you're me, so don't pull any of that fainting-virgin stuff. I'm not suggesting you do anything you really don't want to, but in public ask yourself, 'What would Sharlayne do?'" She turned toward the door with a wink. "Then don't do anything I wouldn't, okay?"

Alice groaned. That certainly left a lot of leeway.

A FIFTYISH WOMAN with the charm of a goatherd let Jed into the old villa. He automatically catalogued what he'd seen so far: a tall brick fence, an enormous and elaborate wrought-iron gate at the street entrance to the property, a long curving drive leading up to the white-walled, red-tile-roofed mansion nestled among palms and flowering shrubbery.

All very substantial and prosperous. A nice place to visit, but he wouldn't want to live here.

The woman, a stereotypical old-maid schoolteacher if he'd ever seen one, offered her hand. "I am Tabitha Thomas," she said in a chilly tone. "I am Ms. Kenyon's personal assistant."

"Jed Kelby." He took her hand in a firm but brief grip. "S. J. Spade Insurance Agency."

"The bodyguard."

He grimaced. The agency preferred *insurance agent* or *security expert* or even *personal security*

consultant. Nevertheless, he said, "Yes, ma'am."
He glanced around the majestic entryway, noting
the antique tile, the Moorish shapes of windows and
doors. "Is Ms. Kenyon available?"

"She's—"

"Right here."

The low timbre of the new voice sent shudders
of anticipation down Jed's spine. He was watching
Tabitha and therefore caught the look of shock that
touched her face before it was quickly gone. For a
moment he couldn't be sure of the identity of the
newcomer, but then he turned, bracing for this first
encounter with his employer.

He had no idea why until he saw her standing
there—posing there, actually—in the arched doorway. Pictures of Sharlayne Kenyon didn't do her
justice, had not prepared him for the reality. Blond
and beautiful and sleek and sexy would do for starters. She simply took his breath away, which annoyed the hell out of him.

This was business, damn it. He wouldn't let her
distract him from his duty.

He stepped forward, thrusting out his hand in a
businesslike manner. "Ms. Kenyon? I'm Jed Kelby.
The agency sent me."

She batted those clear blue eyes. "Ms. Kenyon?" She duplicated his questioning tone. "Are
you suggesting you're not sure?"

Tabitha Thomas stirred. "Not to worry, Mr.

Kelby," she said with perfectly flat inflection. "She often has this effect on strangers."

"Yeah, well…" Jed almost felt left out of the conversation, for some reason. "I've only seen pictures."

A fast smile tilted Sharlayne's lips. "I shouldn't tease you," she said. "I'm really quite relieved you're here. Please, come into the living room, where we can talk." She half turned. "Tabitha, could you send Juan to make drinks. It is almost cocktail hour." She tossed Jed a mischievous glance.

"Not for me," he said quickly. "I don't drink on the job."

"But you're not on the job yet." She gave him a pretty pout. "You don't officially start until tomorrow."

He simply shook his head: no.

"Wine, then." Those soft lips set in a stubborn line. "Surely you can have a glass of wine. We— I've just put in a case of fabulous Kelby-Linus chardonnay—" She stopped short, her beautiful eyes widening. "But—are you connected to *those* Kelbys?"

This wasn't going the way he expected. He didn't want any personal relationship with this woman. Neither did he want to lie to her, so he simply said, "Yes."

"Then that's what we'll have," she said happily, clasping her hands with pleasure. A bejeweled bracelet encircled her wrist, and her nails were long and gracefully shaped. "If you please, Tabby?"

Tabitha's mouth turned down at the corners, but she nodded and walked briskly away. There was nothing for Jed to do but follow Sharlayne wherever she might lead.

ALICE THOUGHT she might faint, she was so anxious about this first test of her false identity. Tabitha hadn't helped, either. The woman had made no secret of her dislike for Alice, but to snipe in front of the bodyguard was completely uncalled for.

Then there was that bodyguard himself. If she'd sat down to outline her ideal man, she'd probably have come up with Jed Kelby.

In the first place, he was tall. She liked tall. Tall, dark and handsome, just like the stereotype. Great, athletic body; easy way of moving, erect posture that hinted of a military background.

If all that wasn't enough, he had close-clipped black hair and clear hazel eyes that showed a changing pattern of green and gold. The guy was, quite simply, a knockout. And *that body*...

She picked up two glasses of wine and offered one to him. "Cheers," she said, sipping.

"Cheers." He barely sipped the wine before setting the glass on the huge carved wooden coffee table. Apparently, he really didn't intend to drink on duty.

To hell with that. Alice needed all the courage

she could get, however false. She took another swallow. "Did you have a nice drive?" she asked.

He nodded brusquely. "Why do you need a personal security specialist, Ms. Kenyon?"

She blinked in surprise. "Why...I don't know. It just seemed like a good idea at the time."

He frowned. "Are you in any kind of danger?"

"Not at all." She got hold of herself then, and switched back to the official line. "That is, unless you call the press a danger. To be perfectly frank, I've become such a media target that sometimes I feel I'm in danger just appearing in public." That much was true; she had no idea how Sharlayne stood the constant scrutiny and interference.

He shrugged, broad shoulders moving beneath navy-blue knit. "Guess it goes with the territory," he said without so much as a trace of sympathy. "I understand you've only recently moved into this house."

"That's right. A few days ago, as a matter of fact."

"Then the first order of business is for me to check out your security system." He stood up abruptly. "If you'll tell me where to stash my gear—"

"Wait a minute. Not so fast." She frowned. "There'll be plenty of time for that. Let's talk about the rest of it."

His dark brows rose. "What rest of it?"

"How we're going to...relate to each other."

"You lost me," he said. "You're my employer. I'm here to do the job you hired me for—protect you."

"That's all well and good, but I don't want anyone to know I've hired a bodyguard. That would be like inviting every crackpot in town to take a shot at getting through my security."

"Okay. Then we won't tell anyone."

"Exactly. But sooner or later someone will wonder who the handsome man living in my house might be." She gave him her best come-hither look, which obviously wasn't all that good, judging by his lack of response.

If he noticed the compliment, he failed to let on. "Okay, tell 'em I'm your cousin. I don't care."

"Really, Jed. Do you think anyone would believe *that?*"

"Why wouldn't they?"

"Because I'm Sharlayne Kenyon, silly." She drained her glass. "If someone asks, you're my new boyfriend. Since I'm between close personal friends at the moment, they'll believe that. Can we use your real name?"

"Sure. Why not? But I don't think the boyfriend story will fly."

"It's the only story that *will* fly. With it we can spend every minute together and no one will think anything about it. You see? It's the only way."

"I see you *think* it's the only way. I'm not so sure."

She patted his strong jaw. "Lighten up, Jed. This will be a walk in the park for a man in your line of business. I wouldn't want to think you'll find it *too* difficult to pretend to have…feelings for me."

"I never lighten up on the job," he said. "Your safety is my only concern."

Was that a challenge?

ALICE MADE IT all the way into Sharlayne's master suite and collapsed on the chaise longue before succumbing to a bad case of shakes. "I'm dying!" she gasped. "That's the scariest thing I ever did. I kept waiting for him to stand up and shout, *'Imposter!'*"

Sharlayne and Tabitha regarded her with varying degrees of sympathy: none from Tabitha and very little from Sharlayne.

"Brace up," Sharlayne said. "He bought it, didn't he?"

"Apparently, although he did give me a start or two." Alice pulled herself together sufficiently to stare at her employer.

"My God." She gaped. "Is that a wig?"

Sharlayne touched the nondescript brown head covering and frowned. Her face was free of makeup and she wore sensible shoes and a dress that actually fit like a dress, not a banana peel. "Awful, huh?"

"Not really. In fact, you look a lot like me."

"I guess that's the point." **Sharlayne turned her**

laser gaze on Tabitha. "What do you think? Did she do all right?"

Tabitha's lip curled. "She barely got by. If she'd been trying to fool anyone who actually knew you—"

"That won't happen," Sharlayne cut in impatiently. "Now, both of you listen. Wilbert's waiting for me at the service entrance. If you have any questions, this is the time to speak up."

Alice asked quickly, "Where will you be?"

"That's strictly top secret."

"But what if I have to get in touch with you?" Alice felt a touch of panic at the prospect of being completely stranded and on her own.

"Tabitha will always know where to find me. She'll also handle all the credit cards. Anything you want, up to but not including a mink coat, go to her."

That didn't sit well. Not that Alice had a hankering for a mink coat; she just didn't have a hankering to go begging to Tabitha. "I don't like it," she said unhappily.

Tabitha said with malice aforethought, "Too bad. That's the way we've worked it out."

"Easy." Sharlayne gave her senior assistant a warning glance. "Try to get along, will you? We want Alice to enjoy this experience, after all."

"She's already enjoying it too much." Tabitha's gaze was malevolent. "Flirting with that bodyguard—"

"Great!" Sharlayne looked delighted. "That's exactly what I want her to do—act just like me." She smiled at Alice. "Relax, honey. You did just fine or Tabitha wouldn't be so annoyed."

"This time," Alice conceded. "But when I run into someone who already knows you—and I inevitably will—all the artful makeovers in the world...all the designer clothing and glittering jewels and fabulous surroundings...won't get me through. I have to admit, I figured this could be fun—"

"Not to mention profitable."

"That's true."

"Well, stop worrying about it," Sharlayne said as if her mind had already turned around in another direction. "Do the best you can. Any time you can gain for me will help. I'm going to finish that book if it kills me."

"Okay," Alice said, "but this seems even crazier now that we're into it."

"Alice, listen to me." Sharlayne leaned down to peer into eyes nearly identical to her own. "*People see what they expect to see, not what's actually there.* If they expect to see Sharlayne Kenyon, they will."

"But what if—"

"Alice, you're whimpering." Sharlayne straightened, her manner stern. "Let me remind you what's at stake here—a brilliant tome detailing my brilliant life, and a debt-free future for you. Isn't that worth a little stress and strain?''

"I suppose, but what if I'm found out? What if—''

"Hush and listen to me. You're also getting a chance to live a fantasy most women would kill for. A mansion, a good-looking man at your beck and call, servants, a good-looking man, designer clothes, a good-looking man—''

"Okay, I catch your drift. A good-looking man.'' Alice, who had never in her life been free of money worries or had any male, good-looking or otherwise, at her beck and call, was putty in Sharlayne's hands. But one question still remained. "Why do I even *need* a bodyguard, good-looking or otherwise?''

"You don't,'' Sharlayne said calmly. "Let me explain this one more time. He's just around to keep people away, so they won't get wise to the switch.'' She glanced around the bedroom, clearly impatient. "Now, I really have to get out of here. Last chance for questions.''

Her words reminded Alice of the part of the wedding ceremony where the minister asks if anyone present knows why this couple should not be joined together. This was definitely a now-or-never moment.

She opened her mouth, but no sound emerged.

Sharlayne said, "Good. In that case—ta-ta, ladies. Tabitha, keep me posted. Alice, enjoy yourself.'' With a final conspiratorial wink, she was gone.

Alice turned to Tabitha, who was staring at the door through which her boss had disappeared. ''This is ridiculous,'' she muttered. ''Nobody with a grain of sense or an eye in his head would ever accept you as Sharlayne Kenyon.''

''You better be wrong,'' Alice said, ''because if you're right, we're both up the proverbial creek without a paddle.''

This time, she didn't flinch before Tabitha's glare. She was, after all, Sharlayne Kenyon.

CHAPTER THREE

Nothing ventured, nothing gained; or,
my greatest creation is me

By the time I was twelve years old, I was five foot four and measured 25-22-23. I guess you could say I became something of an overnight sensation in Hog Jaw, Arkansas....

That Book About This Body,
Sharlayne Kenyon

TABITHA JOINED Alice and Jed for dinner at the big hand-carved Spanish table in the formal dining room. This might have thrown a lesser woman into a rage, but Alice was more grateful than anything else. As cute and sexy as this man was, better not to take chances, even in the guise of a wild-and-crazy adventuress.

A maid served the meal: an enormous salad, broiled chicken and assorted veggies. Dessert was an incredibly light lemon mousse. Watching Jed devour the food, she began to wonder if he would starve to death before this job was over.

Meals were planned with Sharlayne in mind: heavy on fruits and veggies, light on meat and carbs. But with Sharlayne out of the picture, Jed could use a little consideration.

At the conclusion of the meal, she leaned forward with a deliberately inviting smile. "Would you care to join me for coffee in the living room?" she asked Jed.

He hesitated, then nodded in his usual brusque manner. "Good idea. I need to report on the results of my security check, anyway."

As if the pleasure of her company wasn't nearly enough.

Tabitha looked spitefully pleased. "I believe I'd like to sit in on this, too, Sharlayne. I'm naturally interested in anything that pertains to your safety."

"Naturally." Alice gestured to the maid, who indicated with a nod that she understood.

In the living room, Alice took a seat on the overstuffed red sofa; Jed chose a chair opposite, while Tabitha hovered near the heavily carved fireplace, her eyes narrowed and watchful.

"Tell us, Mr. Kelby," Tabitha said as the maid poured coffee from a silver pot, "is Sharlayne safe here?"

Jed waited until the coffee had been served and the maid departed before answering. Then he said, "Ms. Kenyon is safe only if there's no threat. There *is* no security system."

Alice gasped. "You're kidding."

"I wish. There's no alarm system, the entry gate doesn't lock, the fence has a number of breaks and none of the windows can be properly secured. There are enough vines and shrubberies around the windows, even on the second floor, that a child could reach them."

Tabitha and Alice eyed each other in confusion. Alice said, "I don't understand."

Jed gave her a long, level look. "Were you told there was a full-fledged security system here when you bought the place?"

"Well, no, but...I just assumed, I guess." Or the real Sharlayne had assumed. Or maybe she knew the truth and didn't consider it important. "This place had stood empty for several years and there were a lot of repairs before we—before I could move in."

Tabitha set her cup on the mantel. "And you were in a hurry and pushed the refurbishment through," she said. She added to Jed, "Would it be very expensive to install what we need?"

"Yes." There was no softening of the word; Jed simply announced his opinion.

Alice felt a cold chill down her spine. "Of course, there's no real threat," she ventured. "Just a media circus to be kept at bay...maybe an occasional groupie. I don't see that this presents a major problem, do you, Tabby?"

"Let me think about it." Tabitha retrieved her cup. "My instinct is that it will be all right for at least a while—perhaps as long as Mr. Kelby is in residence. Speaking of which…'' She was obviously trying for a pleasant expression. ''Which room will Mr. Kelby occupy?''

''I don't know. I hadn't thought that far ahead.''

''I have, and I have a suggestion,'' Tabitha said. ''In light of these new findings, I feel strongly that he should sleep as close to your suite as possible. Perhaps the room across the hall from you?'' She added for Jed's benefit, ''That room is quite pleasant, actually…of reasonable size and not *too* feminine.''

He shrugged. ''Whatever. I agree I should be close, though. The lack of security leaves me concerned if not alarmed.''

''Maybe while you're here, you could prepare a security plan for us,'' Tabitha suggested.

''Good idea.'' He finished his coffee and rose. ''If you'll direct me, I'll pull my stuff inside now.''

''Up the stairs.'' Tabitha pointed. ''Turn left. Your room is the first door on the right.''

''Thank you. Now, if you'll excuse me…''

Alice seethed until he'd had plenty of time to get out of earshot. Then she snarled at Tabitha, ''What the heck are you up to?''

''Me? Not a thing.'' Feline malevolence colored her voice.

''Don't give me that. Why did you suggest that room?''

''Because the man makes you nervous and I like

seeing you nervous,'' Tabitha hissed. ''Installing you in her place is probably the stupidest idea Sharlayne ever had. If I've got to be a party to it, there should be something in it for me, too, even if it's only watching you squirm.''

Alice looked at her with pity. ''Tabitha, that's mean. Even for you, that's mean.''

Tabitha caught her breath, her cheeks flushing. ''How dare you speak to me that way!'' She uttered the words in a hoarse undertone. ''If she heard you, you'd be in a ton of—''

''I'm sorry,'' Jed said from the doorway. ''Am I interrupting anything?'' He stood there with a long canvas bag over his shoulder and a newspaper in his hand.

Had he overheard anything he shouldn't have? A glance at Tabitha revealed that she, too, was concerned about that possibility. His expression was closed and unreadable and giving nothing away.

''You're not interrupting a thing,'' Alice said with false carelessness. ''What can I do for you, Jed?''

''You can explain this item in the newspaper.'' He shook out a copy of the *U.S. Eye,* already turned to the page he wanted, and read: '''We hear that the scrumptious Sharlayne Kenyon is holed up in her new Beverly Hills digs with a bad case of laryngitis. Fortunately for her, she's also holed up with a new main squeeze, a mystery man with the physique of a...''' Here Jed's voice dripped with scorn.

"'Of a'…well, let that go. Either of you care to explain this item?''

Alice turned to Tabitha, incapable of making any plausible explanation. Fortunately, Tabitha was equal to the task.

"That's what we call a planted item,'' she said calmly. "We want to keep people away from Sharlayne. That will help us do it. If she's sick and being attended by a new boyfriend, no one will expect to see her out and about. This sort of thing is done all the time.''

Jed's taut expression didn't relax. "Lying's a way of life, huh? Do me a favor and leave me out of any future flights of fancy.'' He pivoted, disgust in every line of his body, and stalked out of the room.

ALICE DIDN'T SEE Jed again that night before retiring to her suite. Restless, she prowled through the beautiful rooms, turning the television on and off a half-dozen times. For a while, she sat on her balcony, which overlooked the glistening swimming pool below, and wondered why she felt as edgy as a criminal anticipating the long arm of the law.

Finally, she decided that what she needed was a snack. In Sharlayne's small refrigerator behind the wet bar, she found soda, bottled water, three candy bars—bad Sharlayne!—and a small bunch of shriveled green grapes.

She threw the grapes and the candy bars away. What she wanted was...

Yogurt, she decided. Surely there must be some in the kitchen.

If she could find the kitchen.

It took a while, since she really didn't know the huge house all that well. At last she recognized the hall that led to the "working" areas: kitchen, laundry room, pantries and so forth. Poised with her hand on what she felt confident was the kitchen door, she realized belatedly that there was light spilling underneath. Pushing open the door, she stopped short.

And stared.

Jed stood in front of the huge industrial refrigerator, his back to her. His bare back: he wore nothing but a pair of jeans. No shoes, no shirt, no kiddin'. The sleek lines of his well-muscled back caused her eyes to widen even more.

At her soft gasp, he turned to face her.

She said, "Oh, it's you. You scared me."

"Sorry." He closed the refrigerator door without taking anything out. "If you'll excuse me, I'll get back to my room."

"Didn't you come here looking for something to eat? Don't leave until you've found what you want." She moved farther into the room.

He said, "Bad idea."

"No, really, it's all right. I'm looking for a carton

of yogurt myself.'' She brushed past him to open the refrigerator.

"It's not all right," he said. "I'll go."

"I say it's all right and I'm in charge here." She darted him an annoyed glance but couldn't help adding, "Why isn't it all right?"

"Because you're nearly naked, Ms. Kenyon. I'm here to protect your person and your reputation, not compromise either. Or both."

Caught flatfooted, she glanced down at herself.

She was wearing a diaphanous shorty nightgown and matching negligee, if you could call it that, since it left nearly nothing to the imagination. She'd put it on hours ago because it was the most modest thing in the drawer.

But even as mortification heated her cheeks, she reminded herself that Alice Wynn had no reason to be embarrassed by anything Sharlayne Kenyon might do. Watching him over her shoulder, she said, "Don't be a prude, Jed—and don't call me Ms. Kenyon. My n-name is Sharlayne."

He didn't appear to notice her stutter. "I know your name, Ms. Kenyon." He cocked his head and gazed at her, fists planted on his hips just above the low-slung waist band of his jeans. "It occurs to me that this is as good a time as any to get a couple of things straight."

"Do tell?" she purred.

"There's a rule at my agency, which I intend to honor."

"Rules are often made to be broken." By Sharlayne, not by Alice, who always followed the rules. Maybe it was time to change that.

"Not this one. It goes, *Thou shalt not get involved with thy client.* You're my client. That's it. You can't be my friend or my…anything of a personal nature. It's not that I want to seem unfriendly, but…" He was stumbling around, not nearly as decisive as he'd been earlier.

"That's ridiculous." Alice laughed lightly. "We can't live across the hall from each other day after day and not be…something." She put all kinds of subtext in that last word.

He was squirming, really uncomfortable with the turn the conversation had taken. "Yeah," he insisted doggedly, "we can. We will. Now, if you'll excuse me—"

"I won't." She couldn't believe she'd said that, and with Sharlayne's familiar petulance. She softened her refusal with a smile. "We're both hungry. Stay and have a snack with me."

"I'm sorry, I—"

"Look, here's the chicken we had for dinner tonight. Have a sandwich."

"I don't think that's a good—"

"Jed," she teased, "you're supposed to be guarding me. You can't spend the next month running out of the room every time I walk into it. Am I that scary?"

His face was stone. "You think you scare me?"

She shrugged, the negligee sliding artfully off one shoulder. "Something's scaring you. I'm the only other person in the room."

"Give me that chicken." He took it from her hands. "You've totally misunderstood my position—deliberately, maybe. Whatever. If you want to run around half-naked, that's your business. I'm just here to do a job."

"I see." She looked around, located a bread box and pulled out a home baked loaf. "You really are a prude, Jed. I'm covered. Hey, in the old days Greta Garbo used to wander through her garden totally nude."

He paused, a carving knife poised over the chicken. "Great who?"

She laughed incredulously. "Not a big movie fan, I see."

"Only of gratuitous violence and car chases." He sliced easily and precisely through the tender chicken. "Like some of this?"

"I shouldn't." But she did. Suddenly, the thought of yogurt was not very appealing.

"Suit yourself."

How annoying. He could at least try to convince her. She slammed the refrigerator closed. "I find my appetite's suddenly gone," she announced. "I'm off to bed. See you tomorrow, Jed."

He mumbled something around the sandwich.

"We work out at nine."

"Work out?"

"Shar—I've got a minigym and I expect you to work out with me. Whatever else happens, I don't want it said that anyone in my employ went to pot while doing it."

Like there was a chance of him doing that. With a last, lingering look at his beautifully muscled chest, she headed back upstairs, wondering who had gotten the best of that exchange.

JED CHEWED methodically on a chunk of chicken and watched the bewitching Ms. Kenyon sweep through the doorway in her sexy nightwear. Talk about a handful! Any man who'd get mixed up with her would have to have a death wish.

Regardless of that, she apparently found plenty of takers. Frowning, he slapped more chicken on a thick piece of bread, slathered on the mustard, topped that with cheese and another slice of bread and sat down on a stool to eat it.

She was both the same as and different from what he'd expected.

He'd expected beautiful and she was, but he'd never expected her to look so young. Even allowing for retouched photographs, she still appeared at least ten years younger in person. Maybe she'd had a face-lift, he thought; maybe she'd found the fountain of youth.

He'd expected her to be charming and she was that, too, but he hadn't expected the vulnerability he sensed beneath the surface. One minute she seemed supremely confident and the next almost…bewildered by the situation in which she found herself.

He'd expected her to be flirtatious, but not with him. He was the hired help, after all. Didn't she realize that if he was distracted by her attractions, he wouldn't be able to keep his mind on business? Maybe she was the kind of woman who had to flirt with every man she met.

Which wasn't the kind of woman who'd interest him under any circumstances.

Famished, he finished the second sandwich in a few bites. Rabbit food didn't do it for him. He could starve on what he'd had for dinner.

On her, however, it looked good. She was both slender and curvy, strong and supple and sexy— *real* sexy. Obviously, she worked at it, and she expected him to work, too.

Okay, he would. He'd jog with her, swim with her, play tennis with her, eat crummy little meals with her, fetch and carry and do whatever she wanted him to do with her…except embark on any kind of personal relationship. Samantha Spade was watching. He didn't intend to screw up this assignment.

Let Ms. Kenyon give him her best shot. He was ready.

Or would be, as soon as he took a cold shower.

ALICE QUICKLY REALIZED that this was a wonderful life indeed.

Every morning for the next several days, a maid delivered coffee and orange juice and whole wheat toast on a tray. At nine she met Jed at the gym for a hard, fast workout, the same one she'd devised for Sharlayne. Lunch on the terrace usually included Tabitha, unfortunately, but was otherwise enjoyable. In the afternoon, Alice swam, and when she swam Jed swam. He looked even better in a swimsuit than he did in the gym in shorts and T-shirt.

Intermixed with this in coming weeks would be appointments. But instead of her going out, everyone would come to her: masseuse, hairdresser, nail technician—name it and someone would be there in a flash to polish or paint.

This was easy! She could do this.

Sharlayne, Alice decided, was little more than a canvas upon which professionals worked their magic. The basic canvas was good, but what those magicians achieved was true art.

This existence was pure luxury, but nearing the end of the first week, Alice was already wondering if life in a gilded case was life at all.

Rolling over on a canvas lounge next to the pool, she opened one eye. Jed sat on a nearby chair, writing on a clipboard balanced on one bare golden thigh. In repose, his face reminded her of a statue of a Greek god. In repose was the only way she'd seen it since their kitchen encounter.

"What are you doing?" she asked.

Without looking up, he said, "Working on the specifications for a new security system."

"Oh." Bor-ring. "Would you mind rubbing a little more sunscreen on my shoulders? I feel like I'm burning."

He didn't move. "You could get out of the sun."

"Too much trouble." She wiggled deeper into her lounge. "Please? Pretty please with sugar on it?"

"Yeah, sure, whatever you say."

He rose, towering over her, and she closed her eyes. "The sunscreen's right there."

"I see it." A moment's silence and then his hands settled over the curve of her shoulders.

She groaned. "That feels great," she murmured, reveling in the firm manipulations of his hands on her bare skin. "Ummm...don't miss anything. I don't want to get burned."

"Seems unlikely." He withdrew his touch and her eyes snapped open. "If anyone gets burned," he muttered, "it'll be me." He squeezed a glob of sunscreen onto his hand and slapped it on his upper body.

Then he grinned.

She was certain she'd never seen a smile on his face before. Surely she'd remember it, for it carried more sheer star power than she was ready to handle. Lips parted, she watched him turn back to the clipboard.

"If you'll excuse me," he said, "I need to make

a few calls to fill in the blanks on this.'' He waved the clipboard. ''If you need me, just sing out. Otherwise, I'll see you at dinner.''

He moved outside her field of vision with the stride of a lion. He looked so good, so self-contained and in control, that it made her short of breath. Pushing up, she scooted around to plant her feet securely on the redwood deck.

Light reflected off the glittering emerald pool nearly blinded her. Letting her head fall back, she closed her eyes. She was playing with dynamite and she knew it.

Sure, it was fun to flirt with such an attractive and uptight specimen of male pulchritude, especially knowing that whatever she did would be on Sharlayne's head and not her own…so to speak. It kind of freed up the old libido.

But in another way, it made her even more anxious than she'd normally be when confronted with such temptation. Most men she'd met had recognized her lack of sophistication and treated her gently—not that there'd been all that many. Jed wouldn't, because he thought she was Sharlayne and Sharlayne had so much experience with men that she made Cleopatra look like an amateur.

What the hell. Nothing would happen here anyway. There wasn't time for anything to happen. Sharlayne would come back and Jed would leave without ever knowing the difference.

Just then, Tabitha walked through the arched entryway to the pool area, brushing aside the trailing vines that covered it. Alice cringed inwardly as the woman walked quickly toward her.

"I thought I'd find you here."

"And you did."

"Be careful you don't get too tanned. Sharlayne never lies in the sun. It's aging."

"I'm using sunblock," Alice gestured.

"Sunblock has been known to fail."

"Tabitha, are you here to annoy me or do you have something to say?"

"You just got another call from Gina at the *Eye*. I thought you'd want to know."

"Was it a simple hello or did she have something more in mind?"

"She wants to talk about the book. I told her there was no book. She still wants to talk to Shar— to you."

"But I have laryngitis." Alice coughed delicately into her hand.

"She also wants to know the name of your new boyfriend. I denied you had a new boyfriend. She said she'd call back."

"Great. Let her call. I think my throat is getting worse."

"As you say." Tabitha turned away.

"Before you go—"

"Yes?"

"You've spoken to—" Alice hesitated, then said, "*Her*, I take it. How's everything going?"

"She reports progress."

"I don't suppose you'd like to tell me where she is?"

Tabitha laughed.

"Not knowing really makes me anxious."

"You can send messages through me."

"Fine, but did either of you ever consider what a bind I'd be in if anything happened to you?"

Tabitha looked incredulous. "Nothing ever happens to me. I've worked for *her* for ten years and never even had a cold. I sprained my ankle once but didn't miss any work because of it."

Defeated, Alice said, "Ask her to think about it, okay? I'd feel much better."

Tabitha's expression said that how Alice felt was not much of a consideration.

SITTING ON THE TERRACE, Jed watched the exchange between Tabitha and Sharlayne with only mild interest. He couldn't hear what they were saying but the old bat was probably getting the best of it.

Like that first night when he'd charged into the living room, waving the newspaper. *"How dare you speak to me that way?"* he'd heard the assistant say to the celebrity in withering tones. What was up with that? Who was in charge?

Not that he himself would enjoy locking horns with the formidable Ms. Thomas. She could quell with a glance; she could flay with a word. Why the hell did Sharlayne put up with her insolence?

Sharlayne's behavior perplexed him in other ways, too. Why did she come on to him one minute and ignore him the next? After the little encounter in the kitchen, he'd dreaded going to the workout session the following morning. Yet when he had, he'd found a woman minus glamour exercising with a vengeance he wouldn't have believed if he hadn't seen it himself. That woman was willing to sweat for what she had, which was plenty.

Putting aside the clipboard, he picked up the remote phone on the wrought-iron table before him. Quickly he dialed the agency and asked for the boss lady.

It took her a good five minutes to come on the line.

"What's up, sweetheart?"

"Just checking in. Not much going on here."

"Oh, yeah?" Her sneer crossed over the wires clearly. "That's not what I read in the papers."

The hair on his nape prickled. "Care to tell me what you're talking about?"

"Oh, just all the items in the newspaper about Sharlayne and her new boy toy. That's you, babe—the boy toy."

"Very funny." He tried to control his annoyance.

"I'm glad one of us is laughing." And it wasn't her. "How's her laryngitis?"

"She doesn't have laryngitis. She just put out that story in an attempt to avoid the press."

"She should know by now that if you won't talk to them, they'll just make stuff up."

"Apparently. Now about this security survey—"

"You got that finished?"

"Just about. I thought I should pass it on to Jared for final approval and then we can get a few quotes. It's not gonna be cheap, though."

"Yeah, send it along. Jared will get bids for you. I have the feeling you've got your hands full as it is."

"What's that supposed to mean?"

"Touchy! I figured by now she'd have you jumping through hoops."

"Nobody has me jumping through hoops." He added, in the interests of honesty, "Except maybe you."

"Good recovery," she purred. "Just remember that. And this—*Thou shalt not get involved with thy client.*"

"I'll remember," he said. Jeez, maybe he should tattoo it on the back of his hand.

CHAPTER FOUR

Who does she think she is?

She's not accepting calls; she's not venturing
through her front gate; official word is she has
laryngitis, but I'm not buying it. If a delivery-
man hadn't confirmed her existence, I'd think
Sharlayne Kenyon had dropped off the face
of the earth....

Gina Godfrey, *U.S. Eye*

IT DIDN'T TAKE LONG for Alice to realize this wasn't
the life for her.

Dressing up in somebody else's clothes and jewelry, wearing makeup that completely hid her own
identity, flirting with a drop-dead gorgeous man
with impunity—all were heady experiences.

But by the second week, the walls were closing
in on her—the walls past which she had not ventured since her arrival with the real Sharlayne ten
days earlier. Despite the fact that she'd followed her
boss all over the country for the past two years,
Alice had never realized how truly confining fame
could be. It seemed as if the more Tabitha fielded

telephone calls and refused to let anyone speak to "Sharlayne," the more reporters, fans and friends demanded that very thing.

None of this appeared to bother Jed, who remained calm, cool and collected. The less he responded to the furor around him, the more Alice kicked up her campaign to breach his professional indifference.

At least a little…

On this particular night, she felt ready to jump out of her skin. She'd gone all out on her appearance, mostly spurred by boredom and too much time on her hands. She came down to dinner wearing a skintight champagne silk sheath and nothing more. Actually, "more" wouldn't have been possible because the dress wasn't constructed to accommodate it. Sharlayne would never have approved of a visible panty line on her proxy.

Abrupt with both Jed and Tabitha, Alice barely touched her food and excused herself at the earliest possible moment. On the terrace, she leaned against the heavy balustrade and took several deep breaths.

She wasn't cut out for this kind of life. If she'd ever thought she might be, this settled that question for all time. All the goodies simply couldn't make up for the loss of personal freedom. Maybe it worked for Sharlayne, but—

"What's wrong?"

Jed's voice just behind her sent a shiver down

her spine. "Nothing." She turned to face him, resting against her hands. "Everything."

"Island fever," he said.

"What's that?"

"A feeling of confinement so bad you think you'll jump out of your skin."

"That's it, all right."

"I've also heard it called cabin fever."

"Same thing, huh?"

He nodded. There was a growing intimacy about this conversation, inane though the talk might be. He seemed to be responding to her nervous tension by loosening up himself.

He touched her forearm lightly. "You're trembling."

She froze; no trembling now. Her gaze locked with his. She said, "I'm cold?"

"Not cold." He let his hand drop. Turning aside, he braced his hands on the balustrade exactly as she had done minutes earlier. He stared out over a landscape of manicured trees and gardens highlighted by dozens of twinkling lights.

"There's something I've been meaning to tell you," he said.

Her heart gave a little leap, then settled into a steady drumming. "What?"

"I sent my security analysis back to headquarters so our duty expert could check it over. He's given the go-ahead so we can start looking for bids as soon as—"

With an exclamation of disgust, she turned away. "That's what you wanted to tell me—that you're doing your job?"

"Well, yes." He sounded surprised by her attitude but not offended.

"I don't care about that," she said petulantly, just the way the real Sharlayne would have done. She glanced around restlessly. "Maybe I'll go swim laps or something."

"Sure, why not. Or you could just call the whole thing off."

She gazed at him with suspicion and dread. Could he have figured her deception out? She could barely bring herself to ask, "What whole thing?"

"All this." He spread an arm in a wide arc. "Maybe the medicine is worse than the disease, the disease being public attention and the cure being you cooped up in here like a criminal. I thought this was supposed to be rest and relaxation for you, but it doesn't seem to be working out that way."

"That's for sure. If it were up to me—" She cut off the stream of words abruptly. She couldn't go *there*.

"Don't tell me this is all the Dragon Lady's idea."

Tabitha, the Dragon Lady. Alice put a hand over her mouth and giggled.

"Well, is it?"

"Honestly...no. None of this is Tabitha's doing. It's all mine." *Because it was my decision to go along with Sharlayne's goofy inspiration.* "I can't blame anyone else."

He was silent for a moment. Then he said, "Finding someone who accepts responsibility for her own decisions and actions is rare these days."

She shrugged, her arm brushing his and sending a jolt of awareness through her. "*You* do, don't you?"

"I try to." He moved slightly toward her.

"Then why shouldn't I?" She moved slightly toward him.

In the shadowy half light spilling from windows, he looked questioning, almost hopeful. It was as if he were seeing something new in her, something he had never expected to find.

As she was seeing something different in him. His expression was softer, more seeking, than he'd ever allowed her to see. She swayed toward him, her attention caught by the beautiful shape of his mouth—

"Ahemmm."

Tabitha, clearing her throat. Alice leaped back; so did Jed, just as guiltily.

"Sharlayne, you have a call I think you'll want to take," Tabitha said.

"Who—" Alice shook off her confusion. He'd been ready to kiss her. He would have kissed her if Tabitha hadn't butted in. "All right," she said, her voice more controlled. She slanted a glance at

Jed. "Perhaps later we can pick up where we left off."

His laughter was soft and cynical, the old Jed again. "That's more like it," he said. "For a minute I thought you were about to go soft and..."

She waited expectantly, but he just shrugged and turned away. When he'd reentered the house, she faced Tabitha.

"This had better be good."

"It is," Tabitha said. "*She's* on the line."

That was enough. Alice couldn't wait to get at that phone. Snatching it up, she said indignantly, "High time!"

"And a pleasant evening to you, too."

"Where are you?"

"That's for me to know and you to find out. How goes the masquerade?"

"So far so good, except I've got island fever."

"You're not planning to go AWOL, I hope."

"No." The word came with reluctance. "When I make a deal, I stick to it if it kills me."

"Good." Relief colored Sharlayne's tone. "You'll be pleased to know the book's progressing. Tabitha tells me you're doing great, too, and—"

"The hell she did! I'll bet Tabitha said I was a walking disaster."

"Ohhh! Do you know her or what!" Light laughter. "It's my interpretation that you're doing great, based on the fact that the only solid evidence to the contrary is her contention that you're trying to hit on your bodyguard. After seeing him even from afar, I didn't find that hard to believe."

"You don't care? Not that it's true—it isn't. But if it were...he'd believe he was flirting with the famous—" She glanced around, suddenly cautious, but saw no one. Even so, she amended her thought to, "The famous you. Wouldn't that annoy you, at the very least?"

For a moment, there was silence. Then Sharlayne said in a serious tone, "I actually can't answer that. To have some guy I don't know running about convinced he'd slept with me..." Her voice trailed off on a doubtful note. "It's kind of spooky to think about."

"Don't worry, I won't do it," Alice said. "I never intended to."

"Hey, I'm not taking responsibility for any decisions you may make, kiddo. You want him, go get him." The words were uttered cheerfully. "I might make a run at him myself when I get back." Sharlayne laughed lightly, then added, "I feel better having talked to you, Alice. Keep up the good work. Tabitha's there if you need to contact me."

"Don't go! I really have to—"

The line went dead and Alice didn't know any more than she had before, plus she'd lost out on what would undoubtedly have been the kiss of all time.

Sometimes, such as now, life sucked.

AT BREAKFAST the next day, Jed acted as if nothing had happened. Which was true; only, something would have if Tabitha had used a bit of discretion. Alice tried to convince herself that it was for the best but didn't get very far.

She did get considerably further arguing herself into a calmer state of mind. Since she was committed to the project, she might as well relax and enjoy her silken prison. Most women *would* kill to be in her shoes and—

A shriek raised goose bumps on her arms and she sat bolt upright on the lounge beside the empty blue pool. Someone was in a lot of trouble. Where had that cry come from?

Across the pool, she saw Jed sprinting toward her, his long lean legs carrying him forward with power and grace. He looked great in khaki cargo shorts and a white knit shirt. Even from here, she could see the determination on his face.

The cook appeared around the screen of shrubbery shielding the back of the house from view. "Ms. Kenyon, please— We've got to call the ambulance!"

"What's happened?"

"It's Marie! She—" The rest was lost when the cook turned back toward the house.

Naturally, Alice started after her.

"Wait!" Jed roared. "Don't move, Sharlayne!"

"I've got to help." Ignoring him, she sprinted after the cook, nearly running over a curious gardener in the process. What did Jed think she was, anyway? Whatever had happened in the house, she had to help if she could.

JED BURST THROUGH the kitchen door and stopped short. What he saw astonished him so much that his jaw dropped.

Blood everywhere: on the floor, on the island chopping block. Blood on the towel Sharlayne pressed to the head of one of the kitchen helpers. The young woman sat on a stool, her expression blank and her face pale despite olive skin. She looked to be in shock. The cook hovered in the background, her expression agonized.

Sharlayne glanced over her shoulder and saw him. "Call the paramedics," she ordered, her voice crisp and her manner calm. "Hilda, find a sweater or a jacket or something to put around her shoulders—a towel, even. Maria, you hanging in all right, hon?"

The injured woman nodded. "It was stupid," she said in a faint voice. "Hilda told me not to use that stool, but I—"

"Shh. It'll be all right. Jed?"

"Yeah, I got you." He turned to the wall phone next to the door and punched in 911. "What happened?" he asked.

"She fell backward off the step stool and gashed her head on the ceramic tile. I've pretty much got the bleeding stopped, but she's going to need stitches.''

Jed relayed this information to the dispatcher, then hung up the phone. He couldn't believe what he was seeing. He would have expected Sharlayne to faint at the sight of so much blood. He was even surprised that she'd responded to the emergency by plunging right into the middle of it, let alone that she was competent to handle it.

Watching her, he realized she was considerably more than competent. By the time the paramedics arrived and led off the clumsy kitchen aid, she'd impressed him in a way he'd never expected to be impressed by this woman. She was, after all, a play-girl; Samantha had called her an adventuress. Of course, Samantha had said that with a certain amount of admiration, which Jed didn't share.

He'd never felt the slightest bit of interest in so-phisticated women with their own agendas. Not that he'd ever met any; he hadn't. Sharlayne was his first.

With luck, she'd be his last.

She stood on the front porch in a short, brightly colored cover-up she'd yanked over her bikini swimsuit, waving goodbye to the maid being loaded into the back of the emergency vehicle. ''Don't worry about a thing,'' she called, hands cupped around her mouth. ''You'll be fine.'' She turned back to the house and missed a step, apparently surprised to find Jed standing there with his arms folded over his chest.

"You startled me," she said defensively.

"Sorry. You startled me, too." He stepped aside to let her enter, noting the smear of blood on her bare arm.

"How so?" She gave him a questioning glance as she passed.

"I'd have expected you to faint at the sight of blood, not move into action like an emergency room doctor."

She laughed, her clear eyes sparkling. "You don't have a very high opinion of me, do you?"

"It's not my place to have any opinion of you at all. I'm here to guard you, not to judge you."

"Thanks for reminding me. Now, if you'll excuse me, I need to wash—"

Her last word ended on a squawk, for he caught her forearm and swung her around to face him. "I won't excuse you," he said. "Don't ever do that again."

Those incredible eyes were wide and appealing. "What are you talking about? Do what?"

"Run toward danger when I'm yelling at you not to."

"I didn't run toward danger. Someone was hurt. I couldn't ignore that."

"You didn't know what had happened. It could have been a ruse to get you to act in a particular way. You could have been kidnapped or hurt by ignoring my instructions.''

''Oh, for heaven's sake.'' Scornfully she shoved his hand aside. ''I'm not in any danger. I told you that. Your job is just to see I'm not disturbed.''

''My job is to *take care of you.*'' He thundered the last words. ''Let me do it or I'm out of here.''

''Why—why—'' She sputtered to a halt and drew an exasperated breath. ''Oh, all right,'' she relented crossly. ''I'm sorry, but I can't just stand by and let someone suffer if I can do something to help.''

''You can let me handle it,'' he said grimly. ''The next time—''

''I'm sure there won't be a next time,'' she interrupted. ''Okay, I've been properly chastised. Is it all right with you if I get cleaned up now?''

''Yeah, you run along. I'll just—'' He stared across the manicured lawn beyond the driveway. One of the gardeners was hurrying toward the big wrought-iron gate leading to the street.

There was something pretty damned fishy about the way he kept glancing over his shoulder.

''That gardener,'' he said. ''What do you know about him?''

She peered at the man. ''Nothing. I just moved in. Everyone working here is new.'' She stepped up beside Jed. ''What's the matter?''

''Probably nothing. Wait here.'' Leaping down

the steps to the driveway, he hailed the man. "Hey, you! Wait up! I need to talk to you."

Instead of stopping, the man broke into a run. Jed sprinted after him, hoping Sharlayne had the good sense to obey orders this time.

ALICE WAS GOING to stand meekly in the doorway while Jed ran down one of her employees? Not very likely! She took off down the white-gravel driveway.

Quickly realizing this was not a good idea for a barefoot woman, she veered onto the lawn, plunging through the flowers and shrubbery. Even so, by the time she reached the gate Jed had the gardener flat on his back and was rummaging through his pockets.

"You can't do that!" she exclaimed, halting beside the two men. "I'm sure that's against the law."

"What is?" Jed batted aside the man's hands and reached for the small backpack on the ground beside them.

"Well, *that* is." She pointed. "Going through his stuff. People have rights, you know." To the gardener, she added, "I'm really sorry about this. Mr. Kelby is overzealous sometimes."

"Yeah," Jed said, "apologize. After you do, check this out." He held up a single roll of film.

She took a step back. "What—?"

"Photos of you, if I'm not mistaken, doing your

Florence Nightingale thing." He turned on the hapless man beneath him. "Am I right?"

"I don't have to say nothin'," the man blustered. "I got my rights."

Alice herself wanted to hit him. "Did you take pictures of me? Did you? Because if you did—"

"You'll what?" The man sneered, despite his vulnerable position. "You're public property, lady. I go where the money is."

"But you're on my payroll," she wailed. "How could you do this to me?"

"I don't owe you nothin'." The man glared at Jed. "Okay, you got what you wanted. Can I go now?"

"Please, Jed." Alice appealed to his better nature. "Now that we have the film…"

"That would be letting him off too easy. Why don't you press charges?"

She shuddered. That would be just great. Sharlayne would love that kind of publicity. "No, thanks. I'm satisfied."

"In that case—" Jed stood, then hauled the man up by the scruff of the neck. "Get out of here and don't ever come back. Tell your buddies not to waste their time, either, because the next guy we catch on Ms. Kenyon's property will regret it considerably more than you do."

"You made your point." The man scooped up his backpack. With a last surly glance, he trudged toward the gate. The gateman, who'd watched the entire thing without the least interest of getting involved, let him pass.

At which point Alice turned to Jed and said a deeply relieved, "Thank you."

He advanced on her, his expression grim. "Don't thank me. Tell me why you seem unconstitutionally able to obey a direct order."

She backed away. "I couldn't help it. You looked so fierce that I was afraid you'd hurt someone."

"Professional demeanor. Underneath, I'm a pussycat."

That made her smile. "Really, Jed, I—"

"No, let me talk. I don't give you orders because I enjoy it. Instant obedience could be the difference between life and death."

"Isn't that a bit melodramatic?" she scoffed. "Life and death don't enter into it."

"I don't know that and neither do you. What I do know is that I can't properly protect you without your cooperation."

Smiling, she took his arm, pressing her body against it. "Oh, Jed, don't worry about this anymore. It was just a—a silly chain of events. I'll do everything you say in the future, I promise."

His expression said he didn't much trust her promises, but he'd have to settle for what he could get. For the present, anyway.

JED WAITED UNTIL coffee and dessert after dinner to pull the packet of photographs out of his pocket and offer them to Sharlayne, seated next to him at a sedate distance on the red sofa. He'd already seen the pictures, of course: her, covered with blood. Now he was curious to see her reaction.

She didn't disappoint him. First came shock, then disgust and, finally, relief. "At least he didn't get away with it," she said, tossing the pack contemptuously on the coffee table. "I don't know why people do things like this to each other."

"Paparazzi aren't people." Tabitha rose from her chair and walked to the table, where she picked up the photos. "Oh, Sharlayne," she said, "these are terribly unflattering. You look all hot and sweaty and your hair's a mess." She perused the pictures one at a time, tossing each back on the table.

"Thanks for your support," Sharlayne said with a grimace.

"The point is," Jed reminded them, "we don't have to worry about this batch. But I have to wonder…"

Sharlayne turned suddenly stricken eyes in his direction. "What?"

"We didn't find a camera," he reminded her. "What if we didn't get everything?"

She saw the significance of this instantly. "And I made you let him go," she groaned.

"That you did."

Tabitha's eyes narrowed. "Are you saying you

think something may yet show up in some scandal sheet, Jed?"

"I'd say it's a distinct possibility."

Tabitha shot a withering glance at her boss. "Good work, Sharlayne, insisting he let the perpetrator off." She pivoted. "Well, there's nothing I can do about that, so if you'll excuse me, I have a few telephone calls to make."

Jed wasn't sorry to see her go. The woman always left him uneasy. Apparently, Sharlayne felt the same way, for she seemed to relax once Tabitha was out of sight.

She faced him with a melting gaze. "I'm sorry I've made your job harder," she said. "You must hate me."

"Naw," he said, "I don't hate anyone except liars like that so-called gardener. He lied to get the job so he could sneak around and get pictures of you." His frustration showed when he said, "We should have called the cops."

"But it seemed like such a small transgression at the time," she argued, frowning. "And I suppose he had his reasons. Maybe—maybe he was desperate. This might even have been his first offense."

"So? Everybody has a first time, even criminals. How do you think criminals get started, anyway? They begin with little lies that grow into cheating and stealing and sometimes even murder."

She laughed, her full mouth curving up in an enticing line. "Now who's getting melodramatic?

This is an annoying incident, nothing more. Why don't we just hope for the best. We don't know there was more film. Maybe you got everything.''

''Anything's possible, but I doubt it.''

''It's your job to be suspicious, I suppose. You're very good at what you do, Jed. No doubt you've handled a lot of cases where the stakes were much higher—life and death, even. This is something much simpler. I must say, I still take great comfort in your professionalism.''

He didn't squirm, although he wanted to. He'd never been involved with murder or anything else, since he'd been in the protection business for about fifteen minutes. Speaking of liars, he was no slouch in that department himself. ''Actually…'' he began.

She held up a graceful hand. ''No, really. I'm in your debt, Jed. I'll try not to cause you any more grief. I'm just grateful you were here when I needed you.''

He might not be an experienced bodyguard, but he sure knew when a woman was coming on to him, and this one was. This beautiful and famous woman had made up her mind about him, and what she believed was 180 degrees off.

She wasn't in his debt; he was being paid to take care of her, and if what he suspected was true about the existence of more photos, doing a damn sorry job of it. Better he should speak up before she got any more carried away.

''Sharlayne—Ms. Kenyon, I—''

"You called me Sharlayne." Her smile was at once coaxing and teasing. "That's only the second time. Apparently, it takes moments of great stress to make you human."

"It was a slip of the tongue," he insisted, beginning to sweat. "Ms. Kenyon, you should know that I'm not all that you—"

"Shh." She touched one pink-tipped nail to her pursed lips. "Don't say any more." She leaned forward on the red brocade sofa. "Let's just enjoy the moment, shall we?"

And she touched her lips lightly to his.

STANDING JUST OUTSIDE the double doors she'd deliberately left ajar, Tabitha heard the sudden silence and knew before she peeked through the crack to see what was going on. Of all the nerve! That—that *imposter* was using her false identity to trap the unwary Mr. Kelby.

Unfortunately, Jed was no match for the little tramp. He crushed Alice in his arms, powerless to ignore her enticing charms.

Tabitha had seen enough. Turning, she stalked to her office, where she dialed Sharlayne's number in Arizona. Not once did she question her outrage or consider her beloved employer's track record. Sharlayne was a goddess; Alice was a plebian. There was no requirement that Sharlayne abide by the rules that governed the daily life of ordinary mortals, but every outraged fiber of Tabitha's being insisted that Alice, the most ordinary of women, should lead the same constricted life that Tabitha herself lived.

Sharlayne picked up and Tabitha launched into a impassioned account of the day's happenings, sparing Alice nothing.

CHAPTER FIVE

Fortune favors the bold;
or, how I learned early on
to go after what I want.

When I was fourteen, I fell in love. He was
the richest boy in town. He had the most
beautiful big blue eyes and an equally beautiful big white Cadillac convertible. He used
to grope me out behind the high school football stadium and then one night...

That Book About This Body,
Sharlayne Kenyon

"I'M NOT GOING to grope or be groped on the sofa
in your own living room so forget it."

Alice opened hazy eyes and gazed into Jed's indignant face. "Wh-what?"

He said, "Hands off," and looked pointedly
down at *her* hand curved inside the waistband of
his jeans.

"Oh. Sorry about that." But she wasn't. She was
elated that she'd taken such a liberty. Pure puckish-

ness made her add, "That was a very nice kiss, by the way."

"Oh, yeah. That." He tugged at the collar of an unbuttoned Henley shirt as if it were strangling him. "Big mistake."

"Why is that?" This aggressor role was suiting her to a tee. Was this the way Sharlayne operated?

Fat chance. Sharlayne had to fight the men off with a stick.

Jed licked his lips. "We have a rule in our agency—"

"The one you shared with me?"

He nodded. "*'Thou shalt not get involved with thy client,'*" he declared in stentorian tones.

She pouted. "That's not very friendly."

"But a helluva lot safer." He rose abruptly. "So don't do that again."

She assumed an innocent air. "Do what?"

"Make moves on me."

"They're unwelcome, I suppose?"

That stopped him; he frowned, considering. "No," he said finally. "That's just the problem."

"I guess you've never gotten involved with a client before," she suggested, tongue firmly in cheek, because not for a moment did she believe a guy this good-looking could avoid that particular trap.

"That's right." He eyed her levelly. "I never have and I never intend to." He touched the fingers of his left hand to his forehead in a casual salute.

"If you'll excuse me, I think I'll take a walk around the grounds. I'm a little antsy tonight."

"So am I. I'll go with you."

"You will *not* go with me." He fixed her with a fierce frown. "I'll see you at breakfast tomorrow."

"All right."

She sat there demurely until he'd gone, then collapsed back with a sigh. She couldn't believe she'd thrown herself at him. She *could* believe his response, which had been wholehearted; after all, he thought he was being attacked by one of the most famous femme fatales in the world.

When he'd pulled back, had it been because of his agency's stupid rules or because he didn't find Alice all that irresistible? *Maybe I'm not a very good kisser,* she worried. *Something new to drive me crazy....*

THEY ATE STRAWBERRIES and cream on the terrace the next morning, careful to avoid meeting each other's eyes. That would have been a tacit acknowledgment of what had transpired the previous evening, Jed supposed. She seemed much less sure of herself than she had been then, but that might be part of her act.

Because that's what he'd decided it was. The sweet naiveté of her kiss, the awkward fumbling of her hands, her bravado when he'd called her on it—all were carefully calculated to keep him off bal-

ance. It must be a game with her, he'd decided in
the wee hours of the morning. Well, he wasn't playing.

Looking at her across the table now, he felt himself already weakening, and he didn't like it. True,
Sharlayne Kenyon was the most extraordinary
woman he'd ever met. She was beautiful, but he'd
met other beautiful women. No, it was her quick-
silver nature. One minute she flirted and teased; the
next she seemed as unsure of herself as a teenager.

Which brought up another point: if she was forty-
plus he'd eat his hat, if he had one.

She patted luscious pink lips with a linen napkin.
''What are your plans for the day?'' she asked in a
wistful tone.

He shrugged. ''The usual. I'll walk the perimeter,
check all the entrances and exits, call headquarters
for any progress on bids on the new security system—''

''There's no hurry on that,'' she interrupted.

He peered at her through narrowed eyes. ''I'd
think you'd be in a big hurry about that.''

''Well, I'm not.'' She poked vaguely at a strawberry with her fruit spoon, then looked up with a
bright smile. ''What's the hurry, when you're here
to protect me?''

''Which brings up the next point. How long will
you require my services?''

''Indefinitely.''

Why? He wasn't earning his fee now. Mentioning that probably wouldn't be in the best interests of the agency's bottom line, so he refrained. "Whatever you say, Ms. Kenyon."

"I thought we'd gotten past that," she said with a pretty pout. "Sharlayne, please."

Their gazes met and held, neither willing to pull back first. Fortunately, good old Tabitha chose that moment to interrupt.

"Sharlayne, I have the newspapers."

"Just leave them." Sharlayne gestured without breaking eye contact with Jed.

"I think you'll want to see the *U.S. Eye.*"

"That rag?"

Nevertheless, Sharlayne and Jed pulled back simultaneously. Turning toward her assistant, she held out her hand.

Tabitha put the folded paper in it with an expression Jed could only interpret as satisfied.

Sharlayne scanned the page and gasped. Her gaze flew to meet Jed's, and wordlessly she handed over the newspaper. A photograph upper right immediately caught his attention: a picture of Sharlayne wearing a bikini, holding out a bloody hand and wearing an expression that could be either shock or disinterest.

The article read:

Playgirl escapes serious injury. Much-married Sharlayne Kenyon, rumored to be holed up to write a white-hot autobiography, narrowly escaped with her life Wednesday when she was seriously injured in an accident that sent an unidentified friend to the hospital. According to usually reliable sources, more than a dozen stitches were required to close a cut in Ms. Kenyon's left hand and arm. The incident occurred at her new Spanish-style hacienda on Noble Avenue in—

"Jeez," he said. "They did everything short of printing your address."

"I'm doomed," she whispered. "Why, oh, why, didn't I listen to you, Jed?"

He grinned suddenly. "Because you're a stubborn woman."

"That makes you happy?"

"Having something to do makes me happy," he corrected. "We'll have to be on our toes now."

"Oh, great." She slumped. "This day's off to a great start." Turning to the hovering Tabitha, she said, "Have you heard how Maria's doing, by the way?"

"She's back at work."

"Already? Surely she needs a few days off."

"As hard as she works, every day *is* a day off."

"Really, Tabby, you might try being a little more sym—"

An explosion, loud but not too near, stunned her into silence and the trio froze. Before Sharlayne could say anything, Jed was on his feet and moving.

"Stay here!" he yelled at her. "Stay *here,* damn it! And this time, I mean it."

He vaulted the balustrade and disappeared around the corner of the house.

JED DIDN'T FIND a smoking gun, but he did find a smoking car.

People, the guard included, were already gathering to view the vehicle that had smashed through the front gate. It seemed as if everyone was there except the perpetrator.

He went first to the guard. "Are you all right, Mac?"

"Yeah, just barely." The paunchy man was plenty shaken but had no visible injuries. "I saw it comin' and jumped aside before impact."

"Then you saw who did this?"

He nodded. "Some kid, driving around and lookin' for trouble. I don't know if he intended to smash into the gate or was just a lousy driver. Anyway, he bailed out of the car just before it hit and I assume he got away. When I searched afterward, he was gone."

"Have you called the cops?"

Mac nodded, his expression thoughtful. "What do you think, Kelby? Is someone after Ms. Kenyon or…?"

Jed shook his head. "I wish I knew. Hang tight. I'll go see what I can find before the cops get here.

They won't like it if I mess with their crime scene, but—"

Hands on his arm brought him swinging around, to peer into the flushed face of Sharlayne Kenyon herself.

"My God," she cried, "what happened? Is anyone hurt? Maybe I can help."

He grabbed her by the shoulders and shook her. "I thought I told you to stay put!" he bellowed in her ear.

"But if anyone's hurt—"

"So what are you, a doctor? Just because you don't faint at the sight of blood doesn't mean you're Florence Nightingale."

"Jed, you don't understand!" She flailed at him, trying to pull free. "Let me go! I can help if you'll just—"

"Nobody was hurt, Ms. Kenyon," Mac interjected quickly. "We're waiting for the cops now."

"Before they arrive," Jed said, "I want to see what I can—"

A wailing siren cut through the air and he glared at her. "Foiled again," he said. "Whose side are you on, anyway?"

She had the good grace to appear sheepish.

"I'M HAPPY TO SAY we don't think the bomb was aimed at you personally, Ms. Kenyon."

Alice stopped pacing around the living room and faced the two policemen on the red sofa. One was cheery and middle-aged, the other sad faced and older. Both seemed intent upon soothing her.

Jed, on the other hand, had withheld comment. She could feel him watching her, no doubt waiting for her to screw up again.

"Then what?" she demanded. "Cars just don't drive down a quiet residential street with a bomb in the trunk and decide to ram a gate."

The cops exchanged guarded glances. Then the older one said, "We think it was some kind of gang initiation. Your gate was just in the wrong place at the wrong time."

Funny. She managed a strained smile. "You caught the man who did it, then."

"More like the kid who did it. He's sixteen, with a big brother who's already got a rap sheet as long as my arm. Like we said, it looks gang related— arm a kid with a bomb and point him toward some ritzy neighborhood. He was probably supposed to blow up a statue or somebody's BMW. We suspect he panicked and lost control of the car."

Silence settled over the room. After a few moments, Jed said quietly, "That's thin, Officer. Real thin."

The man flushed. "It's our best shot. Take it or leave it."

"We'll run along now," the other officer said. "We've told you all we know, and you'll have to go from here. We don't believe anyone's out to get you, but we'll keep you updated on the investigation.'' He cast an amused glance at his partner, who was *not* amused.

Sharlayne followed the two cops into the large entry hall. ''Then you think I have nothing to worry about.''

''Yes, ma'am.'' The older officer halted by the door, cocking his head questioningly. ''Except maybe that voice of yours.''

''My voice?'' she echoed, completely perplexed.

He nodded. ''I read about your laryngitis. Now that I hear you again—''

''Hear me *again?*'' She felt as if someone had hauled a rug from beneath her feet.

''You don't remember.'' He didn't look surprised. ''No reason you should. I moonlight for a private company that specializes in crowd control. You recall that awards show two, three years ago when you were mobbed trying to get into your car?''

She struggled not to look blank. Obviously, it had happened before she'd started to work for Sharlayne.

They were waiting for her to respond so she nodded hastily, adding, ''We met then?''

''Not officially. When we finally got you through that mob you turned to me just before the door closed and said, 'I can't thank you enough, Officer. I'll never forget this.'''

''That was *you?*'' Thanks a lot, Sharlayne. ''But…you were wearing a uniform, right? Now you're in plainclothes. That's why I don't remember.''

He was pleased. "Yeah, that's probably it. But I remember your voice as clear as if it was yesterday, and it doesn't seem nearly as low now. Must be the laryngitis.''

She resisted the urge to clear her throat and lower her voice. "I'm sure that's it.'' Without seeming to do it, she shepherded the two men out the front door. "Once again I have to say, I can't thank you enough, Officers. I'd appreciate it if you'd keep an eye on this place for a few days, just until I start feeling a little more secure.''

"We sure will. Uh, Sharlayne?''

"Yes?'' Now what?

"I wonder if you…'' He hauled out a notebook. "Could I have an autograph for the wife? She really admires you, says you sure know how to live.'' He offered the book. "I'd really appreciate it.''

"Jeez, Jim.'' The older cop looked completely exasperated. "You're acting like a damned groupie.''

"She doesn't mind. Do you, Sharlayne?''

She sure as hell did. They were all staring at her, expecting her to be gracious, and all she could think was that she wished she'd pretended to have a broken right hand instead of laryngitis.

The officers' expressions were beginning to change, become puzzled. Suspicion might follow if she didn't act.

She smiled. "Of course," she said, taking the notebook. "I'm flattered you'd ask."

The cop gave his partner a "See? I told you she'd be glad to do it" look and fished a pen out of his pocket.

Alice gazed at the lined page, hesitating. She'd seen Sharlayne's signature dozens of times, of course, most often on her paycheck. She licked her lips. "What's your wife's name?"

"Linda."

In great slashing letters that she hoped resembled Sharlayne's, however vaguely, she wrote: "To Linda. You've got a wonderful man here. Hang on to him! Wishing you all the best, Sharlayne Kenyon."

And prayed.

JED SAID, "I think we should get out of this house, at least until I can get security up to par."

"Are you crazy?" Alice demanded, growing cold at the thought of venturing out into the greater world in her disguised state. "I just got here. No way will I—"

"Sharlayne, listen to reason." Jed drained his glass of chardonnay in a single gulp, his manner impatient. "Your security system's virtually nonexistent. The entry gate can't be securely locked. I've already—"

"Get the gate fixed!" She gestured with wildly flailing arms. "What's the big deal?"

"As I was *trying* to explain, I've already contacted the company that made the gate—or I *tried* to contact them. The company went out of business several years ago and the locking mechanism is unlike any *I've* ever seen. It may take a while to locate someone who can rebuild it or replace it."

"Great. Just great." God, would this never end? She pressed the heels of her hands to her temples. She was being hit with one dilemma after the other and she was in no position to resolve any of them. She had no money and no authority—

And there stood Tabitha, observing the exchange like a cat with canary feathers sticking out of the corners of her mouth.

"Tabitha," she said, "what do *you* think we should do?"

"Oh, for—" Jed spun away and walked to the windows overlooking the terrace, his shoulders rigid.

Tabitha spoke serenely. "I'm sure I don't know. It's entirely up to you, Sharlayne."

Sure it was. Alice gritted her teeth, then had a new thought. Maybe it really *was* up to her. Could this be Tabitha's way of saying she'd back any option?

Or was this Tabitha's way of saying that she, too, was worried?

Alice pivoted toward Jed. "You don't agree with the police—that what happened today was just a random occurrence," she guessed.

He turned away from the windows to face her squarely, his expression grim. "I don't know what to think, but I don't want to take any chances. Until the security is upgraded here, I can't be responsible for your safety. It's as simple as that."

"Then what you're really saying is—" Alice bit her lip "—you won't stay on the job under current conditions?"

"Yeah, I guess that's what I'm saying."

"Tell me the rest of it. Exactly what are you suggesting?"

"That you move to a hotel," he said, so promptly that he'd obviously been considering the options. "You can hole up there more safely than you can here while the work is being done. I wouldn't expect it to take more than a week, two at the most, to get the new system into place and either a new gate installed or repairs done to this one."

With both Jed and Tabitha staring at her, Alice averted her gaze. Maybe he was right. She picked up a small crystal bird from a tiled table and turned the shining object over in her hands, trying to decide the best course of action.

It wasn't like her to hesitate. She'd always prided herself on decisiveness, a necessary quality in a good nurse. But she was no longer acting on her own. She was acting for Sharlayne.

Damn it! Sharlayne should make this decision. She faced the two of them with fresh determination.

"Let me sleep on it," she said. "I expect you're right, Jed, but I don't want to do anything hasty. I'll let you know my decision at breakfast—whether I move to a hotel during the security upgrade or stay here."

"If you stay here, it'll be without me," he said flatly. "Of course, you can always call in another security firm."

She recognized a threat when she heard one, but the truth was, she didn't want another security firm. "I understand," she said with a sigh. "I'll see you at breakfast. And Jed…"

He hesitated on the trip to the door. "Yes?"

"Thank you for everything you did for me today. I do appreciate it."

"It's my job," he said shortly. Walking out, he passed Tabitha without a further word.

The woman watched him leave, then said to Alice, "Well?"

Tabitha had no more expression than one of those presidents on Mount Rushmore. Alice gave an exasperated sigh. "Don't you 'well' me. I don't know what I'm supposed to do and I can't call *her* and ask, can I? But you can."

"What exactly do you want me to say?"

"That I'm very uneasy about the things that have been happening here—the photo in that scandal rag, the bomb in the car. The police may be right, but Jed's worried, and he's the professional." Alice chewed her lower lip anxiously. "At first I thought about going to Sharlayne's New York apartment, but that's too visible. Instead, I want authorization for the security upgrade and for the three of us to move to a hotel while the work's being done—you, me and Jed.''

"Why Mr. Kelby? Surely you won't need protection at a hotel."

"Are you kidding? I'll need him more than ever. I'll have to stay completely out of sight. You and he will have to do all the public things, including dealing with the hotel staff, fielding phone calls and visitors, shopping for anything we may need. Plus, he'll be available to supervise the security work here."

"All right, I can see that," Tabitha relented. "I'll try to have an answer for you by tomorrow morning."

"Good."

But which answer would it be?

JED SAT DOWN at the small table on the sun-washed terrace and unfolded a napkin into his lap. "So what's it gonna be?" he asked Sharlayne. "Do you stay or go?"

She looked particularly lovely this morning, despite faint blue shadows beneath those remarkable eyes. "Not even a 'Good morning' first?" she asked plaintively.

"Good morning. So do you stay or—"

She cut him off with light anxious laughter. "After breakfast, Jed. Okay? There's plenty of time to—'' Her gaze rose and he realized that someone was approaching behind him.

He recognized the precise footsteps: Tabitha Thomas. She stopped just outside his peripheral vision. He picked up a fruit spoon and reached for the footed dish of melon balls, all his senses alert.

Tabitha said, ''I have those reservations at the Beverly Pacific, Sharlayne. You have a three-bedroom suite on the top floor. We can check in any time you like today.''

Sharlayne's relief was obvious. ''Very good, Tabby.'' Her eyes went to Jed. ''And Jed can move forward on the security work? Of course.'' She smiled at him almost apologetically. ''As soon as breakfast is over, we can get ready to go. I don't see any point in putting it off, do you?''

''None at all,'' he agreed, thinking about how she'd given approval for the security upgrade—almost questioningly. Perhaps he shouldn't be surprised, though. He really hadn't been sure she'd follow his recommendation. If she didn't, maybe nothing would happen, but maybe something would…something bad. It was nothing more than a gut feeling but so strong that he didn't doubt it.

Better safe than sorry.

''I'll start packing for you now.'' Tabitha turned away.

''Wouldn't you like to join us for breakfast?''

Now that the decision had been made, Sharlayne seemed more at ease.

"I ate hours ago," Tabitha said dismissively. "I'll have the car come around at eleven."

Sharlayne nodded, staring down at her fruit cup. Jed wanted to grab her and shake her. Why the hell did she let that woman bully her?

He stood up abruptly. "I've got work to do before we go."

"But—" she looked up at him, her lovely face concerned "—you have to eat."

"I'll grab a couple of these biscuits." He reached for the bread basket. "Don't worry, I won't starve. See you at eleven."

"See you," she agreed faintly, putting down her spoon as if she'd lost her appetite.

THE BEVERLY PACIFIC HOTEL was so old and so venerable that newcomers often didn't even know it existed. Jed certainly didn't, but when the limousine cruised through towering gates and up the curved driveway lined with graceful palms to a private entrance, he could appreciate the anonymity the place offered. It was a good choice.

He looked at Sharlayne, seated across from him next to Tabitha. She'd wrapped a sheer black scarf around her bright hair and oversize dark glasses shielded her eyes. She'd dressed simply in a sleeveless blouse and plain straight skirt; she could be anyone, which of course she wasn't. Obviously, she was trying to fool the unwary.

He hoped she succeeded. They would be considerably more restricted in the hotel than at her home. If she'd had island fever there, what would happen to her here?

A hotel executive with an army of bellpersons met them at the unmarked door next to the service entrance. After much bowing to Sharlayne, he directed his minions to bring up the luggage while he personally escorted her into a plush paneled elevator that whisked them up with a soft whirr of sound. She hardly said a word, just smiled nervously at the man's chatter. Tabitha picked up any slack, interrogating him closely about their accommodations and special arrangements.

Jed almost felt sorry for Sharlayne. He took her elbow and she gave him a grateful glance.

"Relax," he said. "No one even knows we're here and we'll keep it that way. This is gonna work out just fine."

"I hope so." Her tight voice lacked conviction.

Maybe that was the source of her appeal, he thought, standing there clutching her warm bare arm. That brave little note in her voice, the uncertainty that made him want to gather her into his arms and protect her.

Hell, that was laughable. She was not only considerably older than he, but she also had a world more experience. If there was ever a smart cookie, it was Sharlayne Kenyon.

He'd forget that at his peril.

ALICE STOOD in the middle of the living room of the penthouse suite, awed but trying not to show it. She'd seen luxury before when traveling with Sharlayne but never had it been for *her*.

This place was a wonder. The ceiling must be fourteen feet high; the glowing chandelier could be nothing but crystal; the fireplace was marble or she'd miss her guess. The painting above the green brocade sofa had to be a Ruiz, Sharlayne's favorite painter. Alice wondered if it had been hung there specially for her.

The hotel executive bowed his way from the interior of the suite while Tabitha marched behind him, giving orders: "No publicity, none—you do understand, I'm sure. Ms. Kenyon is not to be disturbed on any account. She will take all her meals here. I'll make all arrangements with the kitchen."

The exec nodded, his expression unctuous as he stole a glance at the imposter, still concealed behind glasses and scarf. "We have many amenities Ms. Kenyon will enjoy," he said, all obsequious hand wringing. "Our gymnasium is world-class and our swimming pool—"

"Under no circumstances." Tabitha ushered him firmly toward the door. "Ms. Kenyon will not be using any of the public facilities in this establishment. In fact—'' she swung open the door ''—*Ms. Kenyon isn't even here!*''

A moment's confusion crossed the man's face. Then he breathed a long, ''Ahh! I understand, Ms. Thomas. You may depend upon us to pro—''

She closed the door in his face and turned to Alice. ''Where's your bodyguard?''

''He said he wanted to check out the hotel before he looked over this suite.''

''Good. Let him earn his keep. I'm going to unpack now. Stay out of trouble, if you can.''

''I'll do my very best, Tabby dear.'' Alice spoke in a saccharine voice, hauling off her scarf and fluffing the blond hair that still surprised her. ''Take your time.''

Glad to be alone for a few minutes, Alice prowled the room, picking up candlesticks and objets d'art, admiring the ornate moldings and robust plants in magnificent brass pots. The real Sharlayne would be right at home here.

Alice, on the other hand, felt like a stranger in a strange land.

With a sigh, she sank onto a velvet chair. It would be fun to stay here if she could participate. Tea in the lobby, exercise classes in the gym, sunning herself by the pool. But she could do none of those things, because someone who knew Sharlayne would show up sooner or later and the jig, as they say, would be up.

The telephone rang.

Alice started, her heartbeat accelerating drastically. Tabitha would answer, but the call had already shattered her peace. The phone rang again; again. Where the hell was Tabitha?

It must be the hotel staff, Alice decided, because no one else knew they were here. On the sixth ring, she snatched up the receiver and said a surly, "Hello?"

A voice she'd never heard before in her life snarled, *"Are you really going to write that book? Because if you are—"*

CHAPTER SIX

Not that she needed it, but...

We have it from usually reliable sources that the beauteous Sharlayne Kenyon has—hold on to your hats!—had a face-lift. Those who've seen her lately—and they're few and far between—say she's never looked younger. Makes you wonder if that's the real reason she's lying low....

Gina Godfrey, *U.S. Eye*

"WHO IS THIS?" Her response was automatic; so was the way her stomach clenched into an anxious knot.

"You know who it is," the male voice responded roughly. "Once and for all, are you really working on that piece of trash you call a book?"

"I—you don't—how did you know—?"

"I know everything you do, Sharlayne."

Not everything, she thought. Not nearly everything, but way too much. "Why do you care about the book?" she demanded, her temper rising. "What are you afraid to see in print? Because—"

Click!

The line was dead. She hung up the handset, staring at it as if it could answer her questions.

It didn't, so she considered the possibilities. Someone from Sharlayne's past obviously didn't want her to write the story of her life. Ergo, that someone was a big or bad part of the story. So what could Alice do about it?

She could keep quiet…or she could tell someone about the call—Sharlayne, Tabitha or Jed.

She couldn't tell Sharlayne, because she didn't know how to contact her.

There was no point telling Tabitha, because she would raise the roof about Alice's having answered the phone. Then she'd pass on whatever she chose to Sharlayne, all of it designed to make Alice look bad.

And she certainly couldn't tell Jed, because he'd ask a lot of questions about damaging incidents from her past and Alice wouldn't have the first idea how to answer.

That meant she had to keep her mouth shut, at least for the time being and hope it was just a crank call. Fair enough; the man had sounded raspy and angry but not vicious or deranged. He hadn't made any threats…although there had been an ''or else.''

She must keep her own counsel. She could always bring it up later. In the meantime, she'd forget she'd ever heard that raspy voice.

INSTALLATION OF THE new security system was set to begin in two days. By then, Alice was practically climbing the walls.

If there was anything worse than being locked up on a spacious estate with Tabitha, it was being locked up in a hotel with Tabitha. Especially a hotel where Alice wasn't allowed outside her own front door. That's exactly what she told Jed when he rose from the breakfast table and announced he'd be gone most of the day to oversee the security improvements.

"I'm going with you," Alice announced.

"No way. It's not safe. You're not to stir out of this suite."

"If I don't get out of here, I'll go crazy," she wailed.

"If you don't cooperate, it could get a helluva lot worse."

"I don't see how," she argued. "I'll just slip out the back door of the hotel and into the car. No one will be the wiser."

"No one except the photographers who've surrounded this place since an hour after you arrived."

She stared at him in amazement. "You're kidding. Why wasn't I told?"

"Because it wasn't important as long as you stayed put." He seemed to think she should have figured that out for herself.

"But..." Maybe wheedling would work. "If I disguise myself—do the glasses and scarf thing and sneak out the service door—'' She eyed him hopefully. ''Please, Jed. I've got to get out of here, even for a little while.''

He gazed at her without expression. ''You're the boss.''

''Well, yes, but I don't want to go against your advice...unless I have to.''

''My advice is, stay here.''

Her temper rose. ''That's my house you're going to. I have a right to be there.''

''True. You're a grown woman and can go or do whatever you please. It wasn't my idea to keep you cooped up, either there or here. In fact...'' He narrowed his eyes thoughtfully. ''I have to wonder why you're doing it, if it makes you so nuts.''

''Wh-why, you know why I'm doing this. I just n-need peace and quiet—''

''That's not the way it looks. It almost looks as if—'' he cocked his head and regarded her assessingly ''—it looks like you're trying to draw *more* attention to yourself, not less. I just can't figure out why.''

She whirled away from him and walked to the door opening onto the balcony terrace. ''That's ridiculous. Why would I do such a thing?'' she asked.

''I don't have a clue. Maybe it's time for you to tell me.''

She'd like to, she realized; she'd like nothing better than to come clean. But she couldn't, of course.

She was being paid to do a job and she wouldn't betray Sharlayne, who'd been nothing but kind.

So she turned back with a bright smile. "You've got me all wrong, Jed," she practically purred. "I plead guilty to wanting my cake and eating it, but that's all. Please, we can at least try. We'll sneak out the back door and no one will ever know."

For a moment he simply stared at her, his expression revealing a disappointment so deep it hurt her. Then he said, "Whatever you say, Ms. Kenyon. You're the boss."

"Don't do it," Tabitha said flatly. "It's a bad idea."

"I'm sorry you disapprove," Alice said, "but I have to do this."

"You'll be seen. You'll be—" Tabitha shot a glance at Jed, who was standing off to one side, appearing disinterested. She wanted to say, *You'll be seen,* you fool. *And if you are, someone may realize what's going on here.* Loyalty to the real Sharlayne precluded that, however, so she substituted, "You'll be setting yourself up for just exactly the kind of publicity you don't want."

"We're sneaking out the back. It won't be a problem."

"Sharlayne!"

"I'm going, Tabby. I'll be back later."

Jed held the door for her and she slipped out into the hall; he followed, closing the door softly. Tabitha stood all alone in the beautiful penthouse. Damn the woman anyway! She was a flake, pure and simple. If she got away with this there'd be more to come.

Tabitha couldn't allow that to happen. Crossing to the telephone, she dialed the desk.

When she hung up, her problem was solved...or made so much worse that it would no longer be hers.

FIFTEEN MINUTES LATER, Alice burst back through the door to the suite, frightened and out of breath. She couldn't believe what had just happened, what else might have happened if Jed hadn't sprung into action.

Tabitha leaped to her feet, dropping the newspaper onto the cocktail table. "My God, what is it?"

"They were there waiting! They ambushed us!" Alice grabbed the back of a chair, trying to catch her breath. The silvery scarf that had been on her head drooped from her hand and she dropped it on the floor; she had no idea what had become of the dark glasses.

"Who ambushed you?"

"Paparazzi! Photographers! Madmen! I just ran up seven flights of stairs to avoid them."

"Where's Mr. Kelby?"

"He—I don't know." Alice glanced around frantically. "He was right behind me."

The door opened and Jed strolled in. Alice wanted to rush across the room and throw herself in his arms.

He stopped just inside the door. "Satisfied?" he drawled, his tone insolent. "I told you it wouldn't work."

"But—how did they find out? I don't understand!"

"Beats me. Maybe someone tipped them off. Maybe they have people posted all over the hotel. Maybe—"

"Maybe you don't know."

"I sure as hell don't. The bottom line is, it doesn't matter. Now, if you'll excuse me, I'm going over to your house to see if the workmen have arrived. Once again, I advise you to lie low. If you choose to ignore me, it's not going to be my problem."

"Oh, *Jed!*"

"I'm outta here."

When he'd gone, Tabitha said, "Good. Now you can tell me what *really* happened."

"Exactly what you predicted. Jed opened the back door and peeked out. The car was there and the coast looked clear. But the minute I stepped out, it was like an explosion in a paparazzi factory— lights flashing, people rushing around, shoving cameras in my face, shouting questions." She shuddered. "It was horrible. How does Sharlayne—how does *she* stand it?"

"She's used to it," Tabitha said matter-of-factly. "She's been dealing with it for years and she knows when to back off. You obviously don't."

"You're so right, I obviously don't." Alice's legs still felt rubbery and she sat down heavily on the sofa. "I'm sorry, Tabitha. I really am. I'm doing the best job I can for Sharlayne, but I'm not used to all this craziness."

"I suppose I can understand that," Tabitha admitted grudgingly. "Perhaps it will make you feel a little better if you know that the book is coming along quite well."

Alice perked up. "I'm glad to hear that. How much longer does she expect it to take?"

Tabitha shook her head. "I have no idea because *she* has no idea. It will take as long as it takes."

"I really need something a little more definitive," Alice pleaded.

Tabitha's expression hardened. "You agreed to do a job and you're being well paid for it. Relax and the time will pass more quickly than you ever imagined."

"I doubt that."

"You could use an attitude adjustment," Tabitha said spitefully. "Is your glass always half-empty?"

"No, my life is half-empty," Alice snapped. She caught herself up short. "I'm sorry. That was really bitchy. I think I'd better go to my room and pull myself together."

"Excellent idea," Tabitha said. "You might also try praying."

"Praying?"

"Praying that once those photos hit the newspapers, you don't have ex-husbands and former lovers crawling out of the woodwork, attempting to renew old acquaintances."

"Not me!" Alice objected. "Sharlayne."

Tabitha said, "Exactly."

WORKMEN CRAWLED all over the Spanish hacienda on Noble Drive by the time Jed finally got there. Already disgruntled by his run-in with the press, he was in no mood to be hit by questions and problems before he even got inside the front door but that's what happened.

Nothing was working out as planned: nothing fit, boxes contained the wrong equipment, items were on back order or not available at all.

It was a drag, all right. In addition, the front gate had fallen completely off its hinges and the night watchman had quit. The first thing Jed had to do was get someone over here to protect the property, even with the owner safely stashed in a hotel.

If she *was* safely stashed. For all he knew, she was planning her next breakout, or might even have launched it. Why should he care? He was the paid help. She could do any damn thing she wanted to do.

He called the hotel to check nonetheless. She was

there, and therefore safe. Time to get this security mess cleared up.

ALICE WAS SULKING.

She realized it but didn't care. It seemed as if her life had spiraled out of control the minute she agreed to do this crazy thing.

Envy was a terrible thing.

The telephone rang constantly. Tabitha handled calls in the small office off the master bedroom, but the sound of a ringing phone always filled Alice with dread. The worst news she'd ever gotten had come by telephone: her mother's accident, her grandmother's death, her lawyer's warning that foreclosure on the family farm was imminent.

When Tabitha entered the living room looking grim, Alice could barely remain seated. Something awful was about to happen; she just knew it.

Tabitha appeared at a loss for words. "I... You're going to have to handle this one," she said at last.

"Handle what?" Aware that her pulse had accelerated, Alice took a deep breath, trying to calm down.

"This telephone call."

"Who is it?"

"Trace Seymour."

"Trace Seymour! The movie star?"

"The ex-husband," Tabitha corrected. "He wants to do lunch and talk about 'that book.'"

Alice felt faint. She also felt sick to her stomach. "Didn't you tell him I'm sick?"

"Of course. He doesn't believe me. Apparently, there's an item in one of the papers suggesting that this is a publicity stunt."

Alice groaned. "If he doesn't believe that, then make something else up. Obviously, I can't have lunch with the guy—an ex-husband? Uh-uh."

"You'd never fool him across a lunch table," Tabitha agreed, "but on the telephone…maybe."

"Bite your tongue! You can put him off. Please, Tabby."

"I don't think so. He says either you talk to him or he's coming over. You know what that would mean—even more press, more attention and more problems. No, you have to talk to him."

"Tabitha, I can't." Not without barfing.

"You can. Listen carefully. Sharlayne and Trace had one of those whirlwind courtships and an equally whirlwind marriage—less than a year, as I recall. He's not going to get into anything intimate…at least, I don't believe he will. You accept the call, cough a lot, mumble, claim illness and let him do the talking."

"Is that the only way?"

"I'm afraid so."

Holding Alice's arm in a firm grip, Tabitha led the quaking imposter back to the office, where Trace waited on hold. "Believe me," she said, "if there was another way I'd jump on it." She picked up the phone, punched a button and said, "Trace? I'll put her on, but be forewarned. She's ill and her voice is just about gone. Be considerate."

She passed the handset to Alice.

Who took it, along with a deep breath. "H-hello?"

"Sweetheart, is that really you? You sound just awful."

"I feel awful."

"And here I thought you were faking it, the same way you did that time in Cannes."

Alice coughed delicately. "This is entirely different," she croaked.

"I guess. Look, honey, we've got to get together."

"I couldn't possibly. I'm much too sick and it's probably catching."

"Ah, that's a shame. Whatever you've got won't kill you, will it? Because the minute you're up and about, I get first crack at you." He laughed as if the phrase had some special meaning.

"Whatever you say. If that's all—"

"Hey, hang on. I could use a little reassurance here."

"R-reassurance? About what?"

"About that damned book. You don't intend to trash me in there, do you, Sharlayne?"

"I..." Alice stifled a groan and her frenzied glance lit upon Tabitha. No help there; the woman had no idea what he'd said. "I'd never trash you, Trace."

A sigh. Then he breathed, "That's a relief." He didn't sound entirely convinced, more like hopeful. "I was afraid you were going to do a hatchet job on me."

"Why on earth would I—" she caught herself and lowered her voice "—would I do such a thing?"

"To sell books, honey. All that sensational Hollywood stuff always sells books."

He sounded so cynical that Alice felt compelled to reassure him. She also hoped to head off an eventual luncheon date she couldn't possibly keep. "I'd never do a hatchet job on anyone," she said, hoping Sharlayne would share that sentiment. "The truth…"

"That's what I'm afraid of, honey, baby, the truth. Just don't forget that what happened in Palm Springs was all a big misunderstanding. I explained all that. I know you didn't believe me at the time, but I told you the truth. Morgan meant nothing to me."

Morgan? Who the hell was Morgan? *What* the hell was Morgan, male or female?

"I believe you." She burst into a spasm of coughing, then finally managed to gasp out, "I…have to go now. We'll talk soon."

Handing the telephone to Tabitha, Alice raced

out of the room to find a glass of water to soothe her offended throat.

"WHO'S MORGAN?"

"I can't answer that."

"What happened in Cannes?"

"If you didn't read it in the papers at the time, I won't be the one to dredge it up."

"Tabitha, you're no help at all."

"You flatter me." Tabitha grimaced. "Actually...you did a good job with Trace."

Alice's eyes widened. "I did?"

Tabitha nodded a little sheepishly. "I was impressed with the way you handled him. Of course, Trace is all looks and no brains, but still..."

Alice burst out laughing. "Talk about damning with faint praise."

"Whatever." Tabitha turned away.

"Before you go—"

"Yes?"

"Why don't we get an answering machine on that telephone? That way we can screen and avoid even talking to the wrong people."

"Not a good idea. What if Mr. Kelby walked in while we were playing messages? Who knows what he might hear? It's safer for me to handle the phone. If I'm not here, let it ring."

"I suppose you're right, but I'm starting to feel terrorized by that instrument."

Tabitha's expression softened just a trifle.

"You've had a difficult few days," she said, "but I'm sure we're past the worst."

Alice was glad *someone* was sure.

JED RETURNED at midafternoon and he wasn't happy. Alice, who shared that state of mind, returned his short greeting in kind.

"You, too?" he said, his brows rising.

She shrugged. She'd been sitting in the middle of the most luxurious hotel room she'd ever seen, reading—or trying to read—a bestseller provided by Tabitha. Although she'd read page three a half-dozen times, she didn't remember a thing.

"What's going on around here?" He crossed to the wet bar and pulled out a bottle of water from the small refrigerator.

She shook her head. Nothing she could repeat. "How about you? I gather the work isn't proceeding well."

"Not very." He took a deep slug of water. "But it will be okay."

"Soon, I hope. I hate it here."

He eyed her with calm indifference. "I thought you spent a lot of time in hotel rooms, traveling and so forth."

"It's the 'and so forth' that gets to me." Looking at him, so big and strong and sure, was doing strange things to her...taking her mind off her troubles but offering new avenues of tension. She laid aside the book. "I could use a little company," she said, remembering belatedly to add a coaxing smile. "I've been cooped up in here all day with Tabitha."

He laughed. "I see your problem, but I'm not exactly—"

The telephone rang. It rang again.

"Where's the Dragon Lady?" he inquired. "Isn't she going to answer that?"

"She went down to talk to the manager."

"I hope it was about getting an answering machine."

"It's about the combination to the wall safe. It's giving her trouble. She said if the phone rings, we should ignore it."

"Easier said than done." He reached the offending instrument in two long strides, grabbed the handset and uttered a surly, "Yes?"

Alice almost had a heart attack.

AN UNFAMILIAR BUT pleasantly female voice said, "I'd like to speak to Alice Wynn, please."

"You've got a wrong number," Jed replied. "There's no one here by that name." He started to hang up, but the voice stopped him.

"Is this Sharlayne Kenyon's suite?"

"Who wants to know?"

"I do. I'm looking for Alice Wynne. She works for Ms. Kenyon," the woman explained patiently.

"There's no one here by that name."

"In that case, may I speak to Ms. Kenyon?"

He glanced at Sharlayne, who was looking a little alarmed. "I'm afraid Ms. Kenyon isn't taking calls."

"At least ask her where I can contact Alice, then. Alice is my cousin and she'd have told me if she'd taken another job."

"Now, lady—"

"If you don't at least ask, I'm calling the police!"

"Jed," Sharlayne said urgently, "what's going on? Who is that?"

Jed said into the phone, "Can I tell Ms. Kenyon who's calling?"

"This is Carrie Wynn. I met Ms. Kenyon several times, so I'm sure she'll remember me."

Jed covered the mouthpiece with his hand. "It's a Carrie Wynn. She says—"

Sharlayne gasped and reached for the phone, pulled back, reached again. "I'll take it," she said, her voice a trifle shrill. She seemed to catch herself then. Squaring her shoulders, she lowered her voice. "Hello, Carrie. This is Sharlayne. What can I do for you?"

She listened intently for a minute or more, then said, "I assure you, Alice is fine." Her voice was tight and controlled and under pressure. "She's on vacation…sorry, I don't know where…I'll be sure to tell her you called when I speak to her."

Sharlayne hung up the phone and turned toward Jed, her face as white as paper. Alarmed, he stepped forward, reaching out automatically to touch her arm.

"Are you okay? You look like you're about to pass out."

"I'm—" she swallowed hard and shook her head "—I'm not cut out for this life, Jed."

"Who is?" He drew her into his arms, which seemed the only decent thing to do under the circumstances.

She sighed and pressed her soft body against his. "I wish Alice were here. She's so...levelheaded."

"That really was her cousin?" He stroked her spine, just to comfort her. Her flesh warmed his palm through her silk shirt.

"That's right. Carrie." She gave a shaky laugh. "You really threw her when you said you knew nothing about her cousin."

"I told the truth."

"Do you always tell the truth?"

"I try to."

"Because you hate liars."

"Don't make a big deal out of it. I hate lots of things. I like lots of things, too."

"Such as...?" She gazed up at him from beneath the silky fan of her eyelashes, her fingertips digging lightly into his chest.

Thou shalt not get involved with thy client. Thanks a lot, Samantha.

"Such as doing my job." He stepped back, holding Sharlayne away from him. "If you're okay now, I have a report to write."

"About me?"

"And your house."

"What will you say about me?"

That you're the sexiest woman I've ever met; the hardest to resist, too. "I'll say you're the stubbornest woman I've ever met and if you keep ignoring my orders—given strictly for your own good—I'm going to have to walk."

She no longer looked so anxious. "If I gave you an order, would you obey?"

Ah, hell. "I would if it was a reasonable order," he said cautiously.

"A reasonable order given at a reasonable time?"

"That's right."

Her smile blossomed. "I'll remember that, Jed."

"You probably will."

On his way down the hall to his room, he wondered where this was all leading. Very possibly, that would depend upon how able he was to juggle the dictates of his boss and his conscience.

ALICE WAITED for him to disappear around the corner before walking out onto the terraced balcony. Living in proximity to Jed was getting to her bigtime. She was falling for the gorgeous bodyguard and she might as well admit it.

At least she'd made up her mind what to do

about it. Inspired by Sharlayne's notorious example, she was going to sleep with him. Why not? She'd get the fun and Sharlayne would get any credit–blame that ensued.

When this was all over, at least she'd have a beautiful memory.

Reaching for the phone on the lacy wrought-iron table, she dialed her cousin Carrie. ''Hi,'' she said cheerfully. ''I hear you called....''

CHAPTER SEVEN

I never told a soul;
or, what's a little secret between friends?

I met Bill Rogers when I was sweet sixteen.
I'd already been kissed, but he didn't know
that. He was so earnest, so cute, that I let
down my guard—I admit it. I didn't want to
marry him because I'd already figured out that
I wasn't good wife material. I mean, I wanted
jewels, excitement, jewels, travel, jewels.
What he gave me was something else entirely....

That Book About This Body,
Sharlayne Kenyon

"ALICE?" Carrie sounded really confused, as well
she might be. "I just tried to call you and some guy
said—"

"I know." Alice gave a long-suffering sigh.
"That's Sharlayne's new boy toy. I only met him
on my way out the door. He honestly doesn't know
I'm alive." Ha-ha.

"Oh, I get it. He's dazzled by the boss."

"Something like that. So what's up?"

"Nothing much. We haven't talked in several months. I'm just checking up on you. In case you're not aware, the story about your boss moving to that hotel has been splashed all over the newspapers, plus it was on *What's Happening, Hollywood* last night."

"Oh, Lord." Alice sat down hard on a patio chair. "What else are they saying?"

"Well...is it true she barely escaped a bomb at her house?"

"No! The police said it was random and had nothing to do with Sharlayne."

"Really?" Carrie sounded disappointed. "Then is it true that she's just had a face-lift and that's the reason she's staying out of sight?"

"No! Where do people get those ideas?"

"According to *U.S. Eye,* she looks really good these days—years younger, in fact. They say—"

"Spare me the speculation. I can guess the rest." And feel darned good about it, too, Alice thought, stifling a smile. Sharlayne wasn't going to like this, though!

"I've always thought your boss was really nice," Carrie said. "I hope everything's all right."

"Everything's fine. Really. With me, too. Nothing to worry about."

"That's good. Give her my best, okay?"

"When I see her."

"Which reminds me, where are you?"

"Traveling. Give Tom and the boys my love."

"I will, but I really ought to know where you are in case—"

"Someone's at the door. I'll call soon, Carrie," Alice lied through her teeth. She pressed the disconnect button.

Another close call...

TABITHA GLARED AT Alice across the cocktail table. "It's not my fault that detective answered the telephone," she said in a frosty tone. "I can't always be here to do it. I told you to let it ring. I can't stay in this suite twenty-four hours a day when somebody has to handle all the day-to-day details."

"I understand that," Alice said, reminding herself that she had promised to give patience a try. "It's just...that telephone is the most dangerous piece of equipment we have. *I* can't answer it and I can hardly stop him from doing it when it's ringing off the wall. This leaves me in a real bind when you're not around."

"Perhaps when I'm out I should contact the desk and request that all calls be held."

"That would be a great relief."

The telephone rang for about the tenth time that day. The two women exchanged glances; then Tabitha picked up the offending instrument and said an abrupt, "Ms. Kenyon's suite."

Her face went white, so pale that Alice half rose, almost expecting the woman to topple over.

Tabitha listened for a moment and a trace of color returned to her face. Then she said, "Of course I know who you are, Mr. Rogers."

Mr. Rogers, Mr. Rogers… Alice understood that name should mean something to her, but at first blush, it didn't. She racked her brain while keeping an ear tuned in on the conversation.

"I see…uh-huh. Yes, she's here, but… You don't understand. She's not seeing anyone." Tabitha listened, darting a nervous glance at Alice. "Uh-huh, but— In the lobby?" Her voice shot up on an uncharacteristic note of panic. "Hold on."

Taking no chances, Tabitha punched the Hold button on the telephone and faced Alice. "It's Bill Rogers. He's in the lobby and insists on coming right up."

"Who the hell is—?"

And then it hit her: Bill Rogers was one of Sharlayne's many husbands. But which one? "Tell him no," she cried in terror.

"I tried. He's being difficult about it."

"Difficult how? If we say no—"

"He says he'll talk to you or to the press, your choice."

"You mean to Sharlayne. *I* can't talk to him, Tabby. He'll realize instantly that I'm not her."

"Maybe not."

"But they were married!"

"A long time ago. Mr. Rogers was her first husband and they were only married for a few months. I don't think she's seen him more than once or twice in the past twenty years."

"Even so—"

"Even so, we'll have to take the chance. If he goes to the press, it could ruin everything for her. I don't know everything that went on between them, but there was something she simply never talked about."

The offended expression on Tabitha's face added, *Even to me.*

Alice's hands were shaking, and she clasped them together in her lap. "This is awful. I'll never fool him."

"You might. We can draw the drapes and keep it dark in here. If you don't say any more than you have to, and if you let him do most of the talking…"

Alice groaned. "This wasn't part of the deal, Tabitha. I'll blow it, for sure."

Tabitha straightened, suddenly all business again. "No, you won't. This is our only chance." Punching the button, she said crisply into the handset, "Mr. Rogers, Ms. Kenyon says you're to come right up. But be prepared, she's been having trouble with her voice and…yes, that's right. She's not quite over a serious bout of laryngitis. Now she seems to be coming down with a cold, but naturally, she's eager to see you."

Hanging up the phone, Tabitha turned to Alice grimly. "Let's get busy," she said. "He'll be here in just a few minutes."

Jed asked from the doorway, "Who'll be here in just a few minutes?"

IF JED HAD EVER seen guilt, he saw it now on the faces of the two women staring at him as though he were a complete stranger.

Sharlayne swallowed hard, exchanged a glance with Tabitha and said, "Uh, I won't be needing you for a while, Jed."

He strolled farther into the room. "How's that?" he inquired coolly.

"Uh…" She looked hopelessly at her assistant.

Who said, "She's expecting a guest."

"Then it's a good thing I'm here." He planted himself in a chair backed by potted palms and other greenery.

"You don't understand," Sharlayne said. "It's, uh, my ex-husband. I mean, one of my ex-husbands."

"Now I know I'm staying," he said. "From what I hear, some of your exes have no reason to look forward to that book you're allegedly writing."

"What do you mean, allegedly?" Her expression was indignant.

"I haven't seen you write a single word."

"That doesn't mean I haven't."

Tabitha said sharply, "We don't have time for this, Sharlayne."

"That's right, we don't. Jed, please—"

"I'm not going anywhere." He crossed his arms over his chest. "For security reasons, I have to be present. It's my job."

She glared at him. "Can't you see I'm nervous enough about this without you horning in?"

"Yeah, and that's one of the reasons I'm staying. Just ignore me. I'll be quiet as the proverbial mouse. You won't know I'm even here."

The doorbell chimed. Sharlayne started and cast a last anxious glance at Tabitha. Then, taking a deep breath, she went to sit in a gold brocade chair before tall draped windows. Reaching up, she turned off the table lamp, then folded her hands sedately in her lap and nodded to Tabitha. In the low lighting, she looked remote and somehow mysterious.

While the assistant answered the door, Jed watched Sharlayne. He could see her breathing deeply, calming herself, preparing herself for what was to come. The question was, why? Why was it necessary to brace herself to face an ex-husband?

None of this jibed with what he'd read about her in the dossier the agency had provided. It simply didn't make a whole lot of sense.

Not much about her did.

She was not the woman he'd expected. She was

both more secretive and more open, less confident and less poised.

And infinitely more appealing.

Tabitha returned, leading a slender man of perhaps forty-two or -three: medium height, thick dark hair, a hesitant manner. He stopped a good fifteen feet from Sharlayne and the two eyed each other.

Uncertainty, Jed thought. This was weird.

Sharlayne said in that throaty voice of hers, "Bill...it's good to see you again."

"Sharlayne." He just stood there staring at her as if he'd never seen her before. "You look..." She seemed to hold her breath, but she didn't turn away from his scrutiny. "You look wonderful."

She let out her breath on a soft gasp. "Thank you, darling. So do you."

The man shrugged and glanced around for a place to sit—and at that point saw Jed. His eyes narrowed.

Sharlayne said hastily, "That's Jed Kelby, by the way. He's...a consultant. I'm having the security system upgraded at my new home and he's—"

"I know who he is," Rogers said. He sat down on the pillow-piled sofa.

"No, really, he—"

"Honey, I read the newspapers." He nodded in Jed's direction. "I'm Bill Rogers."

"She's telling you the truth. I just work for—"

"It doesn't matter," Rogers appeared tired and stressed. "It's been a long time since I had any say in how Sharlayne lives her life.'' He turned toward her, still earnest. ''I don't like talking about our private business in front of all these other people.''

''I'm sorry, Bill.'' She really sounded it. ''This time, it's necessary. But don't worry. Tabitha and Jed are completely trustworthy.''

''I'll have to take your word for that.'' He leaned back against the brocaded pillows. ''I've been following your exploits in the newspapers.''

''I wish you wouldn't refer to my life as *exploits*,'' she said. ''Uh, Tabitha? Could you find something for us to drink, please? What would you like, Bill? Soda, juice, something stronger? We have some lovely California wine—''

''You know I don't drink, Sharlayne.''

''That's right.'' She was embarrassed by her slip. ''I wasn't thinking. Tabitha, I'll have a glass of that white wine, if you don't mind, and pop for Bill. Jed?''

''Nothing for me.'' Her ex didn't drink alcohol and she'd forgotten?

The flurry of activity passed and she turned to Rogers with a bright smile that appeared forced to Jed. ''Tabitha said you were pretty insistent on the telephone,'' she said softly. ''What is it, Bill? After all these years, what's brought you here?''

''I didn't do it for myself,'' he said at last. ''If it was just me, I'd never put myself through this again—seeing you, I mean. You know what it did to me when you left.''

She sucked in a quick breath. "I'm…sorry about that. You don't know how sorry."

"Really?" He looked at her with clear, honest eyes. "That's the first time you ever said that to me—I mean, said you were sorry and sounded like you mean it."

"Well…I…but surely you knew I didn't want to hurt you."

"Yeah, I suppose."

Whatever he'd come to say was giving him trouble. Jed felt for him. It must be hell to love Sharlayne Kenyon, to have her for a little while and then lose her to the next man.

Tabitha returned with the drinks. Peering at Sharlayne's, Jed, who'd spent his life scrutinizing wine, wondered if it *was* white wine or simply white grape juice. She sipped and made a face, darting an accusing look at Tabitha. The woman pretended not to notice, but she did, of course.

She was apparently ready to take her chances to keep Sharlayne sober and at the top of her game in dealing with this man. If Sharlayne *was* at the top of her game.

Rogers took a gulp from his glass. "Are you sure you want me to say this in front of them?" he asked, obviously worried.

"How can I tell, when I don't know what it is you intend to say?" She spoke lightly, but Jed thought he detected a note of concern.

"You know," Rogers said.

"I don't," she insisted. "I really don't."

"God, have you forgotten everything? That's cold, even for you, Sharlayne."

"Damn it, Bill." Her voice rose. "Say what you came to say."

"It's more...I want to ask a favor."

Ah, Jed thought. *Here it comes.*

"What's the favor?" Sharlayne clutched the stem of her wineglass so tightly Jed feared it might snap.

"I want you to promise you won't tell our private business in *that book.*"

Her nostrils flared with the quick intake of breath. "You'll have to be more specific than that."

Rogers eyed her reproachfully. "I hope you're enjoying this," he said. "Like you don't know what I'm talking about."

"Bill..." She spread her hands helplessly.

"All right," he snapped, voice suddenly harsh. "I'll spell it out." He glanced uneasily at Tabitha, then at Jed. "Remember, you made me say this right out. Sharlayne, I'm begging you to keep our secret."

She didn't seem to have any idea what he was getting at; either that or she was a more magnificent actress than past forays into film would indicate. Rogers saw it, too.

His lip lifted in a disgusted curl. "Damn, Sharlayne, don't tell me you've forgotten we have a child."

ALICE STARED at this stranger, unable to respond beyond the visceral reaction that made her faint with dismay. Sharlayne had a child? Incredible!

But even as she thought that, Alice realized that it must be true—perhaps the best kept secret in Hollywood. Tabitha herself looked stunned.

Jed, on the other hand, revealed nothing. *He* probably had no trouble at all believing such a thing.

Bill glanced around. "You made me say it," he accused with some bitterness. "I know we agreed never to speak of her again, especially not in front of others. But you made me, and now I want your promise that you won't say anything about her in that damned book."

"I—" Alice licked her lips. What would a real mother say at this point? Not that Sharlayne had ever been a real mother, apparently. "First tell me h-how she is."

"Ashley's fine, no thanks to you. I've tried not to blame you entirely for what happened, Sharlayne, but the fact remains that you've never once, not in all these years, asked that question."

"How c-could I?"

"You've got a point there. It would be an awful shock to her to know her birth mother is still alive."

"You told her I was dead?" Horrified, she gaped at him.

"Don't try to lay that on me. You agreed that was for the best when you left. Don't cop out on me now. Ash has no idea her mother is alive. If she found out, I don't know how she'd react.''

"M-maybe she'd be glad to learn that—"

"That she has a mother who loves her? Don't make me laugh.'' Bill stood up, shuffled his feet a little and sat back down.

"If she knew the circumstances..." What the hell were the circumstances?

"Oh, yeah, that would make her feel better—discovering she had a mother more interested in *things* than in her."

Alice could see how Sharlayne had fallen for this man. He was such a straight arrow—kind of like Jed, actually. Good-looking, too. Must have been a real hunk when he was young and vulnerable.

"Do you hate me, Bill?" she asked softly.

For a moment he just looked at her. "I could never hate you, Sharlayne," he said finally, his voice gentler. "Hell, I *loved* you."

"I loved you, too." Alice thought that much must be true.

He smiled, albeit reluctantly. "Do you remember the first gift I gave you after we were married? A mixer, and you said—"

"If it's not something to put on *this body*—"

They smiled together, almost as if they really had shared that moment Alice had only heard of.

His smile didn't last long, though. "Sharlayne," he said, "I've never thought you were a bad person, not ever. No matter what I've read or heard about you, I always took your side. But this book…I can't tell you how much damage it could do. Ash is a wonderful girl. She's a computer tech, living in Dallas now. She doesn't deserve this.''

"Of course not.''

"Then you won't mention anything about it? Promise me.'' He gazed at her with utter determination.

How could Alice promise such a thing? She had no idea what Sharlayne intended to write in her book. Finally, because she had to say something, she replied cautiously, "I promise I'll be very careful about anything I say, if and when I ever write the story of my life. Is that good enough?''

He got a stubborn expression on his face. "I don't know….''

"All I can do is ask you to trust me, Bill.'' She held her breath, waiting for his answer, watching his struggle.

After a moment he told her very slowly, "I guess I'll have to trust you, Sharlayne. I don't believe you've ever lied to me, even when it hurt.'' His faint grin was adorably crooked.

"I…tried not to.''

"I don't believe you'd want to hurt our child, either.''

Alice felt her cheeks flame. "I don't want to hurt anyone, if I can help it. That includes you, Bill.''

He rose. "I guess that will have to be good enough, then. I know if you really think this through, consider all the ramifications, you'll do the right thing."

She stood, but didn't move out of her shadowed niche. "I've got a lot of things to think through. Maybe what I need to is get away somewhere to consider everything." *And to get away from any more ex-husbands,* she added silently. "A mountain resort would be nice."

"You always liked the mountains," he acknowledged. "At least, you thought you did. At the time, you'd never seen a big one."

"I have since." He turned toward the door and she added hastily, "Do you mind if Tabitha escorts you out? I do feel as if I'm coming down with something. I wouldn't want to pass it on to you."

"Your voice does sound a little different," he conceded. "Not as low…something." He gave her a level gaze. "Thanks for speaking with me, Sharlayne."

"Anytime. You know that."

"Yeah, well…" His smile was faint. "Remember what I said. If you wanted to be a mother to Ashley, even at this late date… But you don't, so it would be cruel to dredge up all that just to sell a few more books."

"Yes," she agreed, "it would be cruel."

"You were never a cruel woman." Bill glanced at Jed. "Good meeting you."

Jed nodded. "Same here."

Tabitha indicated that Bill should proceed her,

which he did. Their exit left a suddenly strained silence.

"Jed, I—"

"Shh." He shot a warning glance toward the door leading to the entry. Almost as if on cue, Tabitha reentered and stopped short.

"Oh." She looked from one to the other. "When you have a chance, Sharlayne, I'd like to speak to you privately."

Alice nodded. "In a few minutes."

"I'll be in the office." Tabitha crossed the room and exited.

Alice let out a long breath and waited for him to speak. What did he think of all he'd heard?

It didn't take her long to find out.

"WHAT THE HELL kind of woman *are* you?"

She recoiled from the quiet loathing in his tone and countered with, "What the hell kind of *question* is that?"

"Cute response." He rose from his chair and stalked toward her. "You had a child, which you subsequently abandoned. I don't see any way you can put a good spin on that, Ms. Kenyon."

An answering spark of anger leaped into her eyes. "Who are you to judge me? You don't know anything about it. I didn't abandon my child. I left her with her father, with whom, even you must admit, she was infinitely better off."

"Score one for your side."

"Spare me your sarcasm."

He watched her pace to the terrace windows, then back again. She moved like a prowling lioness, all coiled energy and suppressed emotions. The encounter with her ex had obviously unnerved her.

He asked, because he couldn't resist, "Are you going to out your daughter in your book? You didn't actually promise him you wouldn't."

"No, but *he* trusted me, and he certainly knows me better than you do." She stopped short, facing him. "You're rather quick to judge, Jed."

It was true. He'd listened to the conversation and made up his mind on the spot. It wasn't his place to do that; she wasn't his friend or anything like that, only his client. He wasn't here to pass moral judgment.

Ashamed of himself, he turned from her. "You're right, I'm way out of line. There could be lots of reasons for what you've done."

"There are always reasons. Sometimes good reasons, sometimes not so good."

Reaching out, she laid one hand lightly on his forearm, her fingers digging in. He stiffened, his gaze flying to her face. She looked so incredibly vulnerable, not at all like the cool and calculating woman he'd judged her to be. Those unbelievable blue eyes were soft with pain and her full lips trembled in a way that was intimately appealing.

With deliberate slowness, she tightened her grip on his arm. "I asked you not to stay and hear what

Bill had to say. You insisted you had to for security reasons. Don't blame me if you heard something you'd rather not have.''

"I stand corrected."

"In that case, would you care to kiss and make up?"

That was the last thing he wanted to do—intellectually, at any rate. But while he was still thinking of all the reasons he should be strong, he was also pulling her into his arms. She smiled, lifted her face and closed her eyes like a high school girl. Completely confused, he kissed her hard and fast because he didn't dare take his time.

He was obviously outclassed here. He was dealing with a woman who'd had six husbands and God only knows how many lovers, who'd made a reputation and a fortune as one of the world's great courtesans. But when he kissed her, which he'd done twice now, it was like kissing—like kissing a damned virgin. She was a chameleon, changing her coloring depending upon the situation.

The way she'd played that poor sucker Bill Rogers had been masterful. Almost as masterful as the way she was playing Jed Kelby.

He stepped back abruptly. "Sorry about that," he said. "Once again, I was out of line."

She swayed before him. "Don't be sorry," she said in a coaxing voice. "I needed that comfort."

"I've been called many things," he said, "but comforting has never been one of them."

"I didn't intend it as an insult."

"I wonder what you do intend."

Her smile slipped away. "Jed—"

"I don't suppose you've ever met my boss."

She frowned and shook her head.

"She has a cardinal rule for her operatives."

"Do I have to hear that again?"

No, *he* did. "You apparently weren't listening the other times. She says, *'Thou shalt not get involved with thy client.'* I don't intend to."

"You're not involved," she said. "A simple kiss…"

"Maybe to you. It wasn't simple at all to me. There'll be no more kissing and making up, Ms. Kenyon."

"Isn't that carrying your boss's rule to an extreme?" she argued. "'Involved' implies a great deal more than is going on here. I'm not asking for a lifetime commitment, but I wouldn't mind a little good, clean, all-American fun. No strings, Jed. I promise."

He looked at her, so beautiful and so immoral, and thought she must be nuts. No strings with sexy and unpredictable Sharlayne Kenyon?

There were too many strings already.

CHAPTER EIGHT

Accidents will happen;
or, how I became a victim of love

Every pregnancy I ever had was an accident, except that first one, which was insanity. I knew better, even at the tender age of sixteen. But I was swept away and for a little while I forgot everything, even that damned blender....

That Book About This Body,
Sharlayne Kenyon

ALICE STORMED INTO Tabitha's small office in a fury. She found Tabitha sitting at the French-provincial desk, pen in hand. Her expression was almost haunted.

Alice would not be deterred. She marched forward, pressed her palms flat on the desktop and said in a low, angry voice, "I've got to speak to Sharlayne—*now.*"

"Yes, I suppose you do. Unfortunately, she's not available at the moment."

"Damn it, Tabitha!" Alice began to pace. "I've just been through hell and—"

"I know, I know, and you handled it beautifully."

Alice stared at the woman. She didn't sound like herself and she didn't look at all like herself, either.

Tabitha tapped the pen point nervously on a pad of paper. "You did an excellent job with Bill Rogers, Alice, just excellent. You couldn't have handled him better."

"You think so?" Somewhat mollified, Alice sat in the chair beside the desk. "I had no idea what I was doing, you know."

"I'm sure you didn't."

"I suppose you also knew that I had—I mean, Sharlayne had a child."

Tabitha shook her head slowly. "That revelation stunned me. I'm just beginning to realize how many things she's chosen not to share with me."

"She's probably ashamed," Alice suggested.

"Maybe, but I doubt it. More likely she simply wanted to protect the child."

"Anything's possible." Alice made the admission flippantly, since deserting a child was so awful on the face of it.

"The important thing," Tabitha said, "was that you completely fooled Mr. Rogers. He has no idea he wasn't talking to his ex-wife."

"Which doesn't make any sense. Are people blind?"

"People see what they expect to see."

"Sharlayne said the same thing."

Tabitha nodded. "It helped that he hadn't been in the same room with her for a good twenty-plus years. She was only sixteen when she married him. That marriage was very short-lived."

"Sixteen." Alice shook her head in wonder. "She was just a baby herself."

"She told me once that he was the only husband she married strictly for love. I already knew that, of course, since he was a mere garage mechanic at the time."

"What is he now?"

"Now he owns the garage—bought for him by *her*. I'm not sure he's even aware of her part in that. In fact, now that I think about it, I'm sure he doesn't."

Alice's ire was waning. "But to abandon a baby…"

"Let's not go there again," Tabitha said, suddenly brisk. "We have other things to worry about."

Alice groaned. "I'm not up to any more problems—or any more ex-husbands."

"Perhaps you won't be faced with more. What you said to him—"

"Which time? I was so confused and talking so fast I don't even remember the half of what I said."

"About going away somewhere. That's not such a bad idea."

Alice felt a leap of hope. "Things *are* getting a little hot to handle around here. People apparently feel free to drop by or call any old time. It's disconcerting to say the least."

"But if we moved to a cabin in the Rockies, or a beach house on some island, it would surely cut back on the pursuit."

"Yes! Are you going to ask her if we can?"

Tabitha nodded. "I'll strongly recommend it. It's definitely time we got out of here and found someplace to wait until the house is finished. If the media are trying to find you, they won't be bothering you."

"Agreed, but I still want to talk to her myself. I'm in this so deep now that I think I deserve a little more consideration. Plus I'd like to find out what actually happened with Bill Rogers, and whether she's including it in the book."

"All right. I've got a call in to her now and I'll let you know when I reach her. In the meantime, I have to go to the bank."

Alice groaned. "What do I do when the phone starts ringing and Jed makes a dash for it?"

"It won't. I'll stop by the desk and ask them to hold all calls."

"Thank you." Was this the real Tabitha? Alice reacted spontaneously. "And thank you for your sudden change of attitude. It means a lot to me."

"There's been no change in attitude," Tabitha said. "I am as I have always been." She smiled slightly and added, "I'm only interested in protecting Sharlayne. You've proven to me you'll go that extra mile to do the same thing. We can work together. I didn't believe that to be possible until today."

"Whatever your reasons, I appreciate it."

"Yes, well..." Looking uneasy, Tabitha stood. "It's windy today. Do you mind if I grab one of your scarves to protect my hair? I didn't bring any of my own."

"No, of course not."

"On that note, I'll say goodbye. I won't be long. Take care until I return—and don't answer any telephones."

Their gazes met and some new understanding passed between them. Then Tabitha turned and walked away. Alone, Alice lingered in the small pleasant office, thinking about all that had happened this day. A run-in with an ex-husband, discovery of an unknown daughter, a kiss from a stick-in-the-mud bodyguard, a truce with the worst thorn in her side...

It had already been a helluva day and it wasn't even over.

JED AND SHARLAYNE dined alone on the terrace that evening, via room service. He hadn't seen Tabitha since the meeting with the ex-husband hours ago, but Sharlayne was definitely distracted. He could understand why. She'd been exposed in a less-than-admirable light.

Between the soup and the salad, she roused herself to ask how work was progressing on her house.

"Not well," he said bluntly. "At this rate, you'll be lucky to be back in there by Christmas."

"That's encouraging." She did not, of course, look encouraged at all.

"It can't be helped." He buttered a roll. "You should have taken security into account before you moved in there."

"I'm sure you're right. I should have done a lot of things."

She appeared so forlorn that he was ashamed of himself. "Well," he said, "never mind that. That's in the past. We'll get it taken care of eventually."

"I hope so."

The waiter served the chateaubriand and withdrew. She picked at hers.

"Okay," he said, putting down his knife and fork. "Out with it. What's got you so worried?"

"I'm kind of concerned about Tabitha. She should have been back hours ago and I haven't heard a word from her."

"Did you try her cell phone?"

"Yes. No answer. Of course, it might have been turned off."

"Do you know where she was going?"

"To the bank. She said she wouldn't be long and

that when she got back, she had several important things to do for me. I'm starting to worry, Jed.''

''That's not like her, is it?''

''Not a bit. I'm probably just nervous because of the car bomb. I know the police don't think that was personal but I'm not so sure. If anything happened to Tabitha, I—I don't know what I'd do.''

''Let me see what I can find out.'' He rose to fetch a cordless telephone from a table near the door and punched the Dial button. ''What's her cell phone number?''

She gave it to him and he dialed. The other phone began ringing, so at least Tabitha hadn't turned it off. The ringing stopped and he waited for the Dragon Lady's ''Hello.'' He was, instead, greeted by static, then a very faint voice saying, ''Hello?'' over and over.

''Hello, hello? Is someone there?''

Sharlayne leaned forward. ''You got her?''

He shook his head. ''I don't know what I've got, if anything. The connection's screwy.'' He punched the End button and dialed again. This time he got hash.

He tossed the phone onto the cushion of a wrought-iron settee. ''Something's wrong with her phone. I don't think you have anything to worry about, though. The phone was turned on, at least. She probably doesn't even realize you've been trying to reach her.''

''I suppose.''

"Finish your dinner and by then I'll bet she's shown up."

"I hope you're right, Jed." But she didn't look as if she thought he was.

THE DESK CALLED at exactly 9:05 p.m. to announce that a couple of policemen were in the lobby, asking to come up right away. Jed took the call and relayed the information to Sharlayne, who turned white at the news.

"Easy," he said. "This could be anything—even about the car bomb. They might have a lead on that."

"Or it could be about Tabitha."

"Don't borrow trouble, Sharlayne."

She gave him a grateful look, which was when he realized he'd called her by her first name again. She said, "I'm glad you're here, Jed."

"I'm glad I'm here, too." And not just because this was his first foray into the wonderful world of personal protection, either. Sharlayne was an enigma to him, but he sure as hell didn't want anything bad happening to her.

He answered the knock to find two plainclothes cops standing in the hall. They flashed badges and introduced themselves as Frank Steiner and Harvey Culp.

"Jed Kelby." He gestured them inside. "I'm with the S. J. Spade Insurance Agency of San Francisco. We provide—"

"Yeah, we know about you guys." Frank exchanged a quick glance with Harvey. "And here I thought you were the boyfriend."

"Where the hell would you get an idea like that?"

"Hey!" Frank grinned. "We read the newspapers." He saw Sharlayne and stopped smiling. "Ms. Kenyon?"

Like he wasn't sure?

"Yes?" She stepped forward, her chin lifting as if she were bracing for the worst.

"We're sorry to bring you bad news, but—"

"Oh, God, is it Tabitha?"

"Yes, ma'am." Harvey pulled out a small notebook and flipped it open. "Ms. Tabitha Thomas was the victim of a hit-and-run at 5:21 this afternoon while crossing the street in front of the bank of—"

"I don't care what bank! Is she...?"

"She's in the Beverly General Hospital in critical condition."

"Oh, God." Sharlayne sat down hard on a spindly little chair and pressed her palms to her forehead. "I knew something like this had happened."

"You knew?"

Jed stepped forward. "She had a premonition, that's all. Don't get excited, Officer."

"I have to go to her," Sharlayne said.

"All in good time. First we have a few questions."

"First *I* have a question," Jed interrupted. "Why'd it take you guys so long to notify us of the accident?"

"Because we didn't know who to contact. She had a driver's license, but it was pretty messed up— stuff flew out of her purse on impact and we're still not sure we got everything. If somebody hadn't called her cell phone—"

"That would be me," Jed said. "The connection was rotten."

"We used the redial feature on the phone. It wouldn't dial, but the number did come up. We traced the call here."

Sharlayne stirred. "Thank God you found us."

"Yeah, well— What are you doing here, Ms. Kenyon? I read just the other day that you'd moved into a new house."

Jed took the officer's elbow in a firm grip. "Let me fill you in on the details. I think Ms. Kenyon needs a moment to assimilate all this."

"Thank you," Sharlayne said. "I do."

"Okay," Frank agreed, "but then we need a few words with you."

"Of course." She drooped visibly.

Jed ushered the officers into the spacious entryway. "Okay," he said, "let's have it. Was this an accident or...not?"

POOR TABITHA!

Alice sat alone in the elegant hotel room and regretted every uncharitable thought she'd ever had about Sharlayne's right-hand woman. Why had this happened just when they were starting to connect with each other?

She bolted upright in her chair. Why had this happened before she had a chance to speak to Sharlayne? If Tabitha died, God forbid, or even if she was out of her head for any appreciable length of time, what would Alice do? She had no money, no credit cards, no telephone number linking her to the brains of this operation, assuming there *were* any brains in this operation.

First, however, she had to find out what she could do for Tabitha. If the woman was conscious, she would surely realize she had to release her secrets for the good of her beloved boss. If she was unconscious—

Alice shivered. She didn't want to think about that. Better to sit here quietly and calm down. Thank heaven for Jed!

Who now reentered the room to kneel before her, the two cops looming over him. He took her hands in his and looked into her eyes. Bless him, she thought, grateful for the support.

"The police feel it was exactly what it seems— an accident," Jed said.

Vulnerable and frightened, she tightened her hold on his hands. "What do you feel?"

"I have no reason not to agree with them." He sounded evasive, but his eyes narrowed, warning her not to pursue this line of questioning. "They're going to see if they can tie this in with the car bomb, but they don't expect anything to come of that, either."

"I see." What she saw was that Jed would have opinions of his own, independent of the police. She gazed up at the officers. "Is there anything more we can do to help you, gentlemen?"

"Yeah." Harvey pulled out his notebook. "Does Ms. Thomas have any relatives we should contact?"

Alice thought hard, trying to remember anything she might have heard about Tabitha's connections. Finally she said, "I don't believe so. I've heard her mention a very distant cousin, but I don't even know what state he or she is in. If feelings count, I'd say I'm her next of kin. She's been with me for years, and I'll certainly make sure she has nothing but the best in the way of care."

"The hospital will be relieved to hear it." Harvey flipped the notebook closed and shoved it into his jacket pocket. "Kelby here has filled in the blanks, so I'd say that's about it for now, Ms. Kenyon. We're still hoping to catch the guy who hit her, but you never know."

Jed ushered them toward the entry. "We're sure you'll do the best you can. In the meantime, we'll be going over to the hospital to see how she's doing."

"Yeah, okay. Contact us if you think of anyth—"

The trio moved out of earshot and Alice jumped to her feet. There wasn't a second to lose.

Before she saw Tabitha, there was much she needed to know.

JED POUNDED on the door to Tabitha's bedroom. "Sharlayne, what the hell are you doing in there? Come out here. We have to—"

"Just a minute, Jed."

Hell, it sounded like she was moving furniture. He tried the doorknob. It was locked. "Damn it, are you coming out or do I knock down the door?"

Instead, it flew open in his face. "Where's the safe in this suite?" she demanded.

He frowned. "I don't know. We can call the desk and find out later. I've already called for the car to get you to the hospital. You do want to go to the hospital, don't you?"

"Of course." But she appeared wildly distracted. She bit her lip as if considering many options. Taking a deep breath, she straightened her shoulders and repeated with more emphasis, "Of course! What are we waiting for? Let's go."

So they did.

THE NURSE deflected them toward the doctor's office, which didn't seem like a very good sign. By the time the rumpled resident entered, Alice was on tenterhooks.

"Tabitha Thomas is my friend and employee," she said. "Please tell me she's going to be all right."

The young man rubbed a stubbled jaw. "The jury's still out on that, Ms.—" his tired eyes widened "—Kenyon?"

She nodded. "What are the extent of her injuries?"

"*Extent*'s the right word, because her injuries are extensive. The broken bones don't worry me so much, but she suffered a blow to the head and there's internal damage...."

Alice groaned and Jed covered her fist with his hand. "How bad?"

"Bad enough. She's in a coma at the present. There's no way of knowing how long it will last."

"You mean..." Those spectacular eyes widened. "She can't talk to me?"

"Not at the moment," the doctor said with a trace of wry humor. "She may be able to hear you—we're never too sure about that—but she definitely won't be answering any time soon."

"She is to have the best of everything. I'll assume all responsibility for her care."

"That's fine, but you don't need to worry. The police found her insurance card."

"Oh. That's good. May we see her now?"

"Sure. She's in Intensive Care. Don't stay too long." He started to turn away, stopped. "Actually, you won't be able to stay too long. We'll be taking her down for more tests in a few minutes."

Alice nodded. "Thank you, Doctor."

"Try not to worry, Ms. Kenyon. We're doing all we can."

"I pray it's enough."

TABITHA LOOKED very small on the bed, lying in the midst of wires and tubes and monitors. Pristine white gauze encircled her head; her face and hands were scraped and scratched; her left arm, in a cast.

At their entrance, a nurse rose from a chair beside the bed.

"Any improvement?" Alice asked.

The nurse shook her head. "I'm afraid not, Ms. Kenyon. I'm sorry." She moved toward the door. "I'll be right outside if you need me." She slipped out of the room.

Alice took the chair the nurse had vacated. A nurse herself, she had instantly grasped the gravity of Tabitha's situation. Head injuries were tricky. Tabitha could open her eyes and say, "Hello," or she could linger like this for weeks...months.

Not very helpful when Alice had failed to find anything even remotely helpful in the woman's room. She curved her hand over Tabitha's, careful not to move the IV needle.

"Tabitha? Can you hear me, dear? It's Sharlayne."

Nothing.

Behind them, Jed said, "Jeez, she's really a mess."

"Poor thing." Alice sighed. "I wish there were something we could do."

"The doctors are doing everything that can be done."

"I'm sure they are, but it's so frustrating to be this helpless." Alice looked over her shoulder at the tall handsome bodyguard with the surprisingly tender expression. "Jed, would you mind if I had a few moments alone with her?"

"No problem. I'll go see if I can pump that nurse."

"Thank you."

Alice waited until he'd gone before leaning over the still woman on the bed. She had very few expectations that any of her words would sink in, but as the doctor had said, you never knew. There were cases of patients unconscious during surgery who repeated the dialogue of their surgeons upon awakening.

You simply never knew.

"Tabitha!" She made her tone incisive. "Can you hear me?"

Nothing. No reaction at all.

"It's me, Alice. You're in the hospital, but you're going to be all right." Please, God, let it be true. "While you're here, I have to be able to contact Sharlayne. And I don't know where she is or have a telephone number to reach her at.''

Nothing. She squeezed the limp hand tighter and pressed ahead.

''I don't know where the credit cards are, either. I've searched your room and found nothing. When I get back to the hotel I'll ask the manager to open the safe.''

Releasing the hand, Alice touched the cold cheek with gentle fingers. ''Of course, if I can reach Sharlayne I won't need the credit cards. Tabitha, can't you please—''

The door swung open and a young man in white coat burst through, pushing a gurney. He stopped short at the sight of Alice. ''Sharlayne Kenyon, is it really you? Nobody told me *you'd* be in here.''

''Yes, it's me.'' Alice rose wearily. ''You're here to get my friend?''

He consulted a clipboard. ''Ms. Thomas, yes.''

''Take good care of her, okay?''

''Sure.'' A grin creased his sun-browned surfer's face. ''If I do, can I have your autograph?''

''Sweetheart—'' she stepped close then, reached out her hand to cup his chin briefly ''—if you do, you can have a kiss.'' She winked at his stunned expression and walked out of the room.

That was that. Tabitha wouldn't be providing information any time soon. It was up to her alone.

But what was she worrying about? Even if she

didn't find what she needed, Sharlayne would learn of the accident and make contact.

Alice was sure of it.

SHARLAYNE ALMOST collapsed against the plush seat of the limo on the drive back to the hotel. Jed felt sorry for her. She was tired and worried about Tabitha, and perhaps at least a little about herself.

She turned her head where it rested against the seat. "What do you think, Jed? Was it an accident or was someone really after Tabitha...or maybe me? You've had plenty of time to come up with a theory."

She was right; he should have a theory, but he didn't. "The police seem pretty certain it was an accident," he said slowly. "But..." He held out a ragged scarf—the silvery bit of silk Tabitha had borrowed to guard against the wind.

She caught her breath. "That's my scarf."

"I thought I recognized it." He gave her a warning glance. "Which could mean something or nothing. But then there's the car bomb, complicating the situation. Your scarf complicates matters even more."

"That's what I was thinking." Her eyes were wide and vulnerable.

"Why would anyone want to do you harm, Sharlayne?" What the hell; they'd been through enough to be on a first-name basis. "Is it that book you're not writing or something else I don't know anything about?''

She licked her lips. "I can't think of any other reason, but even that…" She sat up straight, shaking her head. "I don't have any enemies that I'm aware of. As for my ex-husbands, they all adore me. They'd never want to do me harm."

"I'm not so sure Bill Rogers adores you."

"He has reason not to, I'll admit, but you should have seen right away that he's not the type to hurt anyone."

"You hope."

She laughed. "I hope. But you met him. Sending out bombs and hit cars are not things he'd even think about."

"No, but husband number six might."

She looked as if she were thinking fast to remember who husband number six was, another indication of her state of mind. "Oh, you mean John?" she said after a moment. "He's dead."

"But his family-with-a-capital-F is very much alive."

"Forget it," she said. "I simply refuse to believe there's actually someone who knows me who'd want to harm me. Of course, there's always the possibility of a deranged fan on the loose." She shivered as if she'd recalled something to support that scenario.

"What is it?" he asked quickly. "You've thought of something."

"Just that I need to get into the safe in the suite."
She leaned back again, but she didn't appear relaxed at all. "Tabitha must have put the cash and credit cards there. I'm going to need them."

What kind of world did she live in where she put all her assets into the hands of others?

He doubted he'd ever know. He knew he'd never understand.

But he would help her in any way he could.

CHAPTER NINE

Love in the NFL;
or, forward passes were to die for

What's it like being married to America's hero? Not all it's cracked up to be, actually. Mike had several very strong points and he knew how to make them count, but his ego was more unbridled than his...

That Book About This Body,
Sharlayne Kenyon

NOBODY COULD OPEN that safe except Mr. Corwin, the hotel manager, and he wouldn't be available until nine the next morning. That meant Alice had hours more to worry and fret.

Jed left her at the bedroom door with a light but encouraging pat on the shoulder, which felt good but not nearly good enough. She paced until nearly two, then went to bed, where she tossed and turned and worried some more until nearly seven. By then she'd come up with a plan...of sorts.

She'd go away. She'd go to the mountains; that

was it. She'd get a cabin in some barely accessible wilderness area and wait out the storm. She'd go alone; she wouldn't need Jed because no one would know where she was.

Or maybe she'd take Jed. There was more than one way to need a man, right? Besides, the media vultures would be looking for her, which would be all to the good since she was supposed to decoy them away from the real Sharlayne.

The first thing Alice did upon arising that morning was call the hospital for an update on Tabitha. There was no change. Hell.

Next order of business was to get herself in shape to face the hotel manager when he arrived to open the safe. A bath in what amounted to a sunken Roman pool didn't help. Nor did seeing her haggard expression in the makeup mirror in the huge marble bathroom. She'd have to be a magician to transform herself into Sharlayne Kenyon this morning. Whatever. All she could do was all she could do.

When Alice walked into the living room, the first thing she saw was Jed with a cup of coffee in one hand and a newspaper in the other. The first thing she heard was a string of curses that ended only when he looked up and saw her.

"Sorry," he said brusquely.

"I'm almost afraid to ask what set you off."

"You *won't* ask, if you're as smart as I think you are." He gestured toward the coffee service, complete with a second fragile china cup. "Help yourself."

"Sorry to disappoint you." She held out her hand for the newspaper. "I'm asking."

"You'll be sorry," he warned, surrendering his copy of the *Eye*.

The paper was already neatly folded to a photograph of Bill Rogers trying to dodge cameras—unsuccessfully. Quickly she scanned the copy:

Sharlayne's ex tells all. Bill Rogers of Hog Jaw, Arkansas, ex-husband number one of multimarried Sharlayne Kenyon, tells the *Eye* that the playgirl of the western world is planning a mountain retreat to escape the glaring eye of media attention. Seems that's the only way the beauteous Ms. Kenyon can find the solitude she craves to write that kiss-'n'-tell autobiography we've been hearing so much about for the past decade. For Gina Godfrey's take on this newest development, see Section C, page 1.

Alice groaned.

But bad news came at her in bunches. Next to the photo was a brief item headlined "Secretary injured" and reporting that Ms. Kenyon's secretary, Tabitha Thomas, had been struck in a hit-and-run and was in critical condition at a local hospital.

Alice tossed the paper aside. So much for her

mountain escape. She'd have to think of something else somewhere else, and it didn't look as if Tabitha was going to be a whole lot of help. But first—

The buzzer announced a visitor. Without a word, Jed went to open the door.

It was Mr. Corwin, the hotel manager. Now Alice would find out how much trouble she was *really* in.

"THANK YOU SO MUCH, Mr. Corwin. If Tabitha hadn't been hurt none of this would have been necessary. She handles all these details for me."

"I quite understand, Ms. Kenyon." Corwin bowed his way out of the penthouse. "Anything we can do to be of service. We've sent flowers to Ms. Thomas, but please offer her our warmest wishes for a speedy recovery."

"You're too kind."

She closed the door behind him and turned, slumping back against it. She felt miserably unhappy.

Jed looked at her with a perplexed expression, and she could practically read his mind. She'd found a credit card, a key, five thousand cash and a mess of jewelry in that safe. What else had she expected, a treasure map?

In a sense, yes. She'd expected—prayed, hoped—to find Sharlayne's telephone number or some other indication of how to locate her, but... nada.

"Now what?" He followed her back into the living room.

"You're the expert. You tell me."

"Okay, I've been giving it a lot of thought and—"

The telephone rang. Without asking, he picked it up and said a surly hello. He listened for a few minutes, with nothing more than an occasional, "Yeah?" or "No kiddin'" or "Uh-huh."

He hung up. "That was the cop shop. They haven't found the perpetrator, but they did find the car that hit Ms. Thomas. It belongs to a guy with a long list of priors. They think he was probably drunk or drugged out, which supports their theory that it was an unfortunate accident." He walked to the breakfast table and lifted a snowy napkin from a silver tray of pastries. "They could be right."

"They could also be wrong."

The telephone rang again. Annoyed and feeling hassled, Alice snatched it up before he could stop her. She said an impatient, "Hello?"

"I hoped you'd answer again, bitch. You don't learn very fast, do you?"

Who was calling her names and why did the slightly raspy voice sound so familiar?

"I told you not to write that book," he continued, "but from what I read in the papers, you don't learn real fast. You head for a mountain cabin and you're dead meat."

Alice's stomach clenched into a panicky knot. "Who is this?" she said in a frightened croak.

"You know who it is. Arrange a news conference. Announce the book is garbage and you can't write your name anyway, so you're calling the whole thing off. Do it or be real sorry." A click heralded the severing of the connection.

Alice simply stood there with the handset clutched in a death grip. Jed reached her in a few long strides and took the phone from her stiff fingers.

"What is it? Sharlayne, what's wrong?"

"It was—I—he said—" She sucked in a deep breath, fighting her fear and anxiety. Jed's face, filled with concern, gave her courage.

Dear Jed. She threw herself into his arms and clung to him, her entire body shaking.

"Who was it? What did he say, Sharlayne?" His tone was hard and dangerous.

She knew she had to tell him this time. She couldn't keep this to herself, not under the circumstances. "I didn't recognize his voice, but he seemed to think I should."

"What did he say? Tell me exactly."

"Let me think." She concentrated hard, gripping his shirt into a ball in her fist. "He said he was glad I answered again and he…called me a bitch. Then he said…exact words—*'I told you not to write that book, but…you don't learn real fast. You head for a mountain cabin and you're dead meat.'''* She shuddered.

"That's it?"

"He also said…when I asked who he was, 'You know who it is.' But I don't, Jed."

"You're sure?"

She nodded vigorously. "His voice is sort of raspy and sneering…."

"Sharlayne, he said *again*. Have you spoken to him on the telephone before?"

"I—" Jed wasn't going to like this. "He did call once already," she admitted.

"When?"

"The day we moved into this hotel."

"And you didn't tell me?" He shoved her out of his arms.

"I assumed it was just some crank. I didn't think too much about it at the time."

"Give me details."

"It was right after we got here. The phone rang, and since no one else was around, I automatically picked up."

"Go on." His tone was icy cold and angry.

"He wanted to know if I was going to write that book. I…asked who it was and he said I knew who it was, only I didn't. I was trying to find out how he knew I'd moved to this hotel and he said—he said—"

"Out with it," he ordered, no longer sympathetic and supportive.

"He said he knew everything I did."

Jed was silent for a long time. Then he said in a calculating way, "Maybe he does."

She wrapped her arms around her waist, seeking her own comfort. "I'm sorry I didn't tell you."

"Why didn't you?"

"I don't know." She turned away, miserable.

"Don't give me that. Of course, you do."

"All right, I didn't tell you because I knew you'd be annoyed I'd answered the phone when I shouldn't have. Plus I didn't lend any credence to what he said."

"Until now," he amended.

She nodded. "I have to admit I'm getting a little nervous. First there's the car bomb, then the phone call, then Tabitha's accident and now another phone call—"

Their gazes met; he and she agreed.

"Fishy," he said.

"Very. What do we do now?"

"What do you want to do now?"

"I guess I want to find a safe place to hide until my house is ready. I was thinking about the mountains."

"Until your ex blew that plan out of the water."

She nodded. "I'll have to think of someplace else." Someplace private and safe, where it would take the media a few days to track her down. She needed to remain in the spotlight just enough to squelch book rumors and fulfill her obligation to

Sharlayne, but not enough to create this kind of frenzy someplace else.

There was also the little matter of some weirdo making cryptic telephone calls. That had to be considered.

"What about Ms. Thomas?" he asked. "Are you willing to leave while she's still in the hospital?"

"I wouldn't if there was anything I could do for her. At the moment, there's not. A coma is a very tricky thing. She could linger like this for months, years in a worst-case scenario, or she could open her eyes today. Until she rounds that corner, there's nothing much anyone can do but wait."

He regarded her. "You sound almost as if you know what you're talking about."

"I do," she said hotly. "Why wouldn't I when—" She pulled herself up short. She certainly couldn't tell him she was a registered nurse in another life.

"When what?" he goaded.

She lifted her chin. "When I've seen 'The Remarkable Brain' on PBS a dozen times—what do you think? Look, I apologize for not telling you about the first telephone call. Believe me, I'm more upset about my lack of judgment than you can ever be."

"I doubt that."

She forced a careless shrug. "Whatever. I'm going to call for the car. I want to go to the hospital and see how Tabitha's doing."

"I'll call the car," he offered. "You get ready to go."

Relieved because she thought perhaps he'd forgiven her, she did as he directed.

THE LIMO DREW UP in front of the hospital. Before they could make the relative safety of the lobby, they were surrounded by flashing lights and shouting reporters.

"Were you there, Sharlayne? Did you see the accident? Are you really going to move to the mountains to write your book? Are you and Jed flying to Las Vegas later today to get married? I have it from a usually reliable source that—"

Jed growled deep in his throat and reached for the nearest offender. Flying to Las Vegas to get married! Jeez! How did she live with all this crap going on around her on a regular basis?

From all he'd heard, she not only lived with it, she thrived on it. Glancing over his shoulder at her now as he tried to clear a path, she certainly didn't look as if she enjoyed it at all. In fact, she looked frightened.

After shoving the last obstacle—that is, the last photographer—aside, he yanked open the hospital door and pushed her through. She almost fell inside and he dragged the heavy door closed, then made an obscene gesture at the yellow journalists banging on the glass. Strobes popped. He resisted the urge to swear.

He was in a hospital, after all.

THERE WAS NO CHANGE in Tabitha's condition.

That's what the doctor said, but Alice could tell that herself. Sitting by the woman's side and holding her limp hand, she wondered again how long it would take Sharlayne to hear about this and call.

Jed slumped in a chair in one corner of the small private room. A couple of bouquets rested on a window ledge next to him. She frowned. One would be from the hotel, but who had sent the other?

"Jed," she said softly, "who are the flowers from?"

Rousing himself, he leaned forward. "This one's from the Beverly Pacific."

"And the other?"

"From…" He dug through the greenery to extract the card and read, "'Best wishes for a speedy recovery. Alice.'"

Alice. Her own name struck right at the pit of her stomach. It was almost as if she and Sharlayne had *really* exchanged identities. Would they ever be able to make this right?

"Is that the Alice who got the telephone call?" Jed inquired.

Mind whirling, she nodded. Wasn't Sharlayne going to make contact even now? "What florist sent those?" she asked on sudden inspiration.

He checked the card again. "Flowers backward-R Us in Beverly Hills."

"Oh." Disappointed, she considered her options.

"Would you mind calling to see if you can find out where the order was placed? I'd really like to get in touch with Alice now that Tabitha's laid up."

"Yeah?"

Was he suspicious or was she simply feeling guilty? "Alice could be very helpful to me, under the circumstances," she said.

"Okay. No problem." He pulled a cell phone from its hook on his belt, checked the delivery card for a third time and dialed.

Heart pounding, she waited, unable to tell anything from his side of the conversation. She didn't have long to wait.

He clicked off. "They don't give out that kind of information. All she'd tell me was that the order was placed on the Internet."

"That's not very helpful."

"Sorry. Look, you take your time here. I'll go see if I can find a back way out of this fishbowl."

"Thank you."

He left. The room was deathly quiet except for the hum of medical equipment. Tabitha never moved.

Alice couldn't be sure she ever would.

THE FIRST THING Alice did upon arriving back at the hotel was place a call to Sharlayne's publisher. Why that hadn't occurred to her before, she couldn't imagine. Linden Wilbert would know where Sharlayne was hidden away. Alice was sure of it.

She asked for Mr. Wilbert.

"I'm sorry, but he's not in the office," his personal assistant said with crisp professionalism.

"Oh. When will he be back? I really need to speak to him."

"I can't say for sure. He's away on business."

"Days? Weeks? Give me a hint!"

The woman laughed. "I wish I could. Under the circumstances, perhaps our Mr. Hilliard could help you. He's taken on all Mr. Wilbert's duties in the interim."

"No, this is personal—and very, very important. Are you sure there's no way I can reach him?"

"I'm sorry." She sounded it, too. "If he calls in, I can give him a message Ms.—?"

"Ms. Kenyon. Sharlayne Kenyon."

"Oh, Ms. Kenyon, please forgive me. I should have recognized your voice. I'll certainly do all I can to deliver the message."

Alice thanked her and hung up, wondering what the hell was going on.

JED WAS WAITING for her when Sharlayne came out of her bedroom. There were decisions to be made and he figured she was the one who'd have to make them.

She stopped short at the sight of him. "What?"

He laughed. "Do I look like the spider waiting for the fly?"

"Sort of." His remark reminded her of how she'd felt that fateful morning when Sharlayne had beckoned her into the room.

"Sorry about that, but I *am* waiting for you. We've got to figure out our next move."

"I know." She crossed to the wet bar, pulled out a bottle of water and looked at him expectantly.

"First of all," he said, "I had the hotel install a new telephone."

"Why? The old one worked fine."

"This one's a speaker phone." He picked up the unit to show her. "That way I can listen in if you get any more threatening calls."

Her eyes widened. "Threatening? I wouldn't call those calls *threatening*…exactly."

"Okay, menacing. Does that make you feel better?"

"Not much." She carried her bottle of water to the sofa and sat. "What else?"

"Are we staying or going?"

She chewed on her lower lip. "I don't know. I feel so…lost. I can't figure out what I should do or where I should go to do it."

"I assume you'd like my recommendation."

"Of course."

"Then this is it—get out of here while the getting's good. This hotel isn't very secure, although it's still better than your house. Isn't there someplace you'd like to go? Someone you'd like to visit?''

She shuddered as if he'd made some kind of faux pas. ''I can't think of anyplace at the moment. The mountains sounded good before the papers got wind of it—solitude and inaccessibility and all that sort of thing. Now...I just don't know.''

''In the meantime, we stay here?''

She shrugged.

''Why are you so indecisive?'' he asked impatiently. ''It's not like you.''

''How do you know what's like me? You don't, Jed.'' Rising, she turned away. ''I'm exhausted. I'm going to take a nap.''

''Good idea. I'll field phone calls, since Ms. Thomas isn't around to do it.''

''Thank you.'' She walked away with perfect posture, even in her current complicated state of mind.

SHE DREAMED she was in a cage, with lions and tigers prowling around outside. She wasn't exactly frightened so much as confused, until Jed appeared to whisper in her ear: *Don't you think it's time to do something? Unleash your tigers.* And he pounded on the bars with both fists—

It was the pounding that awakened her, the pounding on her bedroom door. Sitting up in confusion, she struggled to get her bearings.

"Hey, wake up! There's a phone call I think you'll want to take."

Jed. What was he talking about? There was no one she wanted to speak to except—

Her eyes flew wide. *Sharlayne!* Could it possibly be?

"I'm coming." She stumbled off the bed and to the door, trying to clear her mind for whatever was about to happen. Sharlayne must have disguised her voice somehow. Alice would have to be careful what she said—my God! Jed would be able to hear Sharlayne's part of the conversation on the new speaker phone. How to warn her?

She threw open the door—in Jed's face.

"It's about time," he said. "You've got a call. It's—"

"I know." She brushed past him, intent upon resolving this situation. Pretending to be someone as high-profile as Sharlayne was too much responsibility.

The handset lay beside the phone. Snatching it up, she said, "Hello? Hello?"

Nothing. The line was dead. She looked around frantically for Jed. "There's no one here!"

"That's because you didn't punch the Hold button." He performed that small chore. "Try again."

"Hello, hello?"

"Laynie, honey, it's me."

She drew a blank. Who the hell was behind that sweet Southern male drawl?

His laughter flowed over the wire like melted caramel. "Don't tell me you don't recognize my voice—don't tell me that! It's me, Mikey, your favorite forward passer."

Her brain raced. Mikey? She stumbled through the list of Sharlayne's ex-husbands: Bill Rogers, the mechanic; Johnny Juice, a drugged-out rock musician; Melvin K. Satterfeld, elderly U.S. senator; Mike—

Texas born and bred Mike Murphy, retired NFL quarterback and national hero.

"Mike!" His name was a breathy sigh of relief on her lips. "Oh, Mike!"

"Now, now, honey lamb, it'll be all right," he assured her. "I been readin' about the further adventures of you. I've got t' say, it sounds like you got yourself in a helluva mess out there."

She spared a glance at Jed. He was watching and listening. "You didn't call to gloat," she asked Mike. "Did you?"

"Baby darlin', you know me better than that. I called to help you out."

Her heart gave a hopeful little jump. "I won't deny I could use some of that."

"I figured. See, the thing is, I'm heading to Japan tomorrow to do a couple of weeks of football clinics. I thought maybe you'd like to use my place while I'm gone. Good spot to hole up, since it's kinda on a island."

His place? She didn't have a clue where his place was. "I..." she hedged. "Do you really think—"

"Shore do. Look, I know you've never seen this place and I don't know what you think about Florida in general, but they got all these little ol' islands down here called keys. My place is on one 'a them that's only got three other houses. We got a guard on the bridge, so the only other way to get here is by boat. That should cut back on the paparazzi by a bunch."

"It's sounding better and better." But apparently not to Jed, who didn't appear happy. She turned her back on him. "Are you sure you wouldn't mind?"

"Hell, yes, I'm sure." His chuckle was low and satisfied. "I know why you want to get away and I'm all for it."

He knew? She doubted it. "And that would be—?"

"You want to write that book, a'course."

"That's all right with you?"

"Sure! More than all right. Hell, I want the book written. I'm eager for the whole world to know I'm the best lover Sharlayne Kenyon ever had."

Speechless, she whirled, too late to avoid the sight of Jed standing there with a stunned expression on his face.

Undeterred, Mike continued, his voice forceful on the speaker. "I'm still the champ, ain't I? It's been a while, I realize, but—"

"You're still the champ," she purred. "You'll *always* be my champ, Mikey."

"See?" His tone was triumphant. "There's nothin' bad you could *possibly* say about me."

Except maybe that he was incredibly conceited. But he also sounded incredibly nice. Generous, too. Sharlayne was right about this one; he harbored no ill will toward her.

"Want to take me up on it, then?" he pressed.

"Maybe. Tell you what. My bodyguard is here—"

"Your what?" He sounded thoroughly shocked.

"It's a long story. Anyway, why don't you give him the details of how we get there, and I'll call you back later today and tell you my decision."

"I thought it'd just be you and that Tabby woman." He sounded disappointed; he obviously hadn't heard about the accident.

"Unfortunately, Tabitha is…indisposed. But you'll like talking to Jed. He's a crusty old guy, but he knows his business."

"Old guy, huh?" Mike sounded happy to hear this. "Okay, put the old codger on and I'll give him the info."

She passed the handset to a scowling Jed, thinking this could be the answer to her prayers.

CHAPTER TEN

Philosophical aside;
the men in my life

Let's be honest: I like men. Always have, always will. I'll admit that most have been nothing more than passing fancies, but every once in a while I've run across a keeper. Of course, it usually took an intimate encounter to make me realize this....

That Book About This Body,
Sharlayne Kenyon

"THE IDEA STINKS," Jed said flatly. "Florida is definitely out."

His attitude got Alice's dander up in a flash. "Wait a minute. I was under the impression that *I* was the one making the decisions here."

"You are, within reason. But as far as Florida goes, I have no intention of deliberately leading you into danger."

"Danger? Ha! Mike's house is on an island, for heaven's sake. Nobody will even be able to get close to me." *Except you,* she resisted adding. "Shut up a minute and think of the advantages to these arrangements."

"Ever hear of boats?" he countered. "Or helicopters?"

"Oh, for the love of—get a grip. I'm being harassed for purposes of gossip, not murder."

"You don't know what you're being harassed for. Neither do I. Neither do the cops."

"That's why I have you hanging around." She gave him her sultriest look.

"Really? You think you have me? Maybe not."

Shocked by his blunt assertion, she stared at him. "Is that some kind of a threat?"

"Not at all," he said, obviously satisfied by her response. "I'm just saying that I don't think Florida is a good idea."

"Then what is? Hanging around here like a sitting duck?"

"No..." He said thoughtfully.

"You can't have it both ways, Jed."

A muscle leaped in his jaw. "Don't push, okay? We both need to think about this."

"Agreed." She glanced at Sharlayne's diamond-studded wristwatch, which looked very at home on her wrist. "It's a few minutes past two. Let's get back together at five for drinks and decisions."

"Works for me."

"See you, then."

"See you."

For a moment they stared at each other across the vast recesses of the huge room. Then she turned and walked out.

THE FIRST THING Jed had to do was call his office. It took nearly five full minutes to reach Samantha.

She said, "This better be good, sweetheart."

"I wouldn't say it's good, exactly. More like screwed-up."

"Oh-oh. Tell Mama everything. Did that secretary who got hit by the car pop off?"

"Naw, she's the same. Still in a coma. It's Sharlayne. She—"

"So it's 'Sharlayne' now, is it? Yesterday she was 'Ms. Kenyon.' You haven't forgotten my first commandment, have you?"

He felt like a kid being called onto the carpet. "'*Thou shalt not get involved with thy client—*' no, I haven't forgotten it. It's just that it's hard to stand toe-to-toe and fight with someone and still avoid using her first name."

"You're not supposed to fight—you're supposed to protect."

"You don't think I know that?" Disgusted, he glared around the room on general principles. "She's making it damned hard for me to do my job. I just found out she had a couple of threatening phone calls and didn't bother to mention them until I dragged it out of her."

"How threatening?"

He repeated the gist of the telephone calls. Following a lengthy silence, Samantha said, "My instinct tells me these are not the work of a prankster."

"Yeah, that's how I felt about it."

"What does she think?"

"That everybody in the world loves her and no one would ever hurt her under any circumstances."

"Must be nice," Samantha said dryly. "Nevertheless, it's your job to protect her, Jed."

"Yeah, I know. Problem is, she's got it into her head to go to Florida."

"With you?"

"Yes. She's thinking about staying at the home of one of her many exes. It's on some key or the other. Can't say I'm too crazy about the idea."

"Because…?"

"First of all, I don't know jack about Florida. Never been there, never wanted to go there."

"So? You intend to only accept assignments in your own backyard?"

"No, but…there's the matter of staying on some little island."

"Harder for bad guys to get there," Samantha pointed out.

"Also harder to get off in an emergency."

"True." Another silence. Then she said, "Assuming there's at least a modicum of security, it's still a good idea. If she can sneak out of town so no one will know she's gone—"

"Don't count on it."

"I won't. I read the papers. Look, Jed, my gut instinct tells me that the Florida caper is a good one. Take her there and keep her out of trouble for a week. By then the security system should be up and running at her place and she can go home."

"In a perfect world," he said dourly. "I don't know if we're dealing with incompetents over there or what, but I'm beginning to wonder if that system's just a figment of my imagination."

"Cheer up, sweetheart. At least you're waiting it out in the lap of luxury."

"Yeah, sure." He hung up, thinking that he'd rather wait it out in the lap of...Sharlayne. It was getting harder and harder to keep his cool and his distance.

Thou shalt not get involved with thy client.

Period.

That's what he really had against Florida: alone on an island with Sharlayne Kenyon. It might prove to be more than flesh and blood could bear, even his.

ALICE TOOK A NAP, or tried to. Mostly she lay on the broad expanse of silk-swathed bed with her eyes closed tight while she tried to figure out what she should do next.

She had nowhere to turn, no one in whom she could confide, no one—conscious, anyway—who knew what was going on. Tabitha was in the hospital, Sharlayne was God only knows where, even Mr. Wilbert was out of touch. She was definitely on her own...almost.

There was still Jed. Too bad she had to deceive him, yet there was nothing she could do about that.

A horrible thought struck: what if he bailed out on her? The Florida offer seemed like the answer to her prayers, but Jed didn't like it. What if she told him she was going anyway? Would he wish her "Bon voyage" and head north to San Francisco, leaving her to stumble along on her own?

He couldn't do that, could he? Hadn't Sharlayne signed some kind of contract with his agency? Even so, the agency might simply assign another operative, and then where would Alice be? Cooped up with some stranger in a strange land...

She had to convince Jed to stick with her, that was all. She knew of only one way to do that.

She would seduce him.

She'd decided days ago to sleep with him but had never formulated any particular plan to achieve this. Instead she'd waited for nature to take its course. And where had that led? Nowhere. Left to his own devices, Jed obviously found her eminently resistible.

She wondered how he'd react to the real Sharlayne. Jealousy clawed at her throat. She groaned and rolled over on the big bed.

She was no Sharlayne Kenyon; she was plain old Alice Wynn. Sure, with Sharlayne's help she'd been transformed into a close approximation of a butterfly, but apparently a second-rate butterfly. Clearly, she was much more attracted to Jed Kelby than he was to her.

Still, she must keep him by her side, no matter what it took.

ALICE DRESSED CAREFULLY for what she hoped was to come. She stood for a long time in front of the closet, considering her options. Tabitha had chosen the items hanging neatly on wooden hangers. In fact, every morning Tabitha selected the day's wardrobe and Alice obediently put on whatever was handed to her.

Now she was on her own. After considerable agonizing, she decided on black Lycra leggings and a sleeveless black Lycra top, both so skintight that there wasn't room for anything underneath. Before she walked out the door, she'd throw on a sheer white blouse that buttoned down the front, concealing while revealing.

She applied her makeup with special attention, even though her hands shook so hard she could barely hold the pencils and tubes and brushes. She had never before set out to seduce a man. She wasn't even sure how to go about it.

Maybe if she simply asked herself, *What would Sharlayne do?* The question made her smile. Still, it was worth a shot.

As ready as she'd ever be, she braced her shoulders, ready to advance upon her prey. But first—

She dialed room service and ordered flowers, hors d'oeuvres, a bowl of fresh strawberries and a couple of bottles of champagne. That should help the seduction along.

She found Jed waiting for her in the living room, standing before the French doors and staring out over the balcony at the manicured greenery below. When she entered, he turned slowly, as if reluctant to confront her.

His eyes widened slightly before he dropped his gaze to her feet and began a slow perusal of her body. It took considerable effort on her part not to avoid that disapproving stare. *What would Sharlayne do?* She'd give him a cheeky smile and say just what she did: "Take a picture. It'll last longer."

"Cute," he told her with a faintly reluctant smile. "Maybe I should."

"Maybe I should, too." Now it was her turn to look *him* over—and he looked damned good in khaki-colored trousers and a navy-blue knit shirt that fit nicely. His short dark hair glistened with drops of water; he must be newly out of the shower.

She headed toward the wet bar. "I think I'll try a glass of Kelby-Linus wine," she announced. "Will you join me?"

"Yes. Let me do the honors."

"Not this time." She gave him a lazy smile.

"This time I'd like to serve you, Jed. Why don't you sit down and enjoy it."

His nostrils flared with the intake of a quick breath. "I'm not sure I'm cut out to be served."

"We're about to find out."

She pulled out a bottle of Kelby-Linus cabernet sauvignon from beneath the counter and reached for the corkscrew. She often did this for Sharlayne, so it was a simple matter to extract the cork and pour ruby-dark wine into crystal glasses. She carried both to Jed where he sat on a chair facing the sofa, and offered one.

He took it, held it aloft to examine the contents for clarity and said, "Cheers."

"Cheers," she repeated. They drank.

"Okay," he said, all business again. "We've got to come to some agreement about Florida. I still think—"

She interrupted him with a groan. "Please, Jed, can we work up to that? I'd really like to enjoy my wine first."

He did not look happy. "I suppose, but—" The doorbell pealed and he shot to his feet. "Who the hell?"

"Let me." She laid a light hand on his forearm.

"Not a chance."

"But it's room service. I ordered snacks."

"Oh." He was disappointed. "Even so, I don't want you answering any doors." He backed her up to the sofa and sat her down before turning away.

Minutes later he reappeared, pushing a linen-covered cart with a grand assortments of nibbles, munchies, huge strawberries complete with stems in a crystal bowl and, on the shelf below, two bottles of champagne in silver coolers.

"Champagne?" He raised his brows.

"It seemed like a good idea at the time." She lifted her glass. "I'd like to finish this excellent cabernet first, though."

"Would you know an excellent cabernet from a run-of-the-mill version?" He sat back down in his chair.

She slipped off her sandals and curled her legs up on the sofa. "Probably not," she admitted cheerfully, "but I know what I like." Her words hung in the air provocatively. "I suppose you're a connoisseur of wine."

He shrugged.

"How long have the Kelbys been in the wine business?" Keep him talking; distract him. But she found that she awaited his answer with interest.

"My great-grandfather and his best friend, Mark Linus, started the California winery around the turn of the century," he said. "He married Mark's sister, Veronica, who eventually inherited the Linus part of the business."

"And his children kept up the family tradition?"

"Yes, and so on, generation after generation."

"Until you."

He gave her a sharp glance. "My younger

brother earned the right to carry on family traditions,'' he said.

''Because...?''

''It wasn't enough for me at the time, that's all.''

She set her empty glass on the end table. ''What did you do, instead, Jed?''

''I got it into my head that I wanted something different, so I—'' He stopped short, his eyes narrowing. ''I'm not going to tell you my life story, Sharlayne. There's no need for you to know anything about me beyond my professional qualifications.''

She pursed her lips. ''That's not very friendly. We're in this together, Jed. It's only natural that I'd want to know a little about you.''

''You know enough.''

''I suspect more than I know.''

He looked skeptical. ''What is it you suspect?''

''I suspect—'' she eyed the stiff-necked Jed Kelby, sitting at attention in a brocade chair, and suppressed an impish grin ''—you were in the army, weren't you?''

''Hell, no!'' He appeared first astounded, then disconcerted, and finally, outraged. ''I was in the Marine Corps.''

She laughed at his consternation. ''You ex-Marines are all—''

''Not ex,'' he interrupted quickly. ''Former. There are no ex-Marines, only former Marines.''

''Once a Marine, always a Marine?''

"Something like that."

"I'll start over. I knew a Marine once and he had the same kind of arrogance you've got, the kind that comes with thinking you can handle anything. It's not unattractive."

"Thanks, and it's not merely thinking. We *are* the best."

But now he was grinning, apparently amused because she'd figured something out about him. "Okay, turnabout is fair play," he said. He popped a ripe red strawberry into his mouth, then reached for the first bottle of champagne. "Tell me something about you I don't know."

"I'm sure you know everything about me," she said. "I'm sure everybody knows everything about me."

"I didn't know you had a daughter. That seems to be some kind of big secret."

She could hardly say, *I didn't know it myself.* She looked down at her hands, with their long shapely nails. "You must think very badly of me."

He popped the champagne cork without spilling a single drop of the golden liquid. "I did at first."

She glanced up hopefully. "At first?"

He poured wine into a crystal flute. "It eventually sank in that some women aren't cut out to be mothers. You probably *did* do the kid a favor by leaving her with her father."

She grimaced. True of Sharlayne, obviously, but not of Alice. "If there'd been a better way... But there wasn't, Jed. Other women face other choices, but that was a very hard one for me.'' She exchanged her empty glass for one with champagne. ''Won't you join me?''

''I haven't finished this.''

''Oh.'' Disappointing. She wanted him with her.

''Ms. Thomas doesn't have any children, either, I take it.''

''No, nor does she want any. She was married once and it didn't work out.'' She added with sudden inspiration, ''Alice, on the other hand—''

''Alice? The woman who got the phone call the other day from her cousin?''

She nodded. ''I think you'd like Alice.'' She *hoped* he'd like Alice. ''She's a registered nurse who came to work for me after I was in an auto accident. She stayed on to set up an exercise program for me, and then she took over meal planning, and then—'' She laughed. ''She made herself indispensable.''

''Why isn't she here now?''

''Oh, because—'' She blinked, realizing she had no story at the ready. ''She...she, uh—she's on vacation. Yes, that's where she is, on vacation,'' she said, reiterating an earlier explanation.

''Is she coming back any time soon? Will I be meeting her?''

''Oh, well— Yes, sure. Of course you'll meet her. Unless something comes up,'' she concluded vaguely.

"Such as?"

"With Alice, you never know. She's such a soft touch. Before she came to work for me, she spent years caring for an ill grandmother. It kind of stunted her social growth. You understand how it is."

"Not really."

This was kind of fun, talking about herself in the third person. It was also revealing; she'd never before acknowledged that her social growth had been inhibited.

"Alice is…really naive," she ventured.

"Unlike you."

She lifted her chin. "Maybe I'm not exactly what you think I am."

"Then again, maybe you are."

"I have a softer side," she protested. "I have feelings that get hurt. There are things I want that I can't have."

"Such as?"

She stared at him, then slowly swung her legs over the edge of the sofa. "You know what I'm talking about," she said in a tone that sizzled.

"Sharlayne—"

"No, really, Jed, why are you so distant?" She rose, dropping the sheer overblouse off her shoulders, not caring where it landed. "We're in this together. We're all we've got."

His gaze slid over her, almost like a touch. "You're a client, nothing more."

"I think I'm considerably more." She drifted across the space between them and put her hands on the wooden arms of his chair. "I know you're more than just a bodyguard to me."

"Security expert." His voice sounded tight and under pressure.

She was making him nervous. That knowledge pleased her enormously. She leaned down to look directly into his face. "We're here alone," she murmured seductively. "Just you and me, not even Tabitha around to get in our way. We're free to say and do whatever we want."

"Stop it, Sharlayne." He spoke roughly, but his hands on her forearms were gentle as he held her back. "You don't have to come on to me to guarantee my loyalty."

"You think that's what I'm doing?" Drunk with power and possibilities, she pressed a lingering kiss on his temple. "I've wanted to do that for a long time. And more—"

Dipping lower, she pressed her mouth to his. Eyes closing, she concentrated on the kiss, her hands moving to his lean cheeks to hold him exactly where she wanted. She was enjoying herself so much, felt so powerful, that it took a while to realize he wasn't participating.

She hauled back her head and stared at him. "What is it?"

"I can be bought, but I can't be had."

The remark hit her like a bucket of cold water in

the face. She straightened. "What's that supposed to mean?"

"That you don't need to do this."

"Need to do what?" She stared at him boldly. "What do you think I am, anyway?"

"A spoiled woman accustomed to getting her own way."

"Well, thanks so much." She backed off, her hands clenched at her sides. "There are a lot of men out there who'd kill to be where you are right now." Or so Sharlayne had often said. "Don't be so self-righteous."

"Sorry if I offended you. It would be dishonorable of me to take you up on your generous offer, under the circumstances."

Alice had never been so insulted in her life. "You're making a big mistake, buster." She whirled around and headed for the sanctuary of her bedroom.

"Wait a minute. We haven't discussed Florida."

"Screw Florida," she said over her shoulder. "And for the record—you're fired!"

"You can't fire me. I have a contract."

"I *can* fire you and I just did." She slipped through the doorway to the bedroom and turned to slam the door in his face. Unfortunately, he barged through before she could do it.

"Be reasonable," he said. "Just because I don't like aggressive women doesn't mean—"

"Aggressive women!" She faced him in outrage.

It hadn't been easy for her to throw herself at him that way. To be criticized as aggressive was more than she could handle.

"Calm down." He held up his hands in a placating gesture. "You can't deny it. The minute you walked out in that getup I knew what you were up to."

"What's wrong with this getup?" She looked down at herself, exposed by black Lycra. *Alice* would never flaunt herself this way.

"You're borderline naked, for openers."

"I am not! I'm completely covered." Pivoting, she dashed for the bathroom, figuring he wouldn't follow her in there.

She was wrong; he followed her without hesitation into the marble wonderland. Deliberately ignoring him, she busied herself by turning the water on in the sunken bathtub to full blast. Surely he'd take the hint and leave.

He didn't. "About Florida—"

"I won't discuss Florida with you. Why should I? You've made your feelings perfectly clear. Now, if you'd leave, I'd like to take a bath."

"We've got to discuss Florida."

"Jed, you're in my bathroom! Will you kindly get out?" She pointed a rigid finger at the door.

"I can't do that, Sharlayne." He had that stubborn expression on his face again. "You've got to listen to me. I've decided—"

"You've decided! Like I care what you've decided." She pressed the heels of her hands over her ears to blot out his voice. "Go away."

"Not until we get a few things straightened out."

He reached for her and she yanked away. Catching a foot on the low rim around the sunken tub, she flailed for balance. He tried to grab her, but she was more intent upon avoiding him than in avoiding a fall.

"Damn it, Sharlayne. Let me help you! Don't—"

Too late.

She already had.

CHAPTER ELEVEN

I play the field;
or, maybe the field was playing me.

I never—repeat, never—took on the entire
Johnny Juice Joy Band in a single evening. In
the first place, it wouldn't have been possible,
since most of them were stoned at any given
moment....

That Book About This Body,
Sharlayne Kenyon

SHARLAYNE HIT the water with a huge splash and
immediately began to choke and thrash about. She
needed rescuing and Jed could see only one way to
do that: go in after her—literally dive in, since the
rapidly filling "bathtub" was more like a swimming pool. When he'd first walked in here and seen
the sunken marble monstrosity, he'd immediately
thought of Roman orgies and Olympic races.

Sputtering and flailing, she tried to stand up,
slipped backward and went under again. That's
when he jumped.

He landed next to her, feet first, with an enormous splash that compounded the splash from open faucets. After fishing around, he grabbed a handful of something and hauled her to the surface in hip-deep water.

She struck at him blindly with both hands and at least one foot. Wet blond hair lay plastered around her face, and her eyes were tightly closed.

But not her mouth. "What are you trying to do, drown me?"

"I'm trying to save you." He caught her wrists and held her arms wide in self-defense.

She stumbled to her feet, water streaming down her body—her *body,* because the tight black stuff she had on was virtually transparent. She was like an angry goddess rising from the sea, full breasted and glorious in her rage.

"Are you trying to save me or just make me crazy?" she shouted at him.

"I'm trying to—"

And then he forgot what he was trying to do, because she surged forward and he surged forward and they came together in an explosion of pent-up desire. Right there in the middle of the bathtub in the penthouse of the Beverly Pacific Hotel, they kissed and kissed again. Ripping at each other's clothes, they struggled not to break the contact of their hungry mouths.

"Damn," he gasped, shocked by her slick hands on his bare back, "I never intended—"

"Shut up and kiss me," she ordered in that throaty voice, "because I *did* intend."

"Can you reach the faucets? We're about to flood the room." He kissed his way down her cheek to her throat, then pulled away just enough to drag the sodden shirt over her head.

"I think so." She had to lean across him to do it, which brought those luscious breasts within easy reach of his mouth. She groaned and pressed against him, her legs opening to lower her body onto his lap. "There," she gasped. "At least we won't wash the hotel into the Pacific."

"I don't know," he muttered, rolling her nipple with his tongue. "The evening's young...."

So much for Samantha's lousy commandment.

JED AWAKENED sometime later in Sharlayne's big canopied bed. She lay on her back beside him, naked as the day she was born. Her light but steady breathing told him she slept soundly.

As he should be. Sex with Sharlayne Kenyon should satisfy the most discriminating lover, and, if her publicity was to be believed, *had*. So why was he lying here staring up at the satin canopy?

Because he was a damned fraud. He'd prided himself on his strong moral fiber and set himself up as some kind of paragon of virtue. Then, in a flash, all that vaunted self-control disappeared in a steamy bathtub. He'd fallen upon Sharlayne like a starving dog on a bone.

The fact that she'd fallen upon him with equal fervor was neither here nor there. She was who and what she was and at least had been acting in character. He, on the other hand—

Hell, he'd acted completely out of character. He never lost his cool, never lost control. If he was going to, it certainly wouldn't be with a woman as worldly as this one. He liked simple women—not simple-dumb but simple as in not complex and complicated. Yet here he was in bed with the most complicated woman he'd ever stumbled across.

He had to get out of here. He couldn't think straight with that beautiful naked body gleaming in moonlight streaming through the French doors. It would be so easy to reach out and touch those full breasts—

She moaned and turned toward him—when had his thought become action? Her flesh throbbed warm and resilient beneath his palm and only when she slid her knee between his thighs did his own nudity register. Without ever opening her eyes, she placed one small but surprisingly strong hand on his chest, her fingertips tightening on his flat nipple.

"Ummm..." Leaning closer, she flicked her tongue across his skin, and at that point, he decided he'd stay just a little while longer.

JED ROLLED from the bed and slipped out of Sharlayne's web at first light. Samantha wasn't going to like such an early call, but he had to get this straightened out now.

He was involved with a client. That meant all objectivity was down the tubes.

He awakened his boss, but that couldn't be helped. "It's me. Jed," he said brusquely. "I've got to talk to you about—"

"It damn well better be about your trip to Florida."

"Not exactly. It's about my client. See, she's—"

"Damn it, Jed, I don't have time for this. You're the fourth operative who's called in the past twenty-four hours to whine. Nobody promised you an easy assignment, as I recall. Don't tell me Sharlayne Kenyon is difficult to get along with, because I don't care. It's your job to get along with her so you can protect her."

"I understand that, but if you could just assign someone else and give me another job—"

"I don't have anyone else! Don't you get it? We're overextended to the max. Look—" She gave an impatient little growl. "Is it that you're not up to it? This is your first assignment. Can't you do the job?"

"I can do the damned job." It stung him to think she could doubt that.

"Then do it. We're in a bind here. Shut up and do your job, okay?"

He gritted his teeth. "Yeah, okay. If that's the only way."

"It is." Her relief was clear. "So you've got a difficult client. Trust me, she won't be the last. Do what you need to do to get along."

"I guess I'll have to." Within reason.

Samantha's laughter conveyed relief. "At least I don't have to worry that you'll get personally involved with her. You're just about the only guy on my payroll I can say that about and mean it, by the way. You're an iron man, Jed. Thank God for you!"

He hung up feeling like a total fake.

Sharlayne appeared just about the time he was pouring his second cup of coffee. She looked radiant in a shimmery white dress that wafted around her bare feet. She didn't hesitate, just walked straight up to him, took the cup out of his hand, sat down uninvited on his lap and kissed him.

Then she nuzzled the side of his neck and murmured, "I'm so glad you're here."

He felt all kinds of body parts reacting to her seemingly artless actions. "Yeah, well, about that—"

She sat up, her arms still loosely around his neck. "Yes?"

"What happened last night—"

Her laughter cut him off. "What *happened?*"

"Can't happen again," he pressed on doggedly.

"Says who?" She kissed his lips lightly.

"Says me." He breathed through his nose, reveling in the scent of her: something light but sophisticated.

"Because…?" Her full lips tilted up roguishly. She obviously wasn't taking him seriously.

"Sharlayne, any kind of a personal relationship between me and a client is…it's unethical. It compromises the quality of my work."

"Don't start that again," she said petulantly.

"Got to. It's the first commandment of my agency. *'Thou shalt not—'*"

"I know all about the shalt nots." She made a face. "I thought we were past all that."

"Not by a long shot. I lost my head last night, but I'm okay now. Either you go along with me on this or I'll have to swap assignments with another operative." Risky, but he was desperate. If she kept coming on to him, he'd crack sooner rather than later. Even iron men had their limitations.

She pouted. "I thought you were right there with me." She traced the line of his set jaw with a fingertip.

He licked his lips. "Yeah, but that's beside the point. If we're going to get you to Florida and safety—"

"Then you've changed your mind about Florida?"

"Yeah, I have. I'm ready to make the plane reservations."

"First class," she purred.

"Okay, first class. The sooner we get out of here the better."

"I'll check on Tabby, then. If there's no change, we might as well go today, provided you can get the reservations." She jumped up off his lap and looked down at him, smiling. "By the way, I understand what you were just trying to tell me."

"You do?"

She nodded. "You mean that while we're out on this limb, it isn't safe to have a personal relationship. But as soon as we get to Florida, we can—"

"That's not what I meant at all. We can't—"

"We can." She blew him a kiss. "I'll call the hospital and then I'll let Mike know we're coming. You call the airline. Use my credit card."

"Okay, but—"

"Say no more, darling." She gave him a playful wink. "I understand *perfectly*."

Somehow he doubted it.

JED SENT the luggage down the back stairs and then tried to sneak Sharlayne out behind it. No dice. A pack of paparazzi waited, so he took her boldly out the front.

Mr. Corwin, the hotel manager, did his best to shoo the waiting celebrity watchers out of their way, but his success was meager. By the time Jed and Sharlayne got past the glass doors, Corwin was shoving people aside while Jed hustled her to the waiting limo.

He should have recognized the man waiting alone on the curb beside the long black automobile. He was famous, after all, even years past his prime as a rock musician. He looked like hell at the moment, with a thin bearded face and shaved head, dirty jeans and a black T-shirt covered with graffiti. Small round dark glasses concealed his eyes.

Johnny Juice, head man of the legendary Johnny Juice Joy Band, drugged-out rock star who'd squandered a brilliant career and several beautiful women, including the one clinging to Jed's arm now.

Sharlayne stepped up beside Jed and her gaze followed his. When she spotted Johnny, she went absolutely still.

Johnny pushed away from the limo. "Sharlayne, I've got to talk to you about that book."

"I—please, not now. This isn't the time to—"

"Got to be now." His voice rose and he reached out to grab her arm. "Don't you get it? I can't have you—" He stopped speaking and peered at her, his lips parted foolishly.

Jed shoved the rocker's hand away. "We've got to go, fella. Call her later."

"Call *who?*" Johnny's voice cycled up and he made another grab for her. "Who *are* you and what have you done with Sharlayne?"

Drugged out. The words circled around them, uttered by the onlookers in various combinations. Jed pushed Johnny Juice aside, hating to do it but appallingly aware just how much the rock legend had deteriorated. When he tried to move Sharlayne toward the car, she hung back as if reluctant to leave her former husband in such a state.

Jed shoved her toward the limo door held open by the driver. "Get *in*. We've got to hightail it out of here."

His command shook her out of her indecision. "Of course. I'm sorry." She climbed inside, pale faced and shaking. Apparently, seeing a man she'd once cared about so whacked out he didn't even recognize her had been quite a shock.

The car door slammed behind them. Someone banged on the window and shouted unintelligible words. Sharlayne covered her face with her hands and turned away from the sight to press against his shoulder.

She wasn't coming on to him this time; she was seeking comfort. Under those circumstances, he could not do less than respond in kind.

ALICE COULDN'T stop trembling. What an awful thing to do to a person, leave him behind to face pity and scorn for recognizing what everyone else was too blind to see: that she was a fraud. Events had certainly proven the real Sharlayne right. People did see what they expected to.

What had Johnny Juice expected? What had he seen that others hadn't?

Jed patted her hand, which rested on his knee.

"Don't let it get to you," he advised. "That was drug-induced dementia talking."

"I suppose," she said unhappily. "Still..."

Still, there was nothing else she could say, under the circumstances. She longed to tell Jed the truth, the whole truth, but that was out of the question. She'd been paid for her silence and her loyalty and she would give them if it killed her.

Jed, in an apparent attempt to take her mind off what had just happened, asked, "How was Tabitha when you called?"

"The same."

"That's a shame." He looked out the dark-tinted window for a moment, then turned back toward her. "Did you reach Mike Murphy about the house?"

"No, but I reached his housekeeper, so she'll be expecting us. She suggested we rent a car at the airport and drive there."

"Sounds like a plan."

"And it should only take a couple of hours if traffic's not too bad."

"Maybe then you'll be safe," he said. "From everything."

She gave a sad little chuckle. "Do you think so? Do you really think so?"

She wasn't sure she'd ever feel safe again.

THE FLIGHT TO Tampa was blessedly uneventful.

Sporting a scarf over her hair and wearing dark glasses, Alice still garnered way too many curious glances, but at least the photographers weren't already on her trail. Once seated in first class, she turned her head toward the window and pretended to sleep.

With Jed on the aisle and acting as her watchdog, she felt reasonably secure. After they were airborne, he called ahead to reserve a car, explaining in detail how he wanted the transaction handled to avoid undue attention. He also arranged with a flight attendant to whisk Alice off the plane as soon as they landed and stash her in an office while he gathered up the luggage and obtained the car key.

Uncharacteristically, everything went smoothly. She couldn't believe how quickly they were on the freeway heading south through a landscape that was totally foreign to her.

"I've never seen such flat country in my life," she said in wonder.

Jed gave her a curious glance as he steered the convertible through traffic. "But you've been here before," he said.

Had she? That is, had Sharlayne? But of course she would have. "I mean, that's what I said the first time I saw it," she amended. "How about you? Have you been here before?"

"No."

"Do you suppose it's possible ever to get used to the humidity?"

He shrugged. "We'll probably find out. Why

don't you check those directions to St. Margaret's Key. We'll be turning west in a bit.''

Alice obediently pulled out the instructions, but she was wondering how difficult it was going to be to stick to her story in what would be increasingly intimate circumstances. Then she remembered that intimacy was exactly what she was after.

A SECTION OF a long bridge leading to St. Margaret's Key rotated on a fulcrum to allow boats to pass between the island and the mainland—and perhaps keep undesirables away. Jed drove slowly across, then stopped at the gatehouse on the other side.

A uniformed guard sauntered out. He leaned down to glance inside, saw Alice and leaped to attention. ''I was told to expect Ms. Kenyon's party,'' he said respectfully, waving them on. ''Go to the end of this road and turn right. Mr. Murphy's place is at the very end of the key.''

Jed thanked him and drove on. Alice watched with a sense of awe as they moved through a beautifully constructed jungle of palm trees and tropical flowers. She'd never seen a green so brilliant or a sky so blue, even in California. The scene took on the pleasant unreality of a postcard the farther onto the island they got.

''You did say there are houses on this island, didn't you?'' Jed asked after a mile or two.

"I think Mike said three or four—look." She pointed. "There's one."

Or at least the majestic marble gate leading to one. Through the trees she could catch just the faint hint of a red tile roof.

"We're here." Jed nodded ahead.

The road led to an iron gate with a fence winging out on each side; the fence was shaded by palms and covered with vines. Inching forward, they finally spotted a small sign above a discreet control box set into one of the pillars beside the gate: Please Punch the Call Button.

Jed lowered the window and leaned out to follow directions. Before he could say anything, the gate began to swing open and a voice invited, "Please proceed, Ms. Kenyon."

Alice frowned, but Jed explained: "Surveillance camera. Good."

The brick driveway wound through the jungle. Impressive, she thought, whereas Sharlayne, she knew, would take all this in her stride.

Steadying herself, Alice said casually, "Nice little place Mike has here. I think we can be very comfortable for a few days, don't you?"

"VERY COMFORTABLE" didn't begin to describe it. Mike's Italian villa sat on a low bluff overlooking a sparkling white beach and water the color of aquamarines. It came complete with swimming pool, hot tub, tennis court, an exercise room, a media room, a multitude of balconies and wraparound terraces— By this time, Alice was so overcome that she barely responded to the enthusiasm of Theresa, the housekeeper.

A tall, dignified woman, Theresa finished the tour with a flourish—at the green-and-white master suite, with its marble-and-glass bath. "Mr. Mike says you're to make yourself at home, Ms. Kenyon," she said in a voice like honey. "Anything I can do for you, I'll be glad to."

"Do you live here, Theresa?"

She shook her head. "I cross over from the mainland every day, or as often as I'm needed. Mr. Mike leaves that up to you."

"I see." Alice turned to Jed, her expression inviting questions.

"Who else works here?"

"There's the gardener, but he only comes twice a week, same as the pool man. The boats are maintained at the marina two miles down the coast, should you care to use them. I look after the house and do any cooking as required. There are guards at the bridge twenty-four hours a day."

"Do you often see the neighbors?"

Again she shook her head. "Hardly ever. This is a very private way to live."

"Good," Jed said with obvious satisfaction. "Now, if you'll apprise me of the security system... Sharlayne, this won't interest you. Why don't you go get settled in."

Why not, indeed. Jed and the housekeeper moved away and Sharlayne turned to the balcony overlooking the water. Her feet made no sound at all in the thick white carpeting of this beautiful room, with its pale-green accents and mirrored walls. She felt much as her fictional namesake must have felt on that tumble down the rabbit hole.

Already the stress of the past few weeks seemed to be loosening its hold on her. This had been a good decision. No matter Jed's original objections, this was the answer.

A motorboat came into view around the curve of land, moving slowly past the private beach below the house. The motor cut off and the boat began to drift. It looked wonderfully peaceful. She and Jed would have to try out Mike's boats.

And the bed, she thought with a faint smile. Definitely the bed.

THEY SETTLED INTO life at Villa Murphy as easily as if they belonged there.

Which they didn't, Jed reminded himself. Or rather, she belonged and he was just along for the ride.

Everything was in apple pie order so far as the security system went; *her* house should have been so secure. No one would get to her here, if indeed anyone had sinister designs.

He was beginning to think no one did. He'd kept in touch with the California cops, and they were still convinced that Tabitha's accident had been just that. Nor had they found any reason to believe the car bomb had been aimed at Sharlayne.

Unfortunately, he could tell that Tabitha's failure to come out of the coma was preying on Sharlayne's mind. Even so, she was relaxing more each day, becoming easier and more casual in both dress and demeanor.

He was liking her better for it. Although he'd been attracted to her from day one, he hadn't *liked* her all that much. A woman married six times... renowned for liaisons with many of the world's most desirable men...rich from their largesse and multiple divorce settlements...

Yeah, that was Sharlayne; only, now she seemed different. Almost like another person.

The person walking down the steps toward the sugary sand beach where he'd been standing to look out to sea. Her white shorts bared those fabulous golden legs, and a pale-peach shirt tied up in a knot bared a bit more skin. An orange straw hat perched atop her short blond hair. She swung a tote over one arm and her feet were bare.

She looked good enough to eat, but he had to admit she hadn't been making moves on him. In fact, she'd treated him with a kind of diffidence, which he found enormously appealing.

She marched up to him now and stopped, smiling.

"What are you up to?" he asked, suspicious in spite of himself.

"Not much." She pursed those luscious lips. "I just sent Theresa home and told her not to come back until Saturday. That's three whole days."

"Yeah?" He wasn't feeling good about this. "What are we going to eat?"

"Afraid you'll starve?" she teased. "I thought we could go out for dinner tonight and worry about tomorrow when it comes."

"Sharlayne, you know we can't take that kind of chance. Someone will recognize you for sure."

"Not necessarily. I can wear a disguise. Besides, Theresa gave me the name of a wonderful seafood restaurant just on the other side of the bridge. No one will even notice. If people do, they'll be too rich and too polite to make a big deal out of it."

"You're sure about that."

"Oh, come on, Jed." She grabbed his arm and pressed herself against it. "We deserve a little fun."

There was something about the way she said that last word that did not bode well for their professional relationship.

"DON'T YELL AT ME, Samantha." Jed switched the telephone to the other hand. "It wasn't my idea to go off the key, but in the final analysis, she's the boss. Remember?"

Samantha's growl bespoke frustration. "It's part

of your job to convince her to do what's necessary. You endangered her tonight.''

''We were off the island for all of two hours. Nothing happened. I don't think anyone even recognized her. Hell, if I hadn't left with her, *I* wouldn't have recognized her.''

''Yeah, I hope. Anything else going on there?''

Just a whole lot of lusting on his part. He said, ''No. It's quiet as a tomb.'' And shivered.

''Great choice of words. Not to change the subject, but Jared's been checking on the security work at her house. It should be completed within another week, ten days, including the closed-circuit television.''

''I—''

A noise distracted him and he glanced across the airy living room. Sharlayne stood in the doorway, holding two brandy snifters and wearing a teeny tiny bikini and a great big smile. She mouthed a few words: ''Care for a swim?''

''Jed? Damn it, where'd you go?''

He cleared a suddenly dry throat. ''Sorry, I think the connection's breaking up. We've covered everything, anyhow.''

''But I wanted to know—''

''Don't ask, Samantha. Don't even ask.''

He hung up the phone and walked toward Sharlayne as if he were operating on remote control.

CHAPTER TWELVE

If you can't take the heat...;

but on the other hand, who wants to stay in a kitchen, anyway? By the time John Smith came into my life, I thought I'd been there and done that as far as men were concerned. Boy, did I have a wrong number! I know people called John a mobster and worse, and he was the chief suspect in that sixty-seven-million-dollar banana caper, but to me he was just a sweet and loving husband....

That Book About This Body,
Sharlayne Kenyon

THIS TIME Jed and Alice awakened in *his* bed, where she greeted him with a sultry smile and a leg thrown over his hips.

"Good morning, sweetheart."

He stiffened as if she'd insulted him. "Don't call me that."

"Sweetheart? What's wrong with sweetheart?"

"That's what my boss calls me."

"You're having a fling with your boss, but with me you act as if I'm attacking your virtue?"

"I'm not having an affair with my boss." He sat up abruptly, in the process dislodging her leg, and shoved both hands through hair too short to be smoothed. "She calls everybody sweetheart. It's part of her schtick."

"Oh." Mollified, she sat up, too. She was naked; never in her life had she felt so free and easy around anyone else when so exposed. "Are you mad? I only invited you for a swim, you know."

"Mad?" Twisting around, he grabbed her by the upper arms and planted a hard angry kiss on her lips. "I'm mad at me, not at you, even though we both knew what your invitation meant. I'm supposed to be in charge here. I'm supposed to set a good example and all that."

She grinned. "I love it when you get masterful. Do it again."

He didn't look as if he wanted to smile, but he did anyway. "Okay, I hear what you're saying— and I'm not mad at you."

"In that case—" she struggled against a smug smile "—I want to go boating today. Let's call the marina and have them get one of Mike's boats ready."

"Damn it, Sharlayne, that's dangerous. Let's stay right here, where I can keep an eye on you."

She kissed his temple and jumped out of bed.

"You can keep an eye on me easier on a boat. It's smaller."

"But—"

"Come on, Jed." She snatched up the beach towel she'd dropped beside the bed last night and wrapped it around her body, tucking it between her breasts. "It'll be fun."

"We're not here for fun. We're here for—"

"You sound like a broken record! Get ready while I make the call."

"I'll make the call. You stay off the phone."

"Okay, as long as I have my way."

She smiled as she walked back to her bedroom. Things were finally starting to work out to her satisfaction.

JED AND ALICE put-putted happily out into the sparkling waters of the Gulf of Mexico in Mike's party boat. The small refrigerator beneath a bright canvas canopy was stocked, the gas tank was full and there was nothing around them except azure seas and clear skies.

Well offshore, Jed cut the engine and they drifted silently in the sunshine. They could see a few other boats in the distance but were essentially alone in a private world. Nobody said anything. They didn't even look at each other; instead stared out to sea from opposite sides of the flat-bottomed boat.

And suddenly, inexplicably, Alice was struck again by that overwhelming desire to tell him the truth, the whole truth and nothing but the truth: how she wasn't really Sharlayne Kenyon, how she was simply impersonating her boss in the interests of that blasted book, how she'd never meant—

"What the hell's that boat doing?" Jed said abruptly.

She looked around and saw an orange-trimmed motorboat surging toward them. "Oh, good," she said happily. "I love it when we catch the waves and rock around."

"If he doesn't pull up, we may catch a lot more than a wave."

"Don't be silly. Some of them just like to see how close they can get." She bit her lower lip, returning to the subject very much on her mind these days. "Jed, there's something I'd like to talk to you about."

"Sure." He hit a button and the engine sprang to life, shattering the intimacy. "What's on your mind?"

"Turn that noise off and I'll tell you. I don't like to shout."

"I will once that boat gets past." He steered toward shore. His gaze remained on the speeding boat, which almost seemed to adjust course in their direction. "I'm listening."

"Really? In that case, I just want to tell you that I'm a total fraud and you're an idiot to believe a word I say."

"Yeah?" The boat was very near now, its course

still threatening. It was close enough now to see one man at the steering wheel, and another sitting beside him, digging into some kind of a bag or container.

Even Alice was beginning to wonder about the lousy driving, but what she had to say was too important to let it go, now that she'd made up her mind. "Jed!" she said sharply. "What's the point of talking to you when all you do is—"

"Get down!"

He dove at her, knocking her over backward just as something *pinged!* against their boat. Confused, she tried to struggle up, but he pushed her back down and covered her with his body.

"Get up!" she screamed, only belatedly realizing that it sounded like a hailstorm up there, combined with a swarm of bees passing overhead. "Jed, I can't breathe!"

"Lie still and shut up," he barked, not giving her an inch of breathing room. "Don't you get it? Somebody's shooting at us!"

HIS WORDS finally penetrated; he knew because she went limp and uttered an astonished, "Ohhh." The roar of the other boat's engine faded finally and Jed peeked cautiously over the side.

A second boat moved in the distance, at an angle to intercept the orange-and-white boat. What the hell was going on?

He wasn't about to hang around to find out. He

swung up into the captain's chair behind the wheel and revved the engine.

Sharlayne sat up stiffly, rubbing her elbows and looking intensely unhappy. "What happened?" she asked plaintively. "Was someone really shooting at us, or was that just your excuse to knock me down and mash me?"

He grinned; now that the danger was over, he could enjoy the adrenaline pumping through his veins. "Since when do I need an excuse?" He steered back toward the marina, his hand heavy on the throttle.

She rose, bracing against the rocking of the boat, and brushed off her shorts. "You didn't answer my question. Was someone actually shooting at us?"

"Yes."

"Who? What does it mean?"

"I don't know. Calm down. It's all over now."

She sat heavily on the padded vinyl bench running along the side of the boat. "I'm calm. Tell me."

"Tell you what? I don't know who or why. I do know enough not to hang around trying to find out."

She nodded, trembling but composed. "Let's leave, Jed. Let's get out of here—out of Florida, I mean."

"And go where?" They were nearing the marina and he throttled down.

"Anywhere. I—I'll think of something."

They entered the narrow channel leading to the docks. "Maybe it would be best," he said. "That is, if it's all right with the cops."

"The cops!" She stared at him, wide-eyed. "We don't need to bother them about a little thing like this."

He gave her a sharp glance. "Getting shot at isn't a little thing, Sharlayne. We've got to report it."

"Why? If we don't, no one will ever know. If we do, they'll ask a lot of questions...."

"Which we'll answer. What's the big deal? Besides, they'll know whether we tell them or not."

"I don't see how."

A rangy kid trotted onto the dock and reached down to grab the rope off the bow of the boat. His eyes were bright with interest. "What happened?" he called out, wrapping the rope around a large post. "Looks like you've been in a war."

Sharlayne caught her breath. "What?"

"Bullet holes," Jed said. "The boat's riddled with them. We're lucky we're not riddled with them." To the kid, he said, "If the cops come around asking questions, tell them we're staying at Mike Murphy's place. That's—"

"Yeah, I know." The kid straightened, avid interest on his face. "Everybody knows where that is. And everybody knows Ms. Kenyon," he added, giving her a shy but hopeful smile.

"Yeah," Jed agreed, "but not many people

know she's here, so do us a big favor and don't tell.''

The kid frowned. "Everybody already knows."

Jed hesitated, his hand on Sharlayne's arm to help her onto the dock. He was almost afraid to ask, "How's that?"

"It's in today's *U.S. Eye*," the boy said, eager to pass on the news. "If you want to see it, I've got a copy in—"

"Thanks, but no, thanks." Sharlayne bolted and Jed started after her, thinking it had to be that trip to the restaurant last night. Why hadn't he talked her out of it?

Because he hadn't really wanted to. He'd wanted to pretend they were just normal people, free to do whatever they chose. Only, they weren't. He had to remember that.

He caught up with her beside the rental car. Once inside and driving away, he said, "Okay, we made a mistake going out last night. I won't blame you for nearly getting us shot, when I'm the one who's responsible."

"The shots had nothing to do with last night."

"Say what?" She'd sounded so certain. He gave her a frowning glance. "Then how...?"

"I don't know. All I know is, I saw that same boat the day we moved into Mike's house. I saw it from the terrace outside my bedroom. I remember because of the orange markings."

"Then you're suggesting that someone was watching the house," he interpreted.

She nodded. "It wouldn't be too much of a stretch for someone to find out that Mike and I have remained friendly. This is a logical place for me to run, I suppose."

"Yeah," he said dryly. "I suppose." He pulled up to the gated entry and punched in the code. "Any insights into why someone would want to shoot you?"

"No." She twisted on the seat. "Jed, what are we going to do now?"

"I don't know," he said honestly, "but I'll think of something—after we talk to the cops."

For a moment he thought she was going to argue, but then she slumped back against the leather upholstery with a curt nod.

ALICE DIALED the hospital in California with shaking hands. Someone was trying to kill her—or, more accurately, someone was trying to kill Sharlayne, which was small comfort. That someone had already injured Tabitha. What if he went back to the hospital to finish that job?

When she finally reached Tabitha's private duty nurse and was assured that there was no change in Tabby's condition—previously a disappointment but today a blessing, Alice breathed a sigh of relief. "Would it do any good for me to come back?" she asked. "If there's even a chance that she might respond—"

"It's highly unlikely," the nurse said gently.

Alice knew that, but there was always a chance.

"In fact," the nurse continued, "another of your employees was here to see Ms. Thomas just this morning, and there wasn't even a glimmer of consciousness."

Alice's heart stood still. "Another of my—"

"Yes. Alice Wynn dropped by. I understand she's your assistant?"

Alice's stomach constricted into a painful knot at hearing her name used so casually. If she was impersonating Sharlayne, could Sharlayne now be impersonating her? To what end?

"Now that I think of it," the nurse added, "I believe she left a message, to be given to you the next time you called. It was on Linda's shift, but she mentioned something about...just let me look here...."

A knock on the door made Alice jump guiltily. Jed's voice summoned her. "The police are here, Sharlayne. You'd better come on down now."

"I'm on the phone. I'll be right there."

"Here it is," the nurse said. "Shall I read it to you?"

"Yes!"

"'Sharlayne,'" the nurse read, "'I'll contact you at your place in New York. Take care. Alice.'"

"Alice." Incredible.

"Is there anything else I can do for you, Ms. Kenyon? You don't sound so good, if you don't mind my saying so. You've been through a lot, with Ms. Thomas's injury and all, but—"

"Did Alice say where she was staying?" Alice interrupted.

"No. In fact, Linda got the impression she was only in town for the day."

"I see. I don't suppose Linda got an impression where she was going next?"

The nurse laughed. "Alice works for you and you don't know?"

"She's on vacation," Alice lied glibly. "Look, if she should call or drop by again, tell her...tell her..." She fumbled for words that would convey her panic to Sharlayne but not to the nurse.

"Sharlayne!" Jed again, at the door. "We're getting a little annoyed out here."

Alice shouted into the phone, "Tell her that if I don't hear from her in twenty-four hours, she's fired!"

Then she hung up the telephone and went out bravely to face the cops, who would find out a lot more than they expected if they didn't take her at face value.

"Ms. KENYON, I'm a big fan." Jed watched the pudgy detective practically slobber over Sharlayne's limp hand. "I can't tell you what an honor this is."

"You're too kind," Sharlayne murmured, flashing that trademark smile.

Only someone who'd lived intimately with her, as Jed had, would realize that those lush lips trembled. She was scared to death and he felt fresh concern for her.

She gestured gracefully to the two policemen to take a seat, then looked helplessly at Jed for guidance. He gave it smoothly.

"Sharlayne, these gentlemen are here about the gunshots, of course. The second boat we saw was the law. As I understand it, the shooters got away?" He turned to the officers for confirmation.

Both nodded, and one said, "We're relieved no one was hurt. We checked out your boat and you folks are in the clear. Apparently you were just at the wrong place at the wrong time."

"What?" Sharlayne practically lunged from her chair. "They weren't shooting at *us?* I mean, they were, but it wasn't personal?"

"We think it was drug related, Ms. Kenyon. Someone's been using this key for clandestine purposes. We've been watching the shore for a week and today it nearly paid off. We think they mistook your boat for that of one of their accomplices."

Sharlayne said, "My God!" very softly. Her gaze flew to Jed and he gave his head a minuscule shake. *No. Don't say anything more.*

So she murmured, instead, "What a relief. I thought—" She let out a shaky laugh. "Thank you for coming here to tell us this. If there's anything at all we can do…''

''There's one thing.''

Jed braced himself for the worst, which in this case would be orders to remain here until they caught the bad guys. He could tell from Sharlayne's expression that she, too, realized the ramifications.

The pudgy detective's smile was ingratiating. ''If you could spare me an autograph, Ms. Kenyon… My wife just loves you. She says you lead the life she'd lead if she had your guts.''

Her laughter sounded almost normal. ''That's what separates the women from the girls, all right— guts. Of course I'll be pleased to give you an autograph.''

While she signed the slip of paper offered by the cop, Jed wandered to the glass doors and stared out over the terrace. Drugs. Yeah, he could believe that. What he couldn't believe was that there was nothing personal in that attack. Drugs were a convenient cover, convenient to whoever was after Sharlayne.

''Thanks for your help, Mr. Kelby.''

''Thank *you*, Officer.''

When the two men had gone, Sharlayne's casual air disappeared. ''Thank God that's over,'' she said, shuddering despite the heat of the day.

''Yeah. Who were you talking to on the telephone before?''

''Tabitha's nurse.''

''Any change?''

She shook her head, adding, "Are you hungry?"

"Now that you mention it, yes."

"Come into the kitchen and I'll fix something."

"Good idea. We can talk while you do it."

She cast him a slanted glance and nodded. She'd had something on her mind since before the shooting. He was eager to find out what.

ALICE FRIED BACON and made cheese omelettes—cholesterol be damned. The loaf of bakery bread was a bit on the stale side, but cut into thick slices, it toasted beautifully.

When they were seated at the butcher block serving bar with big plates of food before them, she waited for him to broach the subject that must be on his mind as much as it was on hers.

He ate for a few moments in silence, obviously relishing the food. Then he looked up and said, "I don't buy it."

"That it was drugs?"

"That's right."

"Neither do I."

"Think, Sharlayne. There must be someone in your past that you can connect to this."

"I can't, Jed. I swear to you, I have no idea who would do such a thing." Her frustration bubbled over. "It could just be some nut. Any kind of celebrity draws the crazies."

"You should know. Has anything like this ever happened before? **On a minor scale, I mean.**"

Had it? Not in the two years Alice had worked for Sharlayne. She shook her head, hoping it was true.

"How about Ms. Thomas?"

"No change, the nurse said." Should she mention "Alice"?

"What is it?" he asked quickly, picking up on her hesitation.

"Apparently A-Alice visited Tabitha."

"Alice. That's…"

She nodded. "She's on vacation. I told you about her."

"Oh, yeah." He reached for the jar of grape jelly.

"Tabitha didn't respond."

"Which means there's no reason for you to return."

"That's right."

"Now what? Or maybe I should ask where." He put his fork on his empty plate and waited expectantly.

"I think we should go to New York."

"New York?"

"I've got an apartment there."

"Well, I'll be damned. In that case, why did we come here?"

Because I forgot all about it, she thought. *Because I don't have the key—*

Hold on a minute—maybe she did. That could

be the key she'd found in the safe after Tabitha was injured.

"I'm waiting," he said.

"Because that's the first place they'd look—did look, I'm sure. Now it doesn't matter so much, since the newspapers have found us." She shook her head hopelessly. "Is it too much to ask for a little privacy?"

"Maybe you should have thought of that before you became…what you became."

She flinched. "It's never been this bad before," she objected, not sure if she was defending herself or Sharlayne. "It's just that talk of this book has whipped up such a frenzy."

"Why? You know and I know you're not writing a book. You're not writing anything, not even grocery lists. Why don't you just announce that there is no book? Then maybe everyone will go away and forget about it."

"There is a book," she said, stung.

"Who's writing it?"

"The story of Sharlayne Kenyon will be written by Sharlayne Kenyon—what do you think? Just because you don't see it actually being done doesn't necessarily mean—" She flounced off her stool.

He caught her before she could make her escape and held her loosely around the waist. "Don't try to snow me. I can't believe you're enjoying all this craziness. Attention is one thing, but don't you think this time it's out of hand?"

Alice thrust out her lower lip and peered up at him from beneath her lashes, as she'd seen her boss do a hundred times. "You think you've got it all figured out," she complained, "but you don't know nearly as much as you think you do."

"I don't think I know jack about you." He touched her chin lightly, lifting it. "One minute you're exactly what I expected you to be, all sleek and sophisticated and blasé. Then the next minute you're like a naive little girl. I don't know which is the real you."

"Maybe there is no real me."

"That's occurred to me, too."

For a moment they stood there, looking into each other's eyes. Then she shifted restlessly.

"Either kiss me or let me go," she said in her throaty Sharlayne voice.

He didn't let her go.

THEY WENT skinny-dipping at midnight.

After running through the dark house, laughing, teasing, they dove into the free-form pool and came up in each other's arms.

She kissed his throat, her lips cool from the water at first but quickly warming. "You make me forget," she murmured. "Thank you."

He didn't make himself forget, unfortunately. Here he was, acting like some besotted suitor, when he should be maintaining a proper distance. He'd gone to hell in a hurry on this job.

He kissed her back anyway.

She pressed her cool, smooth body against him. "What are we going to do?"

"You said we'd go to New York."

"Do you think that's wise?"

"Under the circumstances, I can't think of anything better." He slipped one knee between her thighs.

She sighed. "Sometimes I wish...sometimes I wish I wasn't Sharlayne Kenyon."

He laughed, reveling in the feel of her spine beneath his caressing hand. "Who would you like to be, instead?"

"I don't know." Her lips brushed his skin with every word. "Not Tabitha. She's in the hospital."

"Definitely not Tabitha." He slid his hand down over her buttocks and squeezed.

"Maybe...Alice. I think I'd like to be Alice."

"Alice. Your personal trainer."

"She's also my friend. She does...many things for me."

"Such as?" Lifting her, he pulled her close. Her thighs parted; her legs surrounded him.

"She, uh..." She settled against him, her flesh welcoming. "Whatever I n-need..."

"Within reason." He began to move inside her, slowly and rhythmically. Her hands gripped his shoulders and her head fell back on the slender column of her throat, her breathing fast and ragged.

"W-would it make a difference to you?" She

lifted her head to look at him in the blue glow of the pool lights. ''If I were someone else, someone...ordinary, would it make a difference to you?''

''At this moment, nothing would make a difference to me.'' He grabbed her hips to facilitate their rhythm. ''If you really want to know, ask me when I...don't...have other things on my mind.''

And then they went over the edge together and that was that.

THE NEXT MORNING when Theresa showed up for work, she found a note:

Thanks for the hospitality. Something's come up and we've moved on. Please give my thanks to Mike and tell him we're sorry about the bullet holes in the boat. Love, Sharlayne

CHAPTER THIRTEEN

The ultimate aphrodisiac;
or, how I made whoopee,
not on the Senate floor but
on the floor with a senator.

I know everybody thinks I married Melvin K.
Satterfeld because he was a rich U.S. Senator,
which was just about the only flavor I hadn't
tried. They're wrong. I married him because
he was sweet. Sure, I know some of you are
still mad at him because he killed all those
education bills and used the money to build
big bridges over drainage ditches in his home
state, and there were all those unfortunate rumors about influence peddling, but I never
held little things like that against him....

That Book About This Body,
Sharlayne Kenyon

THE PHOTOGRAPHERS spotted Sharlayne and Jed at
JFK Airport and followed them all the way to the
front door of her apartment, which was in a building

across from Central Park. Jed had to elbow their
way through a crowd to reach the doorman, but
after that, they were home free.

If there was one thing the Brownley Arms had,
it was security. It also had fawning managers, who
greeted Sharlayne with obsequious bows and drool-
ing flattery.

She looked too frazzled to care—still beautiful,
but completely exhausted. The flight from Florida
had been packed, even in first class. She'd been the
object of all eyes, and several of their fellow pas-
sengers had asked for her autograph.

She'd given it, over his objections. Didn't she
realize that only encouraged people?

But then he supposed that was the point. She
hadn't become famous by accident. Being a celebrity was her job. She might be tired of the frenzy
now, but just let it stop for fifteen minutes and she'd
miss the hoopla.

She sure didn't look as if she would at the moment, though. At the elaborate door in an elegant
hallway studded with greenery and subtly lighted
paintings that appeared to be originals to his untu-
tored eye, she handed him a key and stood back to
wait.

The key slipped easily into the lock and the door
swung open. She sighed with relief, then led Jed
and the bellperson pushing the luggage cart inside.

It was a beautifully decorated place, if you liked
that sort of thing. Jed didn't. It struck him as pre-

tentious and overblown, all modern lines and angles and overly bright colors and lighting.

It was *so* bad he wondered if she'd decorated it herself.

"Stop smiling," she growled, her glance unfriendly. "Just let me sit down for a moment and—"

The telephone, a glass sculpture that exposed the phone's innards, rang. She reached for it, even as he yelled, "Don't! Let me—"

Ignoring his command, she said a terse, "Hello?"

He could almost see the color leave her face. It was *him*. Whoever the hell had harassed her in California—maybe whoever the hell had tried to shoot her in Florida. Shoving a couple of bills into the gaping bellperson's hand, Jed pushed him out the door before grabbing the handset. Then, turning her hand, he put his head close to hers so he could listen, too.

A gravelly voice sneered, "And don't think I can't find you whenever I want to. I'm always a jump ahead of you."

"Who *is* this?" She sounded more angry than intimidated. "You coward, afraid to tell me your—"

"*You know who this is.* Quit playing games, bitch. You also know what I want."

"I don't, I swear it."

"*I want the manuscript.*"

"What manuscript? There *is* no manuscript."

The laughter was nasty. "Don't play games with me, you bimbo. In a battle of wits, you're only half-armed."

"Look, whoever you are, I'm going to call the police. This is harassment, pure and simple. You can't threaten me and get away with it."

"This is not a threat—it's a promise. Either you give me that manuscript or I'll give *you* something you can't hump into submission." He continued over her outraged gasp, his tone cunning. "You've already had some close calls. The next time you may not be so lucky."

The line went dead.

Sharlayne met Jed's gaze, her eyes wide and anguished. "I can't believe it. We haven't been here five minutes and already I'm being threatened."

"Obviously he's watching you, or has someone else doing it. Think, Sharlayne. He seemed absolutely sincere when he said you should know who he is."

"But I don't." She released the handset to press the heels of her hands to her forehead.

He hung up the phone, his implacable gaze following her across the room. "Think hard. This is important."

She whirled. "You don't think I realize that? I didn't recognize the voice, end of conversation."

She whirled away and ran out of the room. He stared after her, brooding. Was she deliberately hid- '

ing the identity of the caller? Why would she protect someone who might be out to kill her?

It didn't make much sense, but at least it made more sense than the only other possibility that sprang to mind: she really *didn't* know who the caller was. Which meant that either he was crazy or she was.

ALICE SAT on the edge of a ridiculous bed that looked more like a flying saucer than a place of repose. She'd seen this apartment only once before, and had been amazed that her boss actually *liked* all this avant-garde stuff.

She had to look up the number of Linden Wilbert's publishing company and figure out how to dial a telephone that resembled a block of ice. Then she had to pass through several levels to reach his secretary.

She succeeded, only to be told, "Mr. Wilbert's out of the country at the moment. Perhaps I can help you."

"You can't. Look, this is Sharlayne Kenyon. It is absolutely essential that I reach him."

"Oh, Ms. Kenyon, he said you might call. He instructed me to take a message, which I'll make sure he gets."

"You don't understand. This is an emergency. I have to speak to him *now*."

"I'm afraid that's quite impossible. If you'll just give me that message—"

"All right, here it is. Are you ready? *Help!*"

Alice banged around on the phone until she found the Disconnect button, then sat there glaring at it. This was a ridiculous situation. Here she was, impersonating Sharlayne, while Sharlayne impersonated her. She couldn't just wait around like a sitting duck until she got bumped off or her boss decided to call, whichever came first. She had to do something even if she did it wrong.

As she sat there brooding, it finally occurred to her that the secretary had been lying.

Of course that was it. Mr. Linden wasn't out of the country at all; he wasn't even out of the office. She was sure of it. He simply didn't want to do anything that would rock Sharlayne's boat and cause her to slow down in the rush to finish the book. That had to be it. He was probably standing right next to his secretary, telling her what to say.

A tap on the door roused her from hostile thoughts.

"Sharlayne, are you all right?"

She stalked to the door and threw it open. "No, I definitely am *not* all right."

"Calm down." Jed frowned. "At least you're safe for the moment. If you'll just stay inside until I get a chance to check everything—"

"Forget it. I'm going out."

"Damn it, Sharlayne—"

"I've got to track down my publisher."

"Jeez! You mean there really *is* a book?"

"I told you there was. Will you call the car?"

"Don't do this," he argued. "It's too danger-ous."

"Better now than later. No one will be expecting me to come out so soon after just getting here. We can probably sneak out the back way without ever being seen."

"Wait until I have a chance to scope everything out."

"Forget it. I'm going now, with you or without you. I can call for the car myself."

"Damn it, just let me—"

But she stormed out of the room, in a fury.

JED CAUGHT UP with her at the back service en-trance. "The car's on its way," he said. "I still don't see why you insist on doing this, though."

She whirled on him. "Because I'm sick and tired of being manipulated."

"Manipulated? That's a strange choice of words."

She shrugged. "That's how it feels. I'm not act-ing, I'm *re*acting, and I don't like it. If I can just talk to Mr. Linden—to Wilbert, I can get this whole thing cleared up."

Now Jed really *was* confused. "What does a pub-lisher have to do with possible attempts on your life? Surely you don't think he's behind any of this."

"No, of course not. It's—it's something else entirely. Trust me, okay?"

She looked so appealing standing there that he wanted to trust her; he really did. Fortunately, he wasn't *that* besotted.

"Sorry, no can do. You're obviously keeping things from me and I can't—"

"There!" She gazed past him and pointed. "There's the car across the street already. Come on."

He made a grab for her. "Give the driver a chance to turn around. There's no need to go running across the—"

"I'm tired of waiting."

She shoved past the heavy glass door before he could stop her. Without checking either to right or left, she dashed out into the street.

Obviously she missed what *he* saw at a heart-stopping glance: a taxicab shooting away from the curb and bearing down on her.

JED GRABBED HER by the waist and swung her around in the street with such force that she lost her footing and nearly took them both down. Something smacked her hip, then she heard the scream of tires. The sights and sounds of a New York City street swirled around her and she struggled to sort out what had just happened.

"Are you all right?"

Finally focused, she watched the taxicab that had

hit her disappear in traffic. "That cab—somebody tried to run me down," she said incredulously, rubbing her throbbing hip.

Jed looked furious, but he kept his voice in check. "If anyone's to blame, it's not the cabbie. You tore out into the street without paying attention."

"You blame me, after all that's gone on?"

"Hell, I've got eyes. Your carelessness nearly got you killed. Everybody knows about New York cabbies."

"Thanks a lot." She turned her back on him. "If you knew half of what you think you know—"

"Remarks like that are starting to piss me off." He glared at her. "What are you keeping from me this time?"

"Nothing—or maybe just that although *you* may be used to danger, I'm not. I'm scared, Jed. Can't you be at least a little sympathetic?"

His expression softened. "Okay, I will admit you have a right to be scared. Let's head back inside now, where it's safe."

She shook her head, refusing the yield. "I'm going to find that publisher. Are you coming with me?"

For a moment he hesitated, and then his lip curled. "Yeah, sure, why not, but I want it on the record that I'm doing this under duress. This is your party, not mine."

The limo had made the turn and glided up to the

curb. Jed and Alice climbed in, at which point she collapsed against the soft leather seat. *Linden Wilbert,* she thought with almost hysterical determination, *you won't get away from me this time.*

TWO HOURS LATER they were back at the hotel and Linden Wilbert had indeed gotten away from her. Could his underlings actually have told the truth? she wondered, stepping off the elevator on her floor. But to claim he was out of the country—

She stopped so short that Jed stepped on her heels with a mumbled apology. Mr. Wilbert *was* with Sharlayne! If Alice found one, she'd find the other.

Out of the country? She shivered, praying it wasn't true. He was her only lead.

Jed opened the door for her and she walked inside with dragging steps. He was cross with her, and she was sorry about that. She'd love to level with him, tell him the whole sordid story, but that moment had passed on the boat.

"You've got a message," Jed said, looking at the flashing light on the telephone.

Her heart stopped beating. "Ignore it."

"We can't do that." He punched at the ridiculous telephone and finally found the correct button.

A strange voice came on: "Ms. Kenyon, you have a visitor. He's on his way up now. I thought I should warn you, since there was no stopping—"

The rest was lost in a rap on the door, followed by the pealing of the doorbell. She looked at Jed with dread, wondering what new calamity awaited her.

He must have felt sorry for her, for he said, "I'll handle this. Go on into your bedroom and calm down."

"Stop saying that! I'm calm!"

"You look like a Roman candle about to go off." He turned her toward the hallway and gave her a little shove. "Do as I say, Sharlayne."

"Sexist pig." But she was glad to let Jed do the strong-male-protector thing.

That's what he was being paid for, wasn't it?

JED RECOGNIZED Melvin K. Satterfeld at first glance. The eighty-plus-year-old U.S. Senator was often in the news, a familiar figure because of the decades he'd spent in what was alleged to be public service.

That he'd ever gotten hooked up with Sharlayne boggled Jed's mind, however.

A frail but erect figure, with snowy hair and more wrinkles than a prune, the senator was accompanied by a reedy middle-aged man sporting what appeared to be a perpetual sneer.

Jed said, "Sir," and stepped back respectfully.

The senator said, "How do you do, young man. I'm here to see Miss Kenyon." He walked inside slowly, supported by the flunky at his side. "And you would be...?"

Caught off guard, Jed followed. "I'm Jed Kelby, Ms. Kenyon's..." What? What the hell should he call himself? Bodyguard, lover, gofer...he was all those things.

The senator nodded. "I read the newspapers, sir. I'm well aware of what you are to my former wife." He gestured to the man at his side. "This is Henry Satterfeld, my grandson and assistant."

Henry's dour expression did not change. He led the senator to a chair, then helped the old man sit. When he was settled, the senator looked up with sharp blue eyes.

"Please fetch my ex-wife now, Mr. Kelby."

"I don't think she's in the mood for company at the moment," Jed said uneasily. "She's—"

"Nonsense." The tone sharpened. "She'll see *me*." The senator clasped his hands in his lap, apparently prepared to wait the duration.

Hell, Jed thought, she probably will want to see him. You couldn't turn away an ex-husband like a door-to-door salesman, especially one who was a senator.

He went to fetch her.

"Now what?"

"Who knows? You'll have to take care of this one yourself."

"Damn it, Jed, you're supposed to do my dirty work."

"This time you'll have to do it yourself."

She tried to tug away from him, but he practically dragged her down the hall and thrust her into the living room. A white-haired old man sat in one of those gawd-awful modern chairs, a scowling confederate at his side. He seemed...vaguely familiar, but she had no idea why. She certainly didn't recall ever meeting him.

Confused, she glanced around for guidance from Jed, but he'd turned away, leaving her strictly on her own. She took a diffident step forward.

"You wanted to see me?"

The old guy rose, supported by the other man. "Sharlayne, my love, I am always eager to see you," he said in a pompous, old-fashioned manner. He tottered toward her, holding out his arms.

Did he expect her to hug him? Hesitating, she said, "Uhhh..." and stole a look at Jed.

Who was staring at her with a perplexed expression. It was almost as if he expected her to—

Alice gasped. Now she knew who the old man was: Senator Melvin K. Satterfeld, Sharlayne's third husband. And Sharlayne prided herself on the good relations she'd maintained with all her exes, so there was only one thing to do.

If she could only remember what Sharlayne called the man: Mel? Honey? Senator?

Mel-*vin!*

She said, "Mel-*vin!*" and moved into the circle of his arms. She was a good five inches taller than he, so she hugged him and gave him a kiss on top of his sparse white hair. "How wonderful to see you."

"That's more like it, my dear." Taking her hand in his, he drew her to the monstrosity of a puce sofa, beaming. "Tell me, how have you been since last we met?"

When on earth was that? She searched her memory, which in Sharlayne's case extended for only the past two years. "How do I look?" she asked in her most kittenish tone, wanting to change the subject before old times could get started.

"As if you don't know," he chided. "You look magnificent, as always." Holding both her hands, he glanced around at whoever the other guy was. "Henry, would you fetch me a bottle of water?"

"Oh, Mel-*vin,*" Alice said, "we just arrived. I haven't even looked inside the refrigerator to see if anything's in there."

"Of course there is. That's why I recommended this place to you, my dear. The management is most accommodating when it comes to the little touches, such as keeping all my favorites handy—yours, too, of course. Why, if I sent Henry to check behind that bar, I'm sure he'd find a bottle of my favorite bourbon."

"You know," she said faintly, "I wouldn't be at all surprised. Would you like a drink, then?"

"All I'd like is a bottle of water and a few words with you, my dear. If you could ask your...friend...to give us some privacy...." He glanced pointedly at Jed.

Helpless, she said, "Do you mind, Jed?"

"Not at all." He spun around and marched out with that straight military bearing. Taking a deep breath, she faced her ex-husband—make that Sharlayne's ex-husband; it was getting hard to separate one life from the other—and smiled at him encouragingly.

Which he returned. "Dearest Sharlayne, I read in the newspapers, those bastions of misinformation, scandal and innuendo, that you are busily at work on your memoirs."

"I've...considered it," she hedged, looking down at her hand gripped so firmly in his gnarly fingers.

"That's fine," he said approvingly. "Write the book and sell it. A good politician never gives anything away. I always said you'd make a great politician."

Great politician struck Alice as an oxymoron, but she probably shouldn't say so. "Thank you," she responded demurely.

He patted her knee. "On the off chance that this book will actually come to pass, I wonder if you might accord me a preview. Just for old times' sake, you understand."

"Oh, Mel-*vin,* I don't believe I could do that."

"I wouldn't ask if it wasn't important to me. When we were together, I was a relatively young man...."

She stared at him, wide-eyed. When he was married to Sharlayne, he must have been in his sixties, maybe even his early seventies. Relatively young?

He sighed. "Now that I'm starting to get up there in years, I've become concerned with my legacy. I wouldn't want you to write anything that would reflect badly on that."

"Why, Mel-*vin*." She patted his cheek. "I'm only interested in the truth. With that as my guideline, how could I *possibly* write anything that would reflect badly on you or your legacy?"

This did not bring the anticipated smile to his face. "That is precisely what fills me with trepidation, my love. Fortunately, I am well aware that you are a reasonable woman. The truth can be shaded in many different ways. I merely ask that for old times' sake, you keep that in mind while you are penning what I am confident will be utterly scandalous and utterly delightful memoirs."

"You flatter me, darling," she murmured, trying to be coy. He pressed something into her palm. Surprised, she tried to raise her hand to see what it was, but he restrained her.

"Later," he whispered, his old eyes sharp. He raised his voice. "Henry?"

The grandson–assistant popped into view; he'd obviously been lurking just beyond the door. He carried a small bottle of water, which he hurried to offer to the senator.

Who shook his head. "Bring it along." Rising, he said to Alice, "I believe this concludes our visit. I'm sure we understand each other perfectly."

"Absolutely." Although she understood nothing. She curled her hand more tightly around the piece of paper in her hand. A check? A bill? A threat?

"In that case, we will bid you farewell. Give our best regards to your...friend."

"I will." She followed them in their slow progress toward the door. "It was lovely seeing you again, Mel-*vin*. Do drop by anytime."

"I shall, my love. I shall." She leaned over so he could kiss her cheek. His arm moved unerringly around her waist—dropped lower so he could deliver a teasing pinch on her derriere.

She yelped and recoiled. He laughed, winked one watery eye and allowed Henry to escort him out the door.

Only then did she uncoil her fingers and look at what he'd pressed into her palm.

She found herself staring at a bank deposit slip. Apparently Senator Melvin K. Satterfeld had deposited one hundred thousand dollars into the account of Sharlayne Kenyon.

JED HAD HEARD everything, of course; no way did he intend to leave her alone with that old lecher.

Now he stepped into the foyer, arms crossed over his chest. "How much?" he inquired.

She glanced up, startled, and her hand closed convulsively. "None of your business, darling."

"You really let him buy you off, then." He followed her into the huge living room.

"Certainly not." She stuffed the piece of paper into the pocket of her skintight leather jeans.

"Sharlayne," he said, "you disappoint me. Are you adding lying to all your other sins, or have you been lying all along and I was too dense to realize it?"

"Oh, Jed." All the starch went out of her and her shoulders slumped. She looked suddenly very young and very confused. "Please don't compound my problems."

"I'm here to solve problems, not add to them. But I do have to wonder…"

He saw her struggle; she didn't want to say what she now said: "Wonder what?"

"Wonder how to connect the woman I thought I was starting to know with a woman who'd desert her child and take bribes from ex-husbands."

She winced. "I'm sorry you feel that way."

"Care to explain it all away?"

"I can't," she said. "I would if I could, but I can't. I have no justification for any of it, or for all the other things, things you know nothing about." She gave a bitter little laugh. "Things *I* know nothing about."

"Selective memory, then."

"Not exactly. Maybe. I don't know." She stood there, looking vulnerable and unhappy. "Jed, I don't understand what's going on. I can't explain things I don't understand myself. Can't we just put all that aside and—and carry on?"

"Carry on where?"

"Wherever." She walked to him and slid her arms around his neck, rested her cheek on his chest. "I couldn't have made it this far without you. You know that, don't you? I've been difficult and I'm sorry. I never intended to be."

He didn't want to let his hands settle on her waist, but they did anyway. "This is no good, Sharlayne," he said, his voice gruff. "I'm already too involved with you. It isn't safe."

"It's the safest thing in my life," she whispered, gazing at him with eyes clear but somehow unfathomable. "It's the only thing that's kept me going. Can't we forget everything and everybody outside that front door and just be happy for a little while?"

His answer was an unqualified, although unspoken, *yes.*

CHAPTER FOURTEEN

Putting it all together;
or, things I've learned the hard way

Writing the story of your life is no walk in
the park. You have to take a long, hard look
at a lot of things you'd just as soon remain
forgotten....

That Book About This Body,
Sharlayne Kenyon

THE TELEPHONE RANG a few minutes after two in
the morning.

Alice knew, because she'd been lying cuddled up
against Jed, his soft breathing in her ear, while she
stared at the illuminated dial of the bedside clock.

She'd been trying to figure out how to tell him.

She couldn't stand this deception any longer—
promises be damned. He deserved to know. But
was there a way to tell him without losing his re-
spect completely?

She slid to the edge of the bed and grabbed the
telephone before it could get out the second jarring

ring. This had to be bad news. God, was it Tabitha? Alice's "Hello?" was filled with dread.

"Darling! We speak at last!"

Sharlayne's lilting tone cut through Alice like a laser. She sat up abruptly, all too aware that Jed's breathing had changed in some subtle way.

"Shar—uh…" She cleared her throat. "Alice? Is that you?"

Sharlayne laughed. "Ever the little trooper," she said. "Or…can it be that you're not alone?"

"That's right."

"But, darling," Sharlayne purred, "it must be the wee hours in New York. Whoever can you be trysting with?"

Alice struggled to pull her thoughts together. She'd waited for this call for so long that she mustn't let her boss off the hook. "Let's move on to the important stuff," she snapped. "Where are you and why has it taken you so long to contact me?"

"Now, don't get all testy with little ol' me. I've been monitoring the situation. There's been no need to contact you until now. I mean, you have everything well in hand, do you not?"

"I'm not sure I'd go that far."

"I would. As for poor Tabitha, there was nothing anyone could do for her. I realized that after I saw her."

"As—" Alice stopped before she added "me."

Sharlayne laughed. "Yes, as you. I thought that a rather brilliant stroke on my part."

"What about Mr. Wilbert? Is he with you?"

"As a matter of fact, yes. Clever of you to figure that out."

"Not really. I've been trying to reach him, without success. When are you coming back, *Alice?*"

"I'm not."

"You can't do this to me!"

"Calm down. You're coming *here,* you and your handsome bodyguard."

"Where is here?"

"Linden's LW Ranch. It's right outside Phoenix. Rent a car and ask directions."

Alice's stomach contracted into a knot of anxiety. "When?"

"Today. ASAP. That witch from the *Eye* has been snooping around, apparently on a tip from some malcontent at Linden's office. With any luck, you can get here ahead of the deluge and we can make the switch without anyone being the wiser."

Alice glanced at Jed. He was braced on one bent arm, little more than a silhouette.

An intently interested silhouette. She lowered her voice and switched the phone to the other ear, away from him. "Uh, I think it's time I...you know, I..." How the hell did you say *Tell Jed* without using either word?

"Forget it," Sharlayne said flatly, as if reading

minds was a sideline. "There are a lot of things going on that I can't get into over the phone."

"That goes double here," Alice snapped. "You have no idea—"

"But I do. I may not have all the details but I do have an idea. For your own good—for your own safety—come as fast as you can. Don't say anything to anybody about your reasons. That includes your hunky bedmate."

"You don't know what you're asking." But she probably did, Alice conceded silently. "Can't I just…?"

"Absolutely not. *Come*."

"All right, I'll get there as fast as I can."

"Good. See you in a few hours."

The line went dead.

Alice hung up and sat there, staring at the telephone, realizing that this was the beginning of the end of her adventures among the rich and famous. No regret accompanied that thought, with one exception.

It was also the beginning of the end with Jed.

Who stirred and reached across the bed to caress her thigh. "I take it that was Alice What's-Her-Name."

"That's right."

"We're going somewhere?"

"Yes. She's found a p-place she thinks is safe. It's in Arizona."

"I see." He slid his warm palm over the roundness of her leg. "I wish I knew what was really going on here, Sharlayne."

"Nothing much," she said, her tone light but her heart heavy. "I expect everything will be clear to you soon."

"I'm almost afraid to think about it. I am curious to know why you let your employees jerk you around the way they do, though. Ms. Thomas did it, and now this Alice person." He slid across the bed toward her. "Whatever. I've got more important things on my mind. Come here."

That, she was glad to do.

THE SCANDAL PRESS arrived ahead of them.

"Damn!" Jed said as they rounded the last bend in the road. Television and press trucks cluttered the parking space partially visible in back of the sprawling ranch house, while people, many with cameras, milled around before the large closed gate in the front of a tall adobe wall. "I don't like the looks of this," he understated. "Get down so no one will see you."

Alice slumped low in the passenger seat of the rented car. "If I can just make it inside…"

"You'll make it inside," he promised. "But first, or maybe I should say last—" he glanced at her, his expression grim "—isn't there anything you want to say to me before we throw ourselves to the wolves? Anything at all?" He braked and she resisted the urge to sneak a peak to see where they'd ended up.

"There's a ton of stuff I want to tell you," she said, "but this is not the time or the place." She wanted desperately to spill Sharlayne's beans, but knew she'd waited too long. "Jed," she said desperately, "whatever happens—"

"Hold that thought. No one's spotted us yet, so we'll make a run for it. There's a small gate in the wall back here, but I assume it's locked. Maybe I can boost you over before anyone spots you."

"Yes, let's try that."

He threw open the door to the rental car and stepped out, while she waited for his all-clear. When he opened her door, she crept out, keeping low.

He grabbed her hand. "Let's do it."

Crouching, they ran between the vehicles parked between them and the wall. Anonymity lasted about five seconds.

"Hey!"

The unexpected and dreaded cry made her stumble.

"Wait up, Sharlayne! Where the hell's that photographer?" The cry came from a man just rounding the front corner of the wall.

Jed released her hand and changed course. "I'll try to hold him off, but you'll have to get in on your own," he shouted over his shoulder. Reaching the man, he put out his hands and shoved him back around the corner and out of sight.

Alice rushed to the adobe wall, horrified by this turn of events. Pressing her palms against the rough finish, she looked up at the twelve-foot barrier. There were no handholds, no footholds. No way could she make it over by herself.

But there was that smaller gate. If it was locked, she had to pray someone inside would hear her and open it.

She tried the metal handle of the gate without success. She could hear a growing uproar in front of the house. Jed wouldn't be able to confuse the issue indefinitely.

She'd have to take a chance. "Hey!" she screamed, pounding ineffectually on the wood gate with her fists. "Who's in there? Let me in! Let me in! I—"

The sharp stab of some small blunt object in the middle of her back took her breath away. She flinched and tried to turn but was thrust flat against the gate. Someone held her there while simultaneously jabbing at her with what she instinctively feared was the barrel of a revolver. Panicked, she tried to figure out how best to resist.

A voice hissed in her ear: *"Now you're forcing me to do something I don't want to do."*

She'd know that raspy voice anywhere. Her blood ran cold. "You!" Again, she tried to turn.

He wouldn't allow it. "Bitch! This is a gun, in

case you're too stupid to realize it.'' He yanked her upright and shoved her toward the parking lot. ''Start moving.''

''Jed!''

''He can't hear you. Scream all you want.'' He gave her another shove that sent her reeling forward.

No one could possibly hear her. There was the bedlam in front and who knows what was going on inside.

''Move.'' Her captor herded her forward, punctuating his orders with nudges of the pistol.

Every step pushed her closer to an untimely end. Nothing but cars and vans, sand and sagebrush, lay ahead. If he was going to finish her, she wasn't going to make it easy for him.

Digging in her heels, refusing to be shoved around like a grocery store shopping cart any longer, she grabbed hold of a scraggly bush growing beside the abode wall. Closing her eyes, she waited for the end.

''Damn you!'' The man dragged her away from the bush, and despite herself, her eyes flew open.

The first thing she saw was the raised pistol. The second thing she saw was Henry Satterfeld, Melvin's effete grandson. ''You?'' she cried, hanging on to the bush with all her might. ''You're the one who's been after me?''

''Like you didn't know.'' His voice didn't change tenor. Apparently, he hadn't made any attempt at disguise; he really did have a scratchy and unpleasant voice. "Get ready to die, bitch."

"But...*why?*" Anything to delay the inevitable.

"I can't let you tell all Grandfather's secrets. I can't let you destroy his reputation and the family honor."

"I wouldn't dream of—" Behind Henry, the gate in the tall adobe fence swung open slowly and silently. A figure stepped out: Sharlayne, holding a heavy silver vase with both hands. *Don't stare, Alice!* she warned herself. *Don't tip him off!* "Uh..." She forced herself to look at him. "M-Melvin doesn't know anything about this, I'll bet."

Henry sneered. "Of course not, and he won't."

Sharlayne crept forward on silent feet. She rose on tiptoes, the vase held above her head.

Henry lifted the gun. "After today, you won't be able to hurt anyone again with your lurid tales."

"But you'll be caught," Alice said desperately. "All those people in front—a gunshot—" Sharlayne lifted the vase even higher, while Alice talked louder and faster. "You'll go to jail forever, don't you see?"

Sharlayne brought the vase down on the back of Henry's head, where it struck with a *thunk.* His eyes widened, then rolled back in his head in perfect synchronization with his buckling knees.

Sharlayne, looking like Alice, and Alice, looking like Sharlayne, stared at each other over the comatose form.

The genuine article spoke first. "That slimy little son of a bitch," she said, clearly astonished. "He must have popped his cork and decided to take it upon himself to defend the old guy's honor."

"You've got all your ex-husbands scared spitless, Sharlayne." Fairness made Alice add, "All except Mike, who can hardly wait to read the book."

Sharlayne grimaced. "Why am I not surprised? I'm beginning to realize what a Pandora's box I've opened." She nudged the limp form with a toe. "Now that I think about it, Henry never did like me much. I never dreamed he'd have the balls to try anything like this, though."

Alice wrapped her arms around her torso, weak with reaction and beginning to shake. "Let's get back to basics," she said, her voice as shaky as the rest of her. "I was never so glad to see anyone in my life. I thought I was a goner."

"Heavens, no." Leaning down, Sharlayne pried the pistol from Henry's stiff hand.

"Now what?" Alice glanced anxiously toward the front of the house. "Jed can't keep them busy indefinitely."

"He won't have to," Sharlayne said confidently. "I've got everything figured out. Actually, except for a few minor details like old Henry, here, I had it all figured out before you even got here. Here's what we're going to do, Alice—"

SHARLAYNE'S TERRIFIED shrieks brought Jed charging to the rescue, with that flock of vultures right behind him. Damn! While he'd been holding them back, she'd managed to get herself into fresh trouble.

The sight that met him as he rounded the corner of the adobe wall brought him skidding to a halt. Sharlayne stood over an unconscious man, pointing a pistol at his head with very shaky hands. Looking up, she saw Jed and rushed forward, the gun waving dangerously.

"Jed! He tried to kill me!"

"Easy." He grabbed her wrist in the interests of public safety. Several photographers were already taking pictures of the body, but that probably didn't give her the right to shoot any of them. "Anybody got a handkerchief?" he barked.

"Yeah." A short bald guy passed one over.

Jed took the square of fabric and used it to protect the revolver he removed carefully from Sharlayne's hand. She didn't resist. "What happened?" he asked.

"H-he intended to kill me. That's Melvin's grandson."

"I see that."

"He was behind the phone calls, Jed. When you hear his voice, you'll recognize it right away. It's unmistakable."

"But you didn't recognize it over the phone? Isn't that a bit strange?"

"I can't be bothered with minor details at a time like this," she said indignantly. "Will somebody just call the police?"

"Done." Linden Wilbert walked through the gate. "Please, gentlemen, don't touch anything. This is a crime scene."

At which point, Henry Satterfeld groaned and tried to sit up.

Sharlayne backed away, her expression filled with horror. "Jed, don't let him—"

"Hey!" one of the photographers, squatting next to Henry and flipping through the pages of a little black book, shouted. "This looks like some kind of a diary. It says here he's gonna shut Sharlayne up for good and—"

"Ohhh!" Whirling toward the gate, Sharlayne burst into tears. The publisher took her arm, shot a baleful glance at the ladies and gentlemen of the press and led her past flashing strobes, into the compound, slamming the gate behind them.

Jed didn't blame either of them, even though there was something gut-wrenchingly final about their exit.

"FAST! We don't have much time." Linden steered Alice quickly across a brick patio, into the cool darkness of the house. "Sharlayne's in the bedroom. It's through that door."

Alice responded automatically. Someone else was in charge now; the witching hour had arrived.

The ball was definitely over for Cinderella, and not a moment too soon.

Sharlayne, seated on the edge of the bed, looked up. "Alice! Thank God you're all right. I can see how shaky you are, but we don't have time for that. We've got to hurry."

"Hurry and do what?"

"The first order of business is to get you out of those clothes and into these." She pointed to the articles on the bed. "It's a maid's uniform—sorry about that. There's a brown wig to go with it, and you'll have to take off your makeup, too. I'll put on the clothes you're wearing, then go out to face the lions."

"Whatever you say." Still operating on automatic pilot, Alice kicked off her shoes and wiggled out of the skintight jeans. "You wouldn't happen to know how Tabitha is today? I got so caught up in getting here that I never had a chance to check on her."

Sharlayne smiled. "She's better, I'm happy to report."

"Really?" Alice shook her head in wonder. "Believe it or not, we actually got...almost friendly, there toward the end. I never did understand why she detested me so."

"It was nothing personal, I assure you. She's just an intensely possessive woman. When I found her, she was still getting over the loss of a child and—"

"Tabitha had a baby?" Alice could hardly believe it.

Sharlayne nodded. "I think somehow I came to fill the gap that left in her life. She wouldn't like me talking about it, though. Please don't ever mention it to her."

"Of course not. I'm just relieved she's out of danger now."

"We're all out of danger." Sharlayne took Alice's hand and squeezed. "One last thing. You've got to promise me that you'll keep your mouth shut."

"Forever?"

"Until further notice. I...have several fences to mend before you start dropping bombshells."

"Can't I at least tell Jed?"

Sharlayne shook her head. "Jed was just a hired gun and his part in this is over now. There's no need for him to ever know." Her eyes narrowed. "Unless, of course, there was something going on between the two of you besides a little hanky-panky."

Was there? Alice knew her own feelings but not his.

"Good." Sharlayne shuddered. "If this got out, it would not only screw up all my plans to make many amends, but I'd be a laughingstock. I mean, Gina Godfrey's on my tail now. If she got wind of what we pulled, I'd never rid myself of her."

"I see." Alice didn't want to see, but she did.

"Cheer up," Sharlayne ordered. "We're almost home free. Now, on the assumption that you don't want to miss the final act, put on that maid's uniform. Wearing that, with brown hair and no makeup—" She stopped short, frowning. "Your dark roots are showing, Alice. What are you trying to do, ruin my reputation?"

"Who had time to get a bleach job what with bombs and bullets and—"

"Okay, okay, I apologize. With this wig, you'll pass unnoticed and be able to watch the finale."

"What finale?"

"Wait and be surprised with everyone else." Sharlayne paused, her hands on the buttons of her plain white shirt. Her expression softened. "This has been difficult for you, hasn't it."

"That's an understatement."

"I'm sorry." Sharlayne's smile was actually sympathetic. "It was no picnic for me, either, but it was worth it. I've learned so much."

"So have I." Alice pulled the plain black dress over her head. "The most important being that I wouldn't really trade places with you for all the tea in China."

Sharlayne stepped into the jeans. "And I've learned how painful it is to dredge up the past and try to deal with it in any kind of honest way."

Alice picked up the curly brown wig and looked at it dubiously. "It's been a long time since I've been honest with anyone about anything."

"That's almost over now." Sharlayne frowned at her reflection in the mirror. "What's missing?"

Alice had to laugh. "Just a little thing." She removed the tangle of gold chains from around her neck, the diamonds from her ears, the ruby ring. Once she cleaned away the makeup, the transformation would be complete.

The world would be right side up again.

If that was possible, without Jed.

JED DIDN'T LIKE being kept outside with all the riffraff of the press, but it was Linden Wilbert's house and he got to decide who was allowed where. Besides, Jed had Henry Satterfeld to worry about. Fortunately, the cops arrived within fifteen minutes and took that problem off his hands.

He could see an officer talking to Wilbert, who nodded and escorted him inside. Great. Maybe Jed should just leave.

Hell, he couldn't do that. He had to know how this all played out. Wilbert had already announced that Sharlayne would speak to the assembled throng as soon as the police finished with her. That, Jed couldn't miss.

Would she look for him, seek him out in the crowd? Would she remember the chills and thrills they'd shared, the danger and the kisses?

He would, but would she?

Samantha was right. He never should have gotten

involved with a client. He'd probably pay for it the rest of his life.

Another half hour passed. Finally a servant appeared to invite everyone to congregate on the patio while waiting for the star of the moment. Jed, obviously no one special, went along with the others. Wedged into a corner, he waited while a maid with a frozen expression passed out margaritas.

He was only interested in one woman. When she finally appeared, she leaned on Linden Wilbert's arm, her smile more radiant than ever. The crowd erupted in applause, greeting her like a heroine. Jed kept his hands clenched at his sides. He really wanted to stuff them in his pockets, but Marines didn't do that.

She held up her hands for their attention. Her gaze passed over Jed as impersonally as if she'd never seen him before.

"Ladies and gentlemen," she said in her famous throaty voice, "I apologize for causing you all so much trouble. There's been a lot of upheaval in my life lately, what with that awful man stalking me." She shuddered delicately. "Now, however, I'm finally at a point where I can make a very important announcement." She paused for effect, her timing impeccable. Into an expectant hush, she said, "I've decided not to publish my memoirs after all."

The crowd erupted in disbelief and cries of, "Why? What changed your mind?"

She motioned for quiet. "This decision was

hardly an easy one," she said. "I discovered in the writing that my book dredged up things better left in the past. There are many people, a few of them innocent, who would be hurt by the unvarnished truth, and that's all I could tell. I've decided to spare them."

From the front row Gina Godfrey scoffed indignantly, "You knew that before you started this circus. What *really* changed your mind about writing *That Book About This Body,* Sharlayne?"

Sharlayne's smile was glorious. "I should have known better than to try to put you off with generalities, Gina. The truth is, I've decided not to reveal the story of my life at this point, at the request of my soon-to-be husband. May I present my fiancé and former publisher, Linden Wilbert."

The man came forward, his smile benign. Bright spots of color glowed in his cheeks, as if he were embarrassed by all the hoopla.

"Your *seventh* husband," Gina shouted, "but who's counting?"

"Exactly." Sharlayne joined in the laughter. "There you have it, my friends. I'll take questions now if you'll keep them within reason."

Jed had questions, a million of them, but perhaps none within reason. He stared at Sharlayne in shock as she listened to a query about Henry Satterfeld's skullduggery. How could she do this? Jed wanted to know. What the hell was wrong with her?

He looked closer, leaning toward her where she

stood some twenty feet away. She glanced over, and for an instant, their gazes met.

Hers was only mildly curious.

Jed caught his breath. Who the hell does she think she is? he wondered, because…

That sure as hell wasn't the Sharlayne Kenyon he knew—the Sharlayne Kenyon he loved….

ON THE FRINGES of the crowd, Alice stifled a sigh of relief…and loss. She turned away, her cocktail tray held high. Sharlayne had figured booze would grease the skids and make the ladies and gentlemen of the press less critical of her words.

For Alice, playing a maid wasn't actually all that difficult. She was Cinderella, back in her rags where she belonged.

Jed would never forgive her now. He'd think she'd used him, which of course she had, although at someone else's behest. If only she'd told him who she really was while there was still time. But her loyalty had been too strong and now it was too late.

Even though Jed was just across the patio from her, Alice felt curiously safe. She'd learned a lot these past weeks, not the least of which was the truth of Sharlayne's contention that "People see what they expect to see, not what's actually there."

Unless they're in love…?

"Gimme another one a' them margaritas, babe."

"Babe?" She turned all her disappointment on

the portly reporter who'd been watching the proceedings with a cynical sneer. "*Babe?* Do the words *politically incorrect* have any meaning to you at all?"

"Hey, babe, you're just the maid, not the star of this dog and pony show." He lurched toward the tray, managing to knock it out of her hands.

Three margaritas and four empty glasses hit the brick patio, some shattering and some rolling away. The center of attention now, Alice ducked her head and knelt to grab whatever pieces of broken glass she could.

"Jeez." The boorish reporter looked down at her. "I'll go find someone who's not so clumsy."

She wanted to show him clumsy, but first she had to protect the unwary from broken glass. Gesturing to one of the male waiters, she stood up, unpleasantly aware of all the attention the incident had drawn. Then keeping her head down, she walked quickly toward the door to the kitchen.

She'd seen enough. All she wanted now was to get out of here. Mr. Wilbert's chauffeur would drive her to the Phoenix airport and she'd grab the first plane out.

She'd seen more than enough of Sharlayne in action.

She reached for the doorknob, intent only upon escape. A hand darted out to close over her arm and she glanced around in alarm, fully expecting to find the "babe" reporter.

Jed stood there, his eyes narrow and his jaw tight. "I don't know who the hell you are," he said slowly, "but—"

"Let me go." Her voice squeaked. "I'm n-nobody."

"Very possibly, but I guarded *that body* and I loved *that body*. I'd know it—and you—any-where."

"But—I—you—she—"

"Give it up," he cut her off. "We're going someplace where you can tell me everything." He frowned, and then his eyes widened and he added an incredulous, "Alice?"

She thought she would faint. "Jed—" It was a groan. "It's not what you think."

His lips tilted in a tiny smile. *"Everything,"* he repeated, "that's what you're going to tell me. And you damned well better make it good. You'll have to if you hope to convince me I'm not a total idiot and the most incompetent bodyguard in history."

"You're not incompetent!"

"Yeah, I am, or I wouldn't have fallen in love with my client."

"In *love?*" She stared at him with wonder.

"That's what I said, Alice. You are Alice, aren't you?"

"Do you want me to be?" she murmured, her entire body aching to be in his arms.

"Yeah," he said, "I want you to be. Or hell, maybe you're the real Tabitha Thomas. That's okay. Hell, I don't care. I'm just glad you're not Sharlayne Kenyon.''

He scooped her up and carried her away, and nobody cared because she *wasn't* Sharlayne Kenyon. And sure enough, she told him everything and vice versa, the most important of which was the I-love-yous.

EPILOGUE

Sharlayne who?

Whatever happened to Sharlayne Kenyon, object of a media feeding frenzy a few months ago? Sharlayne had half the men in California sweating bullets over the prospect of her actually writing her scandalous autobiography. The *Eye* has it from a usually reliable source that she's split with her publisher fiancé and plans to move back to Beverly Hills and resume public life. We'll dig up the straight scoop and keep you posted....

Gina Godfrey, U.S. Eye

That Shakespeare was a genius; or, all really is well that ends well

I recognized her the minute I saw her—same blue eyes, same stubborn jaw, same great bod. She was my daughter, all right, but would she let me back into her life? In her place, it wasn't how I'd react....

That Book About This Body,
Sharlayne Kenyon

THE BEAUTIFUL GIRL serving champagne to the Kelbys and the Wilberts was Sharlayne's daughter, Ashley; Alice would have known those splendid good looks anywhere. When the invitation to ''a good old-fashioned book burning'' at the Arizona ranch had arrived three months after the big showdown, not a word about a reconciliation had been mentioned.

But then, Sharlayne was always full of surprises, among them the return of Tabitha Thomas. Recovered and back on the job, Tabitha seemed mellowed by all she'd been through.

Or maybe she was mellowed by the fact that Alice no longer worked for Sharlayne, having quit her job to follow Jed. Or it could be the presence of Sharlayne's daughter, over whom Tabitha fawned.

Relaxed and happy, Alice slid her arm beneath that of her handsome husband, sitting beside her on the wicker love seat on the patio where Sharlayne had faced the press so brilliantly.

Jed's answering grin was conspiratorial, but he'd agreed to let her pick the right moment to make their announcement. Now that he'd given up bodyguarding and had reconciled with his wine-growing family, she knew he was a much happier man.

Of course, Alice liked to think she'd had a little something to do with that.

Flames leaped from the top of the large metal barrel standing in the middle of the patio. A manuscript was neatly stacked on a small cast-iron table next to it. Sharlayne, it appeared, had meant exactly what she'd said in the invitation.

Now she lifted her wine flute. "Cheers," she said. "Cheers to Alice and Jed—may they always be as happy as they are today. And cheers to Linden and me. Seventh time's a charm."

Jed drank. Alice didn't, but no one seemed to notice.

"Cheers to Tabitha, on her recovery, and to my darling daughter, for having a heart big enough to listen."

"Hear, hear!"

"Now for the main event."

Tabitha marched forward and picked up the first page off the stack. She handed it to Sharlayne and stood at the ready.

Sharlayne looked at the page and sighed. "Destroying my book is a crime against nature," she declared. "I put my heart and soul into this and now…"

"Is there some law that says you have to burn it?" Jed asked reasonably. "You could change your mind, you know."

"Not without hurting a lot of people." Sharlayne glanced at her daughter, who watched calmly from the sidelines. "I only waited this long to give Ashley a chance to read it. I felt I owed her that much—assuming she was willing to listen."

"I wasn't at first." Ashley's fingers tightened on the stem of her champagne flute. "It took a little persuasion, but now I'm glad I did.'' Her sudden smile sparkled just like her mother's. ''I probably know more about Sharlayne than anyone in the world.''

''Even me,'' Linden agreed. ''She wouldn't even let *me* read all of it.''

Sharlayne patted his cheek. ''Your understanding nature is one of the many reasons I love you,'' she said. ''Well, let's get on with it.'' Taking a deep breath, she tossed the page into the flames.

Until that moment, Alice hadn't really believed it would happen. Into the silence, she began to clap. After a few perplexed glances, the others joined in.

Apparently the first page was the hardest, because Sharlayne began tossing in pages of deathless prose by the handful. As her frenzy increased, so did the smiles of those watching. It was so *Sharlayne*. She never did anything halfway.

When the final page had been consigned to the flames, she stepped back and drew a breath. ''Well,'' she said, ''that takes care of that. On to other things.''

''Uh-oh.'' Jed glanced at Alice. ''I told you so.''

''What?'' Sharlayne demanded quickly. ''You told her what?''

''That you had some ulterior motive.''

''I do,'' she confessed with dignity. ''I wanted to tell you the final disposition of all the things that happened. The car bomb was exactly as the police thought—a gang thing.'' She ticked items off on her fingers as she spoke. "Tabitha's accident was Henry's doing, because she was wearing my scarf and the idiot didn't know the difference." She made a face. "The boat shooting in Florida was drug related, and the taxi attack in New York City was Henry again."

Jed nodded. "Sounds about right to me. What's going to happen to Henry, by the way?"

"He's been committed to a mental institution, where he's writing his own book, presumably blaming me for the ills of the universe. Melvin says not to worry. He's flushing the pages as fast as his grandson produces them."

"See?" Alice said to her husband. "She's not up to anything."

"Well..."

Everybody looked at Sharlayne again.

"Maybe I'm up to a *little* something. Alice, dear, I'd like to make you an offer you can't refuse."

Jed said, "Forget it."

"Now, you haven't even heard it."

"I think I'm afraid to hear it," Alice said. "You have a long history of talking me into things."

"You make me sound like a master manipulator." Sharlayne pouted. "It's nothing ominous, I assure you. I'd just like you to fill in for me for a month or so to enable my darling husband and me to go on a truly private honeymoon."

"Out of the question," Alice and Jed said simultaneously.

''Don't be so quick to turn me down,'' Sharlayne argued. ''It'll be a piece of cake. You can stay here at the ranch and Tabitha will run interference. When you go out, you go as me, that's all. Simple. In return, I'll buy that overpriced piece of land Kelby-Linus Wines is so hot for, and give it to you as a gift.''

''What piece of land?'' Jed looked stunned.

Sharlayne smiled that mysterious smile. ''Ask your brother, Steve. He knows all about it. So what will it be, kiddies? Are you going to make me sweeten the pot?''

Instead of running screaming from the state, Alice laughed.

''Now?'' Jed asked.

''Now.'' She rose. ''Sharlayne, I couldn't impersonate *that body* again if I wanted to, which I don't.'' Turning sideways, she smoothed her loose-fitting T-shirt over the faint curve of her belly. ''Meet Jed Jr.,'' she said. ''He's due to enter the world in another six or seven months. Guess my career as a stand-in for a femme fatale is behind me.''

''That,'' Jed said to his wife, ''is what *you* think. Someday, with Sharlayne's blessing, we'll write our own book and tell the world who the real femme fatale is.''

And that's exactly what they've done.

HARLEQUIN *Super* ROMANCE

CREATURE COMFORT

A heartwarming new series by

Carolyn McSparren

**Creature Comfort, the largest veterinary
clinic in Tennessee, treats animals of all
sizes—horses and cattle as well as family
pets. Meet the patients—and their owners.
And share the laughter and the tears with
the men and women who love and care
for all creatures great and small.**

#996 THE MONEY MAN
(July 2001)

#1011 THE PAYBACK MAN
(September 2001)

*Look for these Harlequin Superromance titles
coming soon to your favorite retail outlet.*

HARLEQUIN®
Makes any time special ®

*Harlequin truly does
make any time special. . . .
This year we are celebrating
weddings in style!*

To help us celebrate, we want you to tell us how wearing the Harlequin wedding gown will make your wedding day special. As the grand prize, Harlequin will offer one lucky bride the chance to **"Walk Down the Aisle" in the Harlequin wedding gown!**

There's more...

For her honeymoon, she and her groom will spend five nights at the **Hyatt Regency Maui.** As part of this five-night honeymoon at the hotel renowned for its romantic attractions, the couple will enjoy a candlelit dinner for two in Swan Court, a sunset sail on the hotel's catamaran, and duet spa treatments.

To enter, please write, in, 250 words or less, how wearing the Harlequin wedding gown will make your wedding day special. The entry will be judged based on its emotionally compelling nature, its originality and creativity, and its sincerity. This contest is open to Canadian and U.S. residents only and to those who are 18 years of age and older. There is no purchase necessary to enter. Void where prohibited. See further contest rules attached. Please send your entry to:

Walk Down the Aisle Contest

In Canada	In U.S.A.
P.O. Box 637	P.O. Box 9076
Fort Erie, Ontario	3010 Walden Ave.
L2A 5X3	Buffalo, NY 14269-9076

You can also enter by visiting www.eHarlequin.com
Win the Harlequin wedding gown and the vacation of a lifetime!
The deadline for entries is October 1, 2001.

HARLEQUIN WALK DOWN THE AISLE TO MAUI CONTEST 1197
OFFICIAL RULES
NO PURCHASE NECESSARY TO ENTER

1. To enter, follow directions published in the offer to which you are responding. Contest begins April 2, 2001, and ends on October 1, 2001. Method of entry may vary. Mailed entries must be postmarked by October 1, 2001, and received by October 8, 2001.

2. Contest entry may be, at times, presented via the Internet, but will be restricted solely to residents of certain geographic areas that are disclosed on the Web site. To enter via the Internet, if permissible, access the Harlequin Web site (www.eHarlequin.com) and follow the directions displayed online. Online entries must be received by 11:59 p.m. E.S.T. on October 1, 2001.

   In lieu of submitting an entry online, enter by mail by hand-printing (or typing) on an 8½" x 11" plain piece of paper, your name, address (including zip code), Contest number/name and in 250 words or fewer, why winning a Harlequin wedding dre would make your wedding day special. Mail via first-class mail to: Harlequin Walk Down the Aisle Contest 1197, (in the U.S P.O. Box 9076, 3010 Walden Avenue, Buffalo, NY 14269-9076, (in Canada) P.O. Box 637, Fort Erie, Ontario L2A 5X3, Canad

   Limit one entry per person, household address and e-mail address. Online and/or mailed entries received from persons residing in geographic areas in which Internet entry is not permissible will be disqualified.

3. Contests will be judged by a panel of members of the Harlequin editorial, marketing and public relations staff based on the following criteria:

   - Originality and Creativity—50%
   - Emotionally Compelling—25%
   - Sincerity—25%

   In the event of a tie, duplicate prizes will be awarded. Decisions of the judges are final.

4. All entries become the property of Torstar Corp. and will not be returned. No responsibility is assumed for lost, late, illegible, incomplete, inaccurate, nondelivered or misdirected mail or misdirected e-mail, for technical, hardware or software failures of any kind, lost or unavailable network connections, or failed, incomplete, garbled or delayed computer transmission or any human error which may occur in the receipt or processing of the entries in this Contest.

5. Contest open only to residents of the U.S. (except Puerto Rico) and Canada, who are 18 years of age or older, and is void wherever prohibited by law; all applicable laws and regulations apply. Any litigation within the Province of Quebec respecting the conduct or organization of a publicity contest may be submitted to the Régie des alcools, des courses et des jeux for a ruling. Any litigation respecting the awarding of a prize may be submitted to the Régie des alcools, des courses et des jeux o for the purpose of helping the parties reach a settlement. Employees and immediate family members of Torstar Corp. and D. L. Blair, Inc., their affiliates, subsidiaries and all other agencies, entities and persons connected with the use, marketing or conduct of this Contest are not eligible to enter. Taxes on prizes are the sole responsibility of winners. Acceptance of any priz offered constitutes permission to use winner's name, photograph or other likeness for the purposes of advertising, trade and promotion on behalf of Torstar Corp., its affiliates and subsidiaries without further compensation to the winner, unless prohibited by law.

6. Winners will be determined no later than November 15, 2001, and will be notified by mail. Winners will be required to sign an return an Affidavit of Eligibility form within 15 days after winner notification. Noncompliance within that time period may resul in disqualification and an alternative winner may be selected. Winners of trip must execute a Release of Liability prior to ticket and must possess required travel documents (e.g. passport, photo ID) where applicable. Trip must be completed by Novembe 2002. No substitution of prize permitted by winner. Torstar Corp. and D. L. Blair, Inc., their parents, affiliates, and subsidiaries are not responsible for errors in printing or electronic presentation of Contest, entries and/or game pieces. In the event of printing or other errors which may result in unintended prize values or duplication of prizes, all affected game pieces or entrie shall be null and void. If for any reason the Internet portion of the Contest is not capable of running as planned, including infection by computer virus, bugs, tampering, unauthorized intervention, fraud, technical failures, or any other causes beyond the control of Torstar Corp. which corrupt or affect the administration, secrecy, fairness, integrity or proper conduct of the Contest, Torstar Corp. reserves the right, at its sole discretion, to disqualify any individual who tampers with the entry process and to cancel, terminate, modify or suspend the Contest or the Internet portion thereof. In the event of a dispute regarding an online entry, the entry will be deemed submitted by the authorized holder of the e-mail account submitted at the time of entry. Authorized account holder is defined as the natural person who is assigned to an e-mail address by an Internet access provide online service provider or other organization that is responsible for arranging e-mail address for the domain associated with th submitted e-mail address. **Purchase or acceptance of a product offer does not improve your chances of winning**

7. Prizes: (1) Grand Prize—A Harlequin wedding dress (approximate retail value: $3,500) and a 5-night/6-day honeymoon trip Maui, HI, including round-trip air transportation provided by Maui Visitors Bureau from Los Angeles International Airport (winner is responsible for transportation to and from Los Angeles International Airport) and a Harlequin Romance Package, including hotel accomodations (double occupancy) at the Hyatt Regency Maui Resort and Spa, dinner for (2) two at Swan Court, a sunset sail on Kiele V and a spa treatment for the winner (approximate retail value: $4,000); (5) Five runner-up prize of a $1000 gift certificate to selected retail outlets to be determined by Sponsor (retail value $1000 ea.). Prizes consist of only those items listed as part of the prize. Limit one prize per person. All prizes are valued in U.S. currency.

8. For a list of winners (available after December 17, 2001) send a self-addressed, stamped envelope to: Harlequin Walk Down Aisle Contest 1197 Winners, P.O. Box 4200 Blair, NE 68009-4200 or you may access the www.eHarlequin.com Web site through January 15, 2002.

Contest sponsored by Torstar Corp., P.O. Box 9042, Buffalo, NY 14269-9042, U.S.A.

PHWDACONT2

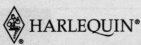

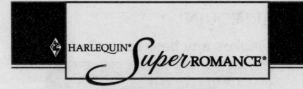